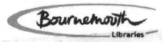

THE ACCORDIONIST

Fred Vargas

The Accordionist

Translated from the French by
Siân Reynolds

Harvill *Secker*

LONDON

1 3 5 7 9 10 8 6 4 2

Harvill Secker, an imprint of Vintage,
20 Vauxhall Bridge Road,
London SW1V 2SA

Harvill Secker is part of the Penguin Random House group of companies
whose addresses can be found at global.penguinrandomhouse.com

 Penguin
Random House
UK

Copyright © Editions Viviane Hamy, Paris, 1997

English translation copyright © Siân Reynolds 2017

Fred Vargas has asserted her right to be identified as the author of this Work in
accordance with the Copyright, Designs and Patents Act 1988

First published by Harvill Secker in 2017

First published with the title *Sans feu ni lieu* in France by Editions Viviane Hamy in 1997

A CIP catalogue record for this book is available from the British Library

penguin.co.uk/vintage

ISBN 9781846559983 (hardback)
ISBN 9781846559990 (trade paperback)

Typeset in India by Thomson Digital Pvt Ltd, Noida, Delhi
Printed and bound in Great Britain by Clays Ltd, St Ives PLC

Penguin Random House is committed to a sustainable future for our
business, our readers and our planet. This book is made from
Forest Stewardship Council® certified paper.

MIX
Paper from
responsible sources
FSC® C018179

THE ACCORDIONIST

Paris, July 1997

I

'PARIS KILLER STRIKES AGAIN! SEE PAGE 6.'

Louis Kehlweiler threw the newspaper down on the table. He'd seen enough and felt no urge to turn straight to page 6. Later maybe, when the whole business had calmed down, he'd cut out the article and file it.

He went into the kitchen and opened a bottle of beer. The last but one. He wrote a big B on the back of his hand in biro. In this July heatwave, you had to increase your fluid intake. Tonight he would sit down to read the latest about the government reshuffle, the rail strike, and the melons that French farmers had dumped on the roads. And he'd keep calm, avoiding page 6.

Shirt unbuttoned, bottle in hand, Louis went back to work. He was translating a huge biography of Bismarck. It was well paid, and he was counting on living for several months off the Iron Chancellor. He carried on for a page, then stopped, his hands hovering over the keyboard. His thoughts had left Bismarck and were focused on a box with a lid, big enough to hold all his shoes and offering one way of decluttering his cupboard.

Feeling rather annoyed with himself, he pushed back his chair, then paced across the room, running his hand through his hair. A shower of summer rain was hammering on the zinc roof overhead. The translation was going well, no reason to get anxious. Thoughtfully, he passed a finger over the back of his pet toad which was sleeping on his desk, snug inside the basket for pencils. He leaned across and read out quietly from the screen the sentence he was in the middle of translating: '*In those early days of May, it is unlikely that the thought had crossed Bismarck's mind . . .*' Then his eyes fell once more on the newspaper, lying folded on the table.

'PARIS KILLER STRIKES AGAIN! SEE PAGE 6.' Never mind, back to work, nothing to do with him. He returned to the screen, where the Iron Chancellor was waiting for him. No need to trouble his head about page 6. Quite simply, it wasn't his job any more. His job, just now, was to translate stuff from German into French, and to say as clearly as possible why, in those first days of May, Bismarck had not yet thought of . . . something or other. A calm, instructive occupation that paid the bills.

Louis typed another twenty or so lines. He had reached: '*For indeed at this stage, there is no evidence that he had taken offence . . .*' when he broke off again. His mind had returned to the box and was obstinately trying to resolve the question of the untidy pile of shoes at the bottom of the wardrobe.

He got to his feet, took the last beer out of the fridge and sipped it standing up. He wasn't fooled. If his thoughts were turning to domestic reorganisation, it was a sign of something. In fact, he knew very well that it was a sign of disturbance. Disturbance to his current plans, with his ideas wandering in trivial directions, a niggling mental blockage. It wasn't so much that he was thinking about his jumble of shoes that bothered him. Anyone could have that kind of thought from time to time, without making a big deal out of it. No, it was that he was actually getting some pleasure from the thought.

Louis took another swig or two. Shirts, too. Yes, he'd thought about sorting out his shirts, no more than a week ago.

No question, this was a serious crisis. Only people who don't know what the hell to do with themselves start thinking about decluttering, for want of being able to set the world to rights. He put the beer bottle on the kitchen counter and went to look at the newspaper. Because, in the end, it was on account of these wretched murders that he was on the brink of a domestic calamity, namely reorganising his lodgings from top to bottom. Not because of Bismarck, no, no. He had no quarrel with a figure from the past who provided him with a living. That wasn't the problem.

The problem was those damned murders. Two women murdered in two weeks, the whole country was talking about it, and he was obsessing about them too, as if he had any right to think about them and their killer, whereas it was absolutely none of his business.

After that affair with the dog and the grill round the tree in the Place de l'Estrapade, he'd decided he was going to give up on crime: it was ridiculous to embark on a career as an *unpaid* criminal investigator, simply on the grounds that he'd picked up bad habits during the previous twenty-five years, carrying out special inquiries for the Ministry of the Interior. As long as he had had an official position, the work had seemed legitimate. Now that he was left to his own devices, the job of private eye seemed somehow sleazy, like being a shit-stirrer or a scalp-hunter. Poking about in crimes when nobody had asked you to, grabbing the newspapers the moment they came out, filing away piles of articles, what else was that but a creepy distraction, and a very questionable way of leading your life?

And that was how Kehlweiler, a man all too ready to suspect himself before suspecting anyone else, had turned his back on being an unofficial private eye, something that had seemed suddenly to veer between the perverted and the grotesque, and to which the most suspect part of himself seemed to be drawn. But now, stoically reduced to the company of Otto von Bismarck, he had surprised his thoughts in the act of turning to domestic decluttering. You start with a plastic box and who knows where you will end up.

Louis dropped the empty bottle into the bin. He glanced over at his desk where the folded newspaper crouched menacingly. Bufo, the toad, had momentarily emerged from his slumber to install himself on top of it. Louis lifted him off gently. He considered his toad to be an impostor. He was pretending to hibernate, at the height of summer what was more, but that was just a ruse: he moved when you weren't looking. Truth to tell, Bufo, having been affected by his state of domesticity, had lost his innate knowledge of hibernation, but refused to admit it, because he was too proud.

'You're a ridiculous purist!' Louis told him, as he put him back in the pencil basket. 'Your phoney hibernation isn't impressing anyone. Just stick to what you *know* about.'

Slowly, he slid the newspaper across the desk towards him.

He hesitated for a moment, then opened it at page 6. 'PARIS KILLER STRIKES AGAIN!'

II

CLÉMENT WAS PANICKING. IF EVER THERE WAS A TIME HE NEEDED TO BE intelligent, this was it; but Clément was stupid, for over twenty years everybody had been telling him so: 'Clément, you're so dumb, just make an effort!'

His old teacher, at his special school, had taken a lot of trouble with him: 'Come on, Clément, try to think of more than one thing at a time, for instance, two things, do you understand? Look, take a bird and a branch. Think about a bird, perching on the branch of a tree – (a) is the bird, (b) is the worm, (c) the bird's nest, (d) the tree, and (e) is *you* sorting out your ideas, you make connections, and you use your imagination. Do you see what I'm getting at, Clément?'

Clément sighed. It had taken him days to work out what the worm was doing in the story at all.

Don't think about the bird, think about today – (a) Paris, (b) the murdered woman. Clément wiped his nose with the back of his hand. His arm was trembling. (c) Try to find Marthe in Paris. He'd been looking for her for hours, asking for her everywhere, going to all the streetwalkers he'd met. At least twenty, maybe forty, well, lots of them anyway. It was surely impossible that any of them could have forgotten Marthe Gardel. (c) Find Marthe. Clément walked on, sweating in the heat of early July, gripping his blue accordion under his arm. Perhaps she'd left Paris, his own dear Marthe, in the fifteen years he'd been away. Perhaps she was even dead.

He stopped abruptly on the boulevard du Montparnasse. If she'd left town, or if she was dead, then he was sunk. Completely sunk. Marthe was the only person who could help him, Marthe was the only person who would hide him. The only woman who had never treated him as a cretin. The only one who ruffled his hair. But what's the use of Paris, if you can't find someone there?

Clément shifted the accordion on to his shoulder. His hands were sweating too much to hold it under his arm, and he was afraid of dropping it. Without his accordion, and without Marthe, and *with* the murdered woman, yes, he was sunk. At the crossroads, he looked around. On a little side street, he spotted two prostitutes, and that boosted his courage a little.

The young woman leaning against a wall in the rue Delambre watched as he approached: a man of about thirty, shabbily dressed, wrists protruding from the cuffs of a shirt that was much too small, carrying a backpack and an accordion, and looking a bit clueless. She stiffened, there were some guys you wanted to avoid.

'Not me,' she said, shaking her head as Clément stopped in front of her. 'Go try Gisèle.'

The young woman jerked her thumb towards her colleague standing three doors further along. Gisèle had been on the game thirty years. Nothing frightened her.

Clément opened his eyes wide. He wasn't offended by being repulsed before he had asked for anything. He was used to it.

'I'm looking for a woman, a friend of mine,' he said awkwardly. 'Her name's Marthe. Marthe Gardel. She's not in the phone book.'

'A friend?' said the young woman warily. 'And you don't know where she works?'

'She doesn't work now, but in the old days she was so pretty! By the Mutualité, Marthe Gardel, everyone knew her.'

'I'm not everyone, and I'm not the flipping phone book either. What do you want her for?'

Clément took a step back. He didn't like people to speak loudly to him.

'What do I want her for?' he repeated.

He mustn't say too much about that, not to arouse suspicion. Marthe was the only one who would understand.

The young woman shook her head. This fellow was some sort of simpleton, no question, and he talked like one. Give him a wide berth. At the same time, she felt a bit sorry for him. She watched as he very gently put his accordion down on the ground.

'This Marthe, if I get you right, she's on the game?'

Clément nodded.

'OK. Stay there.'

The young woman trailed over to Gisèle.

'Guy over there, looking for a so-called pal of his, she used to work Maubert-Mutualité, name of Marthe Gardel, any idea who she is? Not in the phone book.'

Gisèle jerked her chin up. She knew plenty of things that weren't in the phone book, on account of which she took herself rather seriously.

'Lina, my sweet,' said Gisèle, 'if you don't know who Marthe is, you've missed out on your education. The busker over there? Tell him to come over, I don't like leaving my doorway, you know that.'

Lina waved to Clément. He felt his heart start to beat faster. He picked up the accordion and hurried over to the statuesque woman called Gisèle. His steps were clumsy.

'Looks a bit dumb,' Gisèle diagnosed under her breath, drawing on her cigarette. 'And at the end of his tether, I'd say.'

Clément carefully put the accordion down again at Gisèle's feet and looked up.

'You're asking for old Marthe, are you? And what do you want with her? Because you don't just get to see old Marthe like that, let me tell you. She's a classified monument, got to have a permit. And pardon me for saying so, but you look a bit of a weirdo. I don't want any harm coming to her. So what do you want with her, eh?'

'*Old* Marthe?' repeated Clément.

'Yeah, right, she's over seventy, didn't you even know that? Do you really know her, yes or no?'

'Yes,' said Clément, stepping back a pace.

'How do I know that, can you prove it?'

'I know her, she taught me everything.'

'That's her job.'

'No, no, she taught me to read.'

Lina burst out laughing. Gisèle turned towards her with a frown.

'Don't laugh, you ninny. You know nothing about life.'

'She taught you to read?' she asked Clément, more kindly this time.

'When I was little . . .'

'Well, OK, that's the sort of thing she might do. And what do you want? What's your name anyway?'

Clément made an effort. The murder, the murdered woman. He had to lie, invent something – (e) use your imagination. That was the hardest part.

'I want to give her back some money.'

'Well, that might be possible,' said Gisèle. 'She's always short of cash, Marthe is. So how much?'

'Four thousand francs,' said Clément at random.

This conversation was wearing him out. It was all going a bit fast for him, and he was terribly afraid of saying the wrong thing.

Gisèle paused for thought. He did look a bit strange, but Marthe could look after herself. And four thousand francs was four thousand francs.

'OK, I believe you,' she said. 'Now, the booksellers on the embankments, by the river, know what I mean?'

'The river? The Seine?'

'Yes, of course the Seine, dummy. The embankments, there aren't a million of them. So you take the left bank, round about the rue de Nevers, you can't miss her. She's got a little bookstall, this friend got it for her. Because she doesn't like twiddling her thumbs. Can you remember that? You're sure? Because pardon me for saying so, you don't look all that bright to me.'

Clément stared at her without replying. He didn't dare ask her to repeat it. And yet his heart was hammering, he had to find Marthe, everything depended on that.

'OK, I give in,' sighed Gisèle. 'I'll write it down for you.'

'You're taking too much trouble,' said Lina with a shrug.

'Shut up,' said Gisèle. 'What do you know about it?'

She felt in her bag, took out an empty envelope and a stub of pencil. She wrote clearly in capitals, because she did indeed suspect that the young man was not too intelligent.

'There you are, that'll find her. Tell her hello from Gisèle in the rue Delambre. And don't do anything stupid. I'm trusting you, OK?'

Clément nodded yes. He put the envelope quickly into a pocket and shouldered the accordion.

'Hey,' said Gisèle, 'play us a tune, so I can see you're for real. Then I'll feel safer about all this. Sorry to say that, but it's true.'

Clément strapped on the accordion and extended the squeezebox. Then sticking his tongue out a little, and looking straight down at the ground, he began to play.

'Right,' said Gisèle to herself, 'you can be wrong about morons.' This was a real musician. A moron-musician.

III

CLÉMENT THANKED HER PROFUSELY, AND SET OFF TOWARDS MONTPARNASSE. IT was almost seven in the evening, and Gisèle had said he'd have to hurry to catch 'old Marthe' before she shut up shop. He had to ask the way several times, showing the piece of paper. At last: the rue de Nevers, the embankment, and the green wooden boxes perched on the walls, full of second-hand books. He looked at the stallholders, but no one seemed familiar. He'd have to think some more. Gisèle had said 'seventy'. Marthe was an old woman now, he shouldn't be looking for a lady with dark hair, as he remembered her.

With her back to him, an elderly woman with dyed orange hair, wearing brightly coloured clothes, was folding up a little canvas chair. She turned round and Clément put his hand to his mouth. It was his Marthe. Older, yes, but still his Marthe, the one who ruffled his hair without treating him as a cretin. He wiped his nose and crossed on the green light, calling out her name.

Old Marthe examined the man who was approaching her. He seemed to know her. A slightly built man, dripping with sweat, carrying a blue accordion under his arm as if it were a flowerpot. A large nose, blank eyes, a pale complexion and fair wavy hair. Clément came to stand in front of her. He was smiling, he recognised everything, he was safe.

'Yes?' said Marthe.

Clément hadn't imagined that Marthe would fail to recognise him, and he began to panic again. What if Marthe had forgotten him? What if she'd forgotten everything about the past? What if she had lost her memory?

His mind went blank, he couldn't even think to say his name. He put down the accordion and hunted feverishly through his wallet. Taking care, he found his identity card and held it anxiously out to Marthe. He was very attached to his identity card.

Marthe shrugged and looked at the worn piece of card. Clément Didier Jean Vauquer, twenty-nine years old. Well, that didn't mean a thing to her. She considered the man with the vague eyes and shook her head, looking rather regretful. Then she stared again at the card, then at the man, who was panting noisily. She felt she should make an effort, that this person desperately wanted something from her. But the bony, unprepossessing and frantic face in front of her, no, she'd never seen it. And yet the eyes, on the verge of tears, the anxious patience, said something. Blank eyes, small ears. A former client? Impossible, too young.

The man wiped his nose with the back of his hand, the rapid gesture of a child without a handkerchief.

'Clément?' whispered Marthe. 'Little Clément?'

Little Clément, for the love of God!

Marthe quickly closed the bookstall's wooden shutters, locked it, picked up her folding chair, her newspaper and two plastic bags, and nudged the young man's arm urgently.

'Come along,' she said.

How could she have forgotten his last name? Of course she had never had occasion to use it, she'd always called him Clément, just Clément. She dragged him fifty metres further along, to the car park by the French Academy, where she put her stuff down between two cars.

'Quieter here,' she explained.

Clément, relieved, let her take charge.

'You see now, don't you?' Marthe went on. 'I always said you'd end up a head taller than me, and you didn't believe me. So who was right? What a long time ago! You were what when I met you? Nine or ten years old? And then one fine day, my little pal disappeared. You could have kept in touch. I don't want to tell you off, but you *should* have.'

Clément hugged Marthe hard, and Marthe patted his back. He smelled sweaty of course, but he was her little Clément, and anyway Marthe wasn't fussy. She was happy to find him again, the little boy lost whom she'd tried to teach to read and talk properly for about five years. When she'd first known him, hanging about on the street, abandoned by his godawful father, he couldn't even speak normally, he'd just kept muttering, 'Don't care anyway, they say I'm going to hell.'

Marthe looked at him anxiously. He seemed totally desperate.

'So, something's the matter,' she declared.

Clément had sat down on a car bonnet, his arms dangling. He was staring at the newspaper which Marthe had put down with her plastic bags.

'Have you seen the paper?' he managed to say.

'I was just doing the crossword.'

'The woman that was murdered, see that?'

'You bet, everyone's seen about that. What a brute!'

'They're after me, Marthe. You've got to help me.'

'Who's after you, my little pal?'

Clément waved his arm around in a circle.

'The woman that was murdered,' he repeated. 'They're after me, it says so in the paper.'

Marthe hurriedly unfolded her canvas chair and sat down. The blood was pounding in her temples. It wasn't the image of the little boy learning his letters that came to mind now, but all the stupid things Clément had done between the age of nine and twelve. Thefts, fights, as soon as anyone called him an imbecile. Cars vandalised, chalk in petrol tanks, windows broken, dustbins set alight. The skinny little creature had just stubbornly repeated, 'I'm going to hell, my dad says so, see if I care.' How many times had Marthe had to go and haul him out of the cop shop? Luckily, because of her profession, she was familiar with all the police stations in Paris and the men who staffed them. At about thirteen years old, Clément had pretty well calmed down.

'God Almighty, it's not possible,' she muttered after a few minutes. 'It can't be, God Almighty, that they want you for *that*?'

'It's me, they're after me, Marthe.'

Marthe's throat constricted. In her head she heard footsteps clattering on the stairs and the child calling, 'They're after me, Marthe, they're after me,' as he hammered on her door. Marthe would open it, and the small boy would fling himself into her arms in tears. She would let him curl up in bed under her red eiderdown and stroke his hair till he went to sleep. He wasn't very bright, her little Clément. She knew that, but she would have allowed herself to be chopped in pieces before agreeing with anyone else who voiced it. There were plenty of people ready to spit on him as it was. It wasn't his fault, poor kid, he'd get better, he'd learn. And then we'd see what we'd see.

And now, well, we were seeing, as Simon might have said, the old bastard who kept the grocer's shop back then. Always the first to point the finger. He called Clément 'bad blood'. Even thinking about that old b stirred Marthe to get going. She knew what she had to do. She rose to her feet, folded the chair and picked up her things.

'Come on,' she said. 'We can't stay here.'

IV

THESE DAYS, MARTHE WAS LIVING IN A GROUND-FLOOR BED-SITTING ROOM, IN A dead-end street near the Place de la Bastille.

'My friend found this for me,' she said proudly to Clément as she opened the door. 'If it wasn't for all the junk I've got in here, it'd be quite smart. The bookstall by the river, that's him as well, Ludwig he's called. Did you ever think one day I'd find myself selling books? Swapped one pavement for another, see? Anything can happen.'

Clément was only half following this.

'Ludwig?'

'The friend I'm telling you about. Now, he's one in a million. And I know what I'm talking about when it comes to men. Put the accordion down, Clément, you're making me feel tired.'

Clément waved the newspaper at her, he wanted to say something.

'No,' said Marthe. 'Put down your accordion first, then sit, anyone can see you can hardly stand up. You can tell me all about the accordion by and by, no hurry. And listen to me now, my boy: we're going to have some supper, we're going to have a little glass of something, and then you're going to tell me what this is all about, calmly and slowly. Got to do things in the right order. And while I'm cooking, you're going to clean yourself up. And for the love of Mike, put that accordion down!'

Marthe hauled Clément over to an alcove at the back of the room, and moved a curtain aside.

'Take a look at that!' she said. 'A real bathroom. Fancy, isn't it? You're going to have a hot bath, because you should always have a bath, and a hot one, when you've got problems. And if you've got some clean clothes, you put 'em on. You can give me the dirty ones, I'll wash them out tonight. It's so hot, they'll dry quickly.' Marthe ran the water and pushed Clément into the bathroom, before drawing the curtain across.

At least he wouldn't smell sweaty now. Marthe sighed, she felt anxious. She picked up the newspaper without rustling it, and read the article on page 6 again, slowly. The young woman whose body had been found yesterday morning in her flat in the rue de la Tour-des-Dames had been hit on the head, strangled, and stabbed a total of eighteen times with a blade, possibly scissors. A real bloodbath.

'*Help is expected from witnesses living nearby who have all mentioned the presence of a man standing watching the building for several days before the murder.*' The sound of water made Marthe jump. Clément was emptying the bath. She quietly put the paper aside.

'Sit down now, my boy, supper's on its way.'

Clément had changed his clothes and combed his hair. He had never been good-looking, perhaps because of his pug nose, pale skin, and especially the blank look in his eyes. Marthe said it was because they were so dark that you couldn't distinguish the pupil from the iris, but if you were prepared to look carefully, he wasn't so bad, and anyway, what the hell did that matter? As she stirred the pasta, Marthe went over in her head the information from the article: '. . . *enquiries are focusing on a young white man, aged twenty-five to thirty, small and slight or very thin, clean-shaven, with curly fair hair, cheaply dressed, wearing grey or beige trousers and trainers.*'

The police were confident they'd have an identikit picture available in two days at most.

Grey trousers, Marthe remarked to herself, glancing at Clément.

She ladled the spaghetti out on their plates, adding cheese and sliced hard-boiled egg. Clément looked at his food without speaking.

'Eat up,' said Marthe. 'Pasta gets cold quickly, don't know why. But cauliflower doesn't. There's nobody can tell you the answers to things like that.'

Clément had never been able to talk while eating. He was incapable of doing two things at once. So Marthe decided to wait until they had finished.

'Don't think about it, just eat up,' she repeated. 'Empty sacks won't stand upright.'

Clément nodded and obeyed.

'And while we're eating, I'm going to tell you some of my stories, like when you were little, OK? Like the client I had who wore two pairs of trousers, one on top of the other, and I bet you don't remember it at all.'

It wasn't difficult for Marthe to distract Clément. She was capable of telling story after story for hours, and often found she was talking to herself. So she told him the story of the man with the two pairs of trousers. Then the ones about the fire in the Place de l'Aligre, the politician who had two families, something she was the only person to know, and the little ginger cat that had fallen from the sixth floor and landed on its four paws.

'My stories aren't so good tonight,' Marthe ended, pulling a face. 'I'm not concentrating. I'll fix us some coffee and then we'll have a chat. Take your time.'

Clément wondered anxiously where to begin. He couldn't work out which should be (a). Perhaps this morning in the cafe?

'This morning, Marthe, I was drinking coffee in a cafe . . .'

Clément stopped, his fingers on his lips. He felt stupid. How did other people manage to avoid saying things like 'coffee in a cafe'?

'Go on,' said Marthe, 'don't worry if it sounds stupid, I won't mind.'

'So I was drinking coffee in a cafe,' Clément repeated. 'And one of the men in there, he read out from the paper. And I heard the name of the street, "rue de la Tour-des-Dames", so I listened personally, and then they described this murderer. And it was *me*, Marthe. Just me. So I knew I was in trouble after that, I don't know how they knew. I was very scared, so I went back to the hotel and I got my things, and then all I could think of was to find you, so they wouldn't catch me.'

'But what had this girl done to you, Clément?'

'What girl?'

'The one that's dead, Clément. Did you know her?'

'No. I was just spying on her for five days. But no, she hadn't done anything to me, no.'

'And why were you spying on her?'

Clément pressed the side of his nose and frowned. It was very hard to get things in the right order.

'To know if she had a sweetheart. It was for that. And the pot plant, it was me that bought it, and I gave it to her. They found it, fallen over, with all the earth spilled on the floor, that was in the papers too.'

Marthe got up to fetch a cigarette. As a child, Clément had never been smart, no, but neither had he been crazy or cruel. And the young man sitting at her table, in her bed-sitting room, suddenly made her feel afraid. She wondered for a moment about going out to call the police. Her little Clément, oh God Almighty, it wasn't possible, was it? What had she been hoping? That he'd killed someone by accident? Or without realising? No, she'd been hoping it simply wasn't true.

'But, Clément, what came over you?' she whispered.

'For the pot plant?'

'*No*, Clément, why did you *kill* her?' Marthe shouted.

Her cry ended in a sob. Panic-stricken, Clément came round the table and knelt down beside her.

'But, Marthe,' he stammered, 'Marthe, you know I'm a good kid! You said so, you always said so. Isn't that the personal truth? Marthe?'

'I thought so,' Marthe cried. 'I gave you your education. And now what have you done? Do you think that was being a good kid?'

'But, Marthe, she hadn't done anything to me.'

'Be quiet. I don't want to hear any more of this.'

Clément gripped his head in his hands. Where had he gone wrong? What had he forgotten to say? He'd picked the wrong (a) as usual, and like every time, he'd started off in the wrong place. And he had given Marthe a terrible shock.

'I didn't tell you the beginning, Marthe,' said Clément, shaking her shoulder. 'I didn't kill the woman!'

'So if it wasn't you, who was it? Did God strike her dead or something?'

'You've got to help me, Marthe,' Clément whispered, his hands gripping her shoulders, 'because they'll come and get me.'

'You're telling lies, Clément.'

'I don't know how to tell lies, you told me that too. You told me you've got to have ideas to tell lies.'

Yes, she did remember that Clément was hopeless at inventing things. He couldn't make up a little joke or an April fool, still less tell an outright lie. Marthe thought again of the old greengrocer in their street, Simon, who used to spit on the ground and say, 'That boy's got bad blood, he'll end up murdering us in our beds, see if he doesn't.' Tears sprang to her eyes. She loosened Clément's hands from her shoulders, blew her nose loudly in her paper napkin, and took a long deep breath. She and Clément would have to be right, it couldn't be any other way. It was between themselves and that old Simon, you had to make a choice.

'OK,' she said sniffing, 'start again.'

'See, Marthe,' Clément began, breathing fast, '(a) I was watching this girl. It was this job I was asked to do. And the rest is just a . . . a . . .'

'Coincidence?'

'Coincidence, that's it. They're looking for me because I was seen in the street, me personally. I was working. And a bit before that, I was watching another girl. Same thing. Work.'

'*Another* girl?' said Marthe, her voice expressing her fear. 'Do you remember where?'

'Wait,' said Clément pressing the side of his nose. 'I'm trying to think.'

Marthe got up abruptly and went over to a pile of newspapers under the sink. She pulled one out and looked through it quickly.

'Not the Square d'Aquitaine was it, Clément?'

'Yes, that's right!' said Clément with a big smile, relieved. 'That's where the first girl lived. Just a little street, on the way out of Paris.'

Marthe let herself drop on to a chair.

'My poor boy,' she murmured. 'My poor boy, don't you know?'

Clément, still on his knees, was staring at Marthe, open-mouthed.

'It wasn't a coincidence,' Marthe said quietly. 'Someone killed a woman ten days ago in the Square d'Aquitaine.'

'Was there a pot plant?' Clément asked, whispering now.

Marthe shrugged.

'It was a pretty fern,' Clément murmured, 'I chose it myself, personally. That's what I was asked to do.'

'*Who* asked you? Who are you talking about?'

'This man, he phoned me in Nevers, and said he wanted an accordionist for his restaurant in Paris. But the restaurant wasn't ready yet. So he asked me to keep an eye on these two waitresses, he wanted to hire them, but he wanted to know if they were reliable girls.'

'Oh, my poor Clément . . .'

'Do you think someone saw me in the Square d'Aquitaine too?'

'Well, of course they did. In fact, that's why you were sent there, my poor child: to be seen. God in heaven, couldn't you have guessed that it was a very odd job to be given?'

Clément stared wide-eyed at Marthe.

'I'm an idiot, Marthe. You know that.'

'No, Clément, you're not an idiot. And what about the first murder, didn't you hear that on the news?'

'I was in this hotel, I didn't have a radio.'

'A newspaper then?'

Clément lowered his gaze.

'Oh, reading . . . I've sort of forgotten some of it.'

'You can't read any more?' cried Marthe.

'Not very well. It's too small, the words in the papers.'

'Oh dear,' sighed Marthe in exasperation, 'you see now what happens when you don't carry on with your education.'

'I'm caught in a machinery, a horrible machinery.'

'A horrible machination, Clément. You're right. And believe me, this is too much for us.'

'We're sunk?'

'No, we're not sunk. Because you see, my boy, old Marthe has contacts. She knows people who are clever. And that's where education comes in, see that now?'

Clément nodded.

'But first of all,' said Marthe, standing up, 'did you tell anyone you were coming here?'

'No.'

'Are you sure? Think. You didn't mention my name to anyone?'

'Yes, yes I did, to the girls. I asked about forty street girls, trying to find you. I can't read the phone book properly, it's too small.'

'And would these girls recognise you from the description in the paper? Did you talk to them for long?'

'No, they wouldn't even talk to me, personally. Except this one, Madame Gisèle and her friend, they were nice to me. She said to say hello to you, Gisèle in the rue . . .'

'Delambre.'

'That's right. *They* would recognise me. But perhaps they can't read either?'

'Yes, they can, Clément. Everybody can read. You're an exception.'

'I'm not an exception. Just an idiot.'

'Someone who says he's an idiot isn't one,' pronounced Marthe firmly, taking Clément's shoulder. 'Now listen to me, my boy. You're going to sleep now, I'll fix the camp bed behind the screen for you. And I'm going to nip out to see Gisèle and tell her to keep her mouth shut, and the other girl, her pal, too. Do you know the pal's name? Could it be Lina, a young one, working in the rue Delambre just now?'

'Yes, that's it. You're so clever!'

'It's just education, remember.'

Clément suddenly clapped his hands to his cheeks.

'They'll say that I was coming to see *you*,' he whispered, 'and then people will come for me *here*. I must go away, they'll get me.'

'Just stay right where you are. Gisèle and Lina won't say anything, because I'll ask them not to. Rules of the profession, simple as that. But I've got to get a move on, go and see them right now. And you, just stay here, don't go out, whatever you do. Or answer the door. I'll be late back. Go to sleep.'

V

IT WAS PAST ELEVEN WHEN MARTHE TAPPED GISÈLE ON THE SHOULDER. GISÈLE was standing, half asleep, in a doorway. She had the gift of being able to drop off anywhere, like horses do, she said. She was as proud of this as if she was a champion at some sport, but Marthe had always found it a bit sad. The two women hugged: it was four years since they'd seen each other.

'Gisèle,' said Marthe, 'I'm in a hurry. It's about this man who was asking for me this evening.'

'Thought so. Did I make a mistake sending him?'

'No, you did the right thing. But if anyone comes asking, you don't know anything. You might even see stuff about him in the paper. But don't tell anyone anything.'

'The cops, you mean?'

'For instance. He's a little boy belongs to me, I'll take care of it. See what I'm saying, Gisèle?'

'There's nothing to see. I won't tell, that's all. What's he done?'

'Nothing. He's a kid belongs to me, like I said.'

'Hey, it isn't that little lad from way back, is it, the one you were teaching to read?'

'Quick off the mark, aren't you, Gisèle?'

'Well, just since I saw him, the little grey cells have been working,' said Gisèle with a smile, twirling a finger on her temple. 'Though pardon me for saying so, but he doesn't have a lot upstairs, your kid does he?'

Marthe shrugged, looking awkward.

'He's never been able to say the right thing.'

'You can say that again. But if it's your little Clément, well, that's the way it is. Can't change it, can we?'

Marthe smiled.

'You remembered his name?'

'Like I said,' Gisèle went on, finger to temple again. 'Little grey cells at work. You know what it is, you stand round here on your tod, nothing to do, you got to do something, so you get to thinking. As you would know.'

Marthe nodded pensively.

'Work it out,' Gisèle was saying, 'after all, you spent thirty-five years on the street, thinking about things. Adds up.'

'Look, by the end,' Marthe said, 'I was working with a call phone in my room.'

'Yeah, but. You can think just as well if you're sitting in a room. But if you're always busy with your hands, working in the post office or something, you don't get time to think a lot.'

'True, you need a bit of breathing space to be able to think.'

'Like I'm saying.'

'But Clément, you'd better forget about him, please. Don't say a thing. Keep mum, got that?

'Excuse me, you already told me that.'

'Don't take offence, I just wanted to be sure.'

'So he's in trouble, your Clément?'

'He hasn't done anything. But there are all these other people after him.'

'Other people? Who would they be?'

'Stupid buggers.'

'OK, I get it.'

'I'm off now, Gisèle. I'm counting on you, you're pure gold. And tell Lina too. Love to the kids. And get a bit of sleep.'

The two women hugged each other again and Marthe disappeared with short quick steps. She wasn't worried about Gisèle. Even if she was told Clément had killed two women, or saw an identikit picture in the papers, she still wouldn't open her mouth. Or at least not without checking with Marthe first. But trying to convince Ludwig to help didn't look so easy. Just because Clément had been taught to read by her wouldn't seem obvious proof of innocence to him. What was that reading book called? Back into ancient history. She could see the cover now, a farm, a dog, a small boy.

René and his Dog.

That was it, that was what the book was called.

VI

MARTHE LISTENED AT LOUIS'S DOOR BEFORE KNOCKING, IN CASE HE WAS ASLEEP. He was the sort of person who might go to bed at 3 a.m. or be out all night, but you never knew. She was hesitating, since she hadn't warned him she was coming and hadn't seen him for almost three months. People said Ludwig had stopped taking any interest in the kind of crime that got into the papers. And Marthe, who considered herself part of that scene, for rather confused reasons, was afraid that her friendship with the German, as he was sometimes known, might have ended when he gave up his role as Ministry investigator. Ludwig was one of the few men who could impress old Marthe.

'Ludwig,' she called, rapping at the door, 'sorry to disturb you, but it's an emergency.'

Glueing her ear to the wooden panel, she heard the German push back his chair and approach the door with calm steps. He rarely rushed at anything.

'Ludwig,' she repeated, 'it's me, your old Marthe.'

'Well, of course it's you,' said Louis, opening the door. 'Who else would be shouting the house down at two in the morning? You'll wake the whole building.'

'I was whispering,' said Marthe, coming inside.

Louis shrugged.

'Whispering, I don't think you know what that means! Sit down, I'll make some tea, there's no beer left.'

'Have you seen the paper? The second murder? What do you think?'

'What do you want me to say? Nasty business, that's all anyone can say. Come on, sit down.'

'So it's true, is it, what they say? You're not involved any more?'

Louis folded his arms and looked at her.

'Is that the emergency?'

'I'm just asking a question, no harm in that.'

'Well, it's true, Marthe,' he said, sitting down opposite her, arms folded and legs stretched out. 'Back in the day, I was paid to go round stirring up mud. It would be pretty creepy to go on doing it for nothing now.'

'I don't get it,' said Marthe with a frown. 'It's always been creepy, and I'm surprised it's only now you're noticing that. But since you're so good at it, you might as well carry on.'

Louis shook his head.

'For now,' he said, 'all I'm interested in is Bismarck and finding some boxes to store my shoes in. So that won't get us very far.'

'What's that B on your hand?'

'My shopping list: beer, boxes for the shoes, Bismarck. Why have you come?'

'I told you already, Ludwig. This crime. Well, two crimes . . . '

Ludwig poured out the tea with a smile.

'What's the problem, my old friend? Are you scared?'

''It's not *that*,' said Marthe, raising her shoulders. 'It's the murderer.'

'What about the murderer?' asked Louis, without showing any impatience.

'Nothing. Just that he's round at my place. He's asleep. I thought it was important to tell you, interested or not.'

Marthe put milk in her tea and stirred it with concentration, her muscles tense, but trying to seem casual.

Louis, looking stunned, took a deep breath and leaned back. He wasn't sure how to react. He knew Marthe's ways of old.

'Marthe,' he said deliberately. 'What the *fuck* is the murderer doing in your place?'

'Just told you, he's asleep.'

Marthe lifted up her teacup, then put it down, and met Louis's gaze. She examined the green eyes she knew so well, and found in them scepticism, anxiety and at the same time a spark of lively interest.

'Under my eiderdown, on the camp bed,' she added quickly. 'Don't go thinking I'm making this up, Ludwig, I'm not in the habit of wasting your time. And no, I'm not pushing you to get involved again, believe me. If you want to give all that up, fine, that's up to you, although in my humble opinion, it's a waste of your talents. All I can say is he's round at my place and I don't know what to do. The only person I could think of who might get me out of this was you, and even so, I've no idea how you can. And anyway, you don't believe me.'

Louis dropped his head, and sat for a few moments without speaking.

'Why do you say he's the murderer?' he asked quietly.

''Because he's the one they say in the papers they're after. He's the one who was seen hanging around outside the buildings where the two women lived.'

'If that's true, Marthe, why didn't you call the police?'

'Are you crazy? For them to arrest him? When it's my little Clément, like my own son to me?'

'Ah,' said Louis, leaning back. 'I'm not getting the whole picture here, am I? I thought there was more to it. You're not easy to follow tonight, believe me. You're telling me stuff in a muddle. Now be nice, and try to explain to me so I can understand your story about the murderer and the eiderdown.'

'It must be after talking to Clément, it's confused me. He gets every-thing muddled up in his head, he doesn't line things up in the right order, so it's all over the place.'

Marthe fumbled inside her enormous fake leather handbag, brought out a small cigar, mumbling to herself, and lit it conscientiously, screwing up her eyes.

'I'll begin at the beginning,' she said, blowing the smoke out fiercely. 'More than twenty years back, it was, when I worked Maubert-Mutualité, I already told you, I had the whole of the Place Maubert to myself, it was the high spot of my career –'

'I know all that, Marthe.'

'Never mind, high spot is what it was. The whole of the square and the first bit of the rue Monge, and no other girl would've dared pinch a square metre off me. I could pick and choose my clients. I was queen of the Place Maubert. When it was cold, I worked from home, but on fine days I worked the pavement, because that's where you get the real clientele, not on the phone. I wish you could have seen where I lived in those days –'

'Yes, Marthe. But get on with it.'

'I'm getting there, don't rush me. I'm telling you this in order. And it starts with the pavement, because on my pavement there was this little boy, tiny he was,' said Marthe, waving her little finger under Louis's nose. 'From four thirty every day, there he was, on his own. His father, proper bastard *he* was, had rooms somewhere round about, and the kid, well, he just waited for his dad to remember about him, waited for hours, before he could get inside, when the father got back from the racetrack, which is where he worked. Funny kind of work, if you ask me.'

Louis smiled. Marthe was sometimes inexplicably censorious, as if she had spent her life as a respectable churchgoer.

'So little Clément, he just hung about until the evening or even the night, for someone to pick him up. He was eight, nine years old, but his no-good father wouldn't give him a key, seems he kept money in his flat, and he didn't trust the kid, well, that was what he said, and another thing he said was his son was a halfwit and a bad lot, that's what he used to say, if you can call that saying something. Because if you want my opinion, using language like that, it's not right and proper.'

Marthe took another fierce drag on the cigar and shook her head.

'Sack of shit, the father,' she almost shouted.

'Turn the sound down,' said Louis, 'but go on.'

Marthe once more waved her little finger in front of him.

'Tiny he was, this kid, I'm telling you, a shrimp. So of course your heart went out to him. At first we just used to have a little chat. He was wild, a little street rat. I don't know if anyone but me would have got three words out of him. But in the end we got to be pals. I'd bring him a snack at teatime, because I don't know when he got anything to eat after the school canteen. And it got to be autumn and he'd be waiting there in the dark, and the cold and the rain, believe me or not as you like. And one night, I took him home with me. That's how it started.'

'What started?'

'His education, Ludwig. He couldn't read, he could just about write his name. He couldn't do anything, just nod his head or shake it, or get up to mischief. Yes, he was good at that. But he didn't understand anything, not a thing, and at first he would just cry and curl up on my knee. Makes me want to cry now, just thinking about it.'

Marthe shook her head, and pulled bravely on the cigar with trembling lips.

'Let's have a wee drink,' said Louis abruptly, getting up.

He fetched two glasses, opened a bottle of wine, emptied the ashtray, and lit another lamp, before asking Marthe to pour out. Having something to do did her good.

'Get a move on with your story, old lady. It's nearly 3 a.m.'

'All right, Ludwig. So I took him in hand for about five years. I stopped working after four thirty, and took charge of him till the evening, reading, writing, learning poems, keeping himself clean, giving him supper – education. At first, I remember, I had to get him to hold his head up straight when he talked to people. And then how to say what he wanted to say. It took a lot of patience, I can tell you. After a year and a half, he could read and write. Not very well, I grant you, but he managed. Sometimes he stayed overnight and his father never even noticed. Sundays he was with me all day, and I'll tell you something, Ludwig, Clément and me, we loved each other, I was like a mother to him.'

'So what happened next, Marthe?'

'When he was about thirteen, one night, he just wasn't there. And I never saw him again. I found out that the no-good father had left Paris, without telling anyone. That's how it ended. And then, all of sudden,' Marthe went on after a pause, 'this evening, there he is in front of me, and they're after him for these murders. So I got him washed and put to bed and he's asleep. Now do you understand?'

Louis stood up and walked round the room, running his hand through his hair. He had known Marthe for years and she had not once mentioned this boy.

'You never told me about this kid you were mothering.'

'Why would I? I didn't know where he was any more.'

'Well, you know now. And I'd like to know what you think you're going to do, with a murderer in bed in your room?'

Marthe slammed down her glass.

'What I'm going to do, is not let anyone get near him or hurt him, you understand? I'm not going to budge on that.'

Louis shuffled things on his desk and found that day's paper. He opened it at page 6 and slapped it down on the table in front of Marthe.

'You're forgetting something, Marthe.'

Marthe looked at the headline, the photos of the two young women who had died. 'PARIS KILLER STRIKES AGAIN!'

'Look,' said Louis, 'two women, strangled with a stocking, stabbed nearly twenty times with scissors or a screwdriver or something . . .'

'You don't understand,' said Marthe with a shrug. 'It wasn't *Clément* who did all those horrible things. Where did you get that idea? Just remember I had that boy under my wing for five years, educating him. That's not nothing, and do you think he'd have come back to his old Marthe if he had done it?'

'What I'm wondering, Marthe, is if you really know what might go on inside the head of a murderer.'

'And you do, I suppose?'

'Better than you.'

'And you know Clément better than me too, do you?'

'What does he have to say about all this, Clément?'

'That he knew the two women, that he was supposed to be watching them, that he gave them pot plants. He's the one they describe in the paper, that's true, no doubt about that.'

'But these two women, he didn't lay a finger on them, of course?'

'No, that's right.'

'And why was he watching them?'

'He doesn't know.'

'No?'

'No, he says it was a job he was told to do.'

'Who by?'

'He doesn't know that either.'

'Is he an idiot or what, this guy?'

Marthe said nothing for a few minutes, looking tight-lipped.

'Well, OK, Ludwig,' she said at last, awkwardly, 'that's sort of it. He's not, well, he's not very bright.'

She took a sip of wine and sighed. Louis looked at the teacups, from which neither of them had drunk. He stood up slowly and put them in the sink.

'OK,' he said, as he rinsed them out, 'so if he hasn't done anything, why is he hiding under the blankets in your room?'

'Because Clément thinks he *is* an idiot, that the cops will pick him up the minute he shows his face, and he won't be capable of getting himself out of the fix.'

'And you believe everything he says?'

'Yes.'

'No hope you might have some doubts?'

Marthe puffed at her cigar without replying.

'How tall is he, your little boy?'

'Average, metre seventy-five perhaps.'

'Big and strong?'

'Not at all,' said Marthe, raising her little finger again.

'Well, wait for me to come round at about midday tomorrow, and don't let him escape.'

Marthe smiled.

'No, no, old girl,' said Louis, shaking his head. 'Don't be under any illusions. I don't have faith in this guy the way you do, not at all. I find the whole thing a mess, it's melodramatic and grotesque. And I've no idea what to do. But at the moment, it's think about this or think about shoeboxes, nothing else in my head, like I said.'

'They're not incompatible.'

'Are you sure you want to go back home?'

'Of course.'

'Well, if tomorrow, I find you strangled and stabbed, that'll be your own funeral.'

'I'm not scared. He doesn't attack old women.'

'Ah, you see,' murmured Louis, 'you're not as sure as all that.'

VII

LOUIS DIDN'T HAVE THE WILLPOWER TO GET UP AT TEN, AS HE HAD INTENDED. He wanted to see Marc Vandoosler before going round to Marthe's place, and he was going to be late. He imagined Marthe waiting in a state of high anxiety, sitting on a kitchen stool, watching tigerishly over a sort of lunatic murderer. The whole of France was looking for him and Marthe could think of nothing better to do than take him into her nest, as if he were a china dog. Louis groaned to himself and poured out another cup of coffee. To try and extricate this guy from Marthe's protective claws wasn't going to be fun. And it would take time as well, providing plenty of evidence of his crimes until Marthe was sufficiently impressed. And even then he wasn't sure she'd give him up.

Of course, going to the police right away would sort it out. In ten minutes they'd be round at her door, they'd pick up this man, and that would be an end to it.

But it would be a terrible betrayal, and probably the death of old Marthe. No, obviously, there was no question of alerting any cop, for now. Especially since they'd cart Marthe off as well. Louis sighed with exasperation. He was blocked on all sides, protecting a murderer, risking more lives, not counting Marthe who might be done in at any minute, if this guy took a notion against her.

He ran his hand through his hair a few times, in some perplexity. The meeting wasn't going to be easy with this Clément, what with Marthe seeing him as the vulnerable little boy she had loved so much, whereas he, Louis, envisaged a man who had clearly had a damaging childhood and ended up on a terrible trajectory, killing women. Marthe could see only tenderness, he could see only horror. But he would have to find a way of gently removing this monstrous child from her.

Louis finished dressing, thinking of all those hunters who had tried to take a bear cub away from its mother and who had died in the attempt, even if the cub wasn't particularly appealing. From the kitchen drawer, he took out a flick knife and put it in his pocket. Marthe was the only person who would have no misgivings about confronting a scissors killer.

At about midday, he was standing outside the ramshackle building where Marc Vandoosler lived, in the rue Chasle. The neighbours referred to it as 'the dosshouse', in spite of the improvements carried out by Marc and the two historian friends he had recruited to share it with him. There didn't seem to be anyone home, not even Marc's uncle and godfather, Vandoosler senior, who lived up under the eaves and looked out of an attic window if he heard anyone approach. Louis had only been there twice before, and he peered up at the facade. The windows were all shut on the third floor, which he remembered was occupied by Lucien Devernois, a military historian who was perpetually plunged into the study of the blood and guts of the First World War. And no one seemed to be in on the second floor either, where his medievalist friend Marc Vandoosler lived, nor on the first floor, the domain of Mathias Delamarre who studied prehistoric mankind. Louis shook his head, as he contemplated the shabby exterior of this tall building into which the three explorers of times past had carefully inserted themselves in chronological order. They might not have the same social structures or professional perspectives, but at least (at Marc's insistence) they could observe the correct march of Time. So they had stacked themselves on three levels between the ground floor, which was a communal space and represented the primeval swamp, and the attics where Vandoosler senior lived. He was an ex-policeman with a shady career behind him, now mainly concerned with his own time and how best to spend it. And in the end, Louis had to admit, this collection of personalities, with little in common, hastily brought together two years earlier through economic hardship, had lasted better than anyone might have hoped.

Louis pushed the old gate, which was never closed, and crossed a sort of wild garden surrounding the house. He peered through the windows into the large ground-floor room which Marc called the refectory. Empty. And the front door was locked.

'Greetings, my German friend. Looking for the evangelists?'

Kehlweiler turned round and greeted Vandoosler senior who was approaching with a smile, pulling a supermarket trolley full of groceries. The elder Vandoosler had got into the habit of describing his fellow residents as St Mark, St Matthew and St Luke, or the three evangelists for short, and everyone had had to put up with it, since in any case the elder Vandoosler was not about to change his mind.

'Hi, Vandoosler.'

'Haven't seen you for a while,' said the older man, fumbling for his keys. 'Want to stay for lunch? I'm cooking a chicken, and tonight it's gratin dauphinois.'

'No, I'm in a hurry. I'm looking for Marc.'

'Are you on a case? We were told you'd retired.'

Honestly, thought Louis, you can't start contemplating shoeboxes without everyone in Paris knowing and wanting their say. The old policeman's tone had been one of disapproval.

'Look, Vandoosler, don't come the cop with me, OK? You of all people should know, you can't go wallowing in crime all your life.'

'You weren't wallowing, you were investigating.'

'Same thing.'

'Maybe,' agreed Vandoosler, opening the door. 'So what are you doing instead?'

'Thinking how to sort out my shoes,' said Louis sharply.

'Ah. Lowered your sights then.'

'Yes indeed. And so what? You're spending your time cooking gratin dauphinois.'

'But do you even know *why* I'm making it?' asked Vandoosler, with a stern look. 'You just throw off a remark like that, without wondering, "Now why is Armand Vandoosler making a gratin dauphinois?"'

'I don't care why you're cooking a fucking gratin dauphinois,' said Louis. 'I'm looking for Marc.'

'I am spending my time cooking,' Vandoosler went on, opening the door to the refectory, 'because that is my *sphere of excellence*. So I am obliged by my talent, or should I say my genius, to concentrate on gratin dauphinois. And you, my German friend, would have been well advised to carry on with your investigations, whether you're being paid by the Ministry or not.'

'Nobody is obliged to do something just because they *can* do it.'

'I'm not talking about what you *can* do, but about what you *excel* at.'

'Second floor, yes?' asked Louis, heading for the stairs. 'They're still in the same order chronologically, I suppose? Primeval magma on the ground floor, prehistory on the first floor, Middle Ages on the second and Great War on the third?'

'That's right. And me in the attic.'

'And what do *you* symbolise?'

'Decadence,' said Vandoosler with a grin.

'Quite true,' muttered Louis. 'I'd forgotten.'

He went into Marc's room and opened the wardrobe.

'Why are you following me?' he asked Vandoosler, who was watching him from the doorway.

'I'd just like to know why you're rifling through my nephew's possessions.'

'Where is he, your nephew? I haven't seen him for weeks.'

'Working.'

'Ah,' said Louis, turning round. 'Doing what?'

'He'll tell you.'

Louis chose two T-shirts, a pair of black trousers, a woollen jersey, a jacket and a tracksuit top. He spread them out on the bed, examined them, added a belt with a silver buckle and nodded.

'This should do,' he murmured. 'A typical sample of Marc's immature preciousness. Do you have a suitcase?'

'Downstairs in the magma,' said Vandoosler, pointing.

Louis chose a battered case from the back kitchen, folded the clothes carefully inside it and took his leave of the older man. He bumped into Marc Vandoosler in the street.

'Ah, good, I'm glad I met you,' he said. 'I'm just taking away some of your things.'

He balanced the case on his knee and opened it.

'See?' he said. 'You can make a list if you want and I'll get them back to you as soon as possible.'

'What the hell are you doing with my clothes?' asked Marc, sounding annoyed. 'Where are you going? Want to have a drink?'

'No time. An unpleasant interview coming up. Do you want to see where your clothes are going?'

'Something interesting? People say you've retired.'

Louis sighed.

'Yeah, right,' he said. 'I've retired.'

'So now what do you do?'

'Think about boxes to store my shoes in.'

'Really?' said Marc, genuinely astonished. 'And you want to store my clothes too?'

'No, your clothes are to dress a monster who's killed two women,' said Louis harshly.

'Two women? What do you mean? The scissors killer?'

'Yes, you got it in one, the scissors killer,' said Louis, closing up the suitcase. 'So what? Does it bother you that I'm passing him your clothes?'

'What the fuck is going on, Louis? I haven't seen you for weeks, you roll up and take my best jacket, to give to some murderer, and then you start shouting at me!'

'Shut up, Marc! Don't let the whole street hear you.'

'To hell with the street! I don't know what this is all about. Oh, I'm going home, I've got some urgent ironing to do. Take my clothes if it amuses you.'

Louis caught him by the shoulder.

'Marc, this doesn't amuse me at all. We don't have any choice and this whole business is making me feel ill. No choice, is what I said. We've got to shelter this guy, protect him, give him some clothes, get him washed and his hair cut.'

'Like a doll?'

'You said it, that's exactly it.'

It was almost one o'clock and getting hot.

'Look here, you're not making any sense,' said Marc, less angrily.

'I know. It seems this guy makes everyone he comes into contact with feel confused.'

'Who? Him?'

'Him, the doll.'

'But why are you taking this trouble over a doll?' said Marc calmly. 'I thought you'd retired.'

Louis put the case on the pavement, thrust his hands slowly into his pockets and looked at the ground.

'This guy,' he began slowly, 'this guy, the scissors man, the murderer of women, is *Marthe's* doll. If you don't believe me, come along. Come on. She's got him under her eiderdown.'

'The red one?'

'The red what?'

'Eiderdown.'

'Oh, damn the eiderdown, Marc. The point is that he's living there. Are you trying deliberately to misunderstand?' Louis's voice was raised again.

'What I don't *understand*,' said Marc irritably, 'is *why* this guy is Marthe's doll.'

'What's the time?'

Louis didn't wear a watch, he just tried to sense what o'clock it was.

'Ten to one.'

'It'll make us late, but look, come to the cafe and I'll explain why Marthe has this doll. I only found out last night myself. And believe me, it's not a funny story.'

VIII

LOUIS AND MARC WALKED WITHOUT SPEAKING TOWARDS THE PLACE DE LA
Bastille. Now and then Marc carried the suitcase, since Louis limped
a little on account of a knee long ago damaged in a fire, and was tiring
under the heat and the weight of the case. Marc would willingly have
taken the metro but Louis never seemed to remember that it existed.
He preferred to go on foot, or if pressed by bus, and since he could be
pretty annoying when you argued with him, Marc didn't insist.

At about two o'clock, Louis stopped at the door of Marthe's modest
lodgings in the cul-de-sac near the Bastille. He looked at Marc with
drawn features, his eyes at their greenest and most intense. Stiff and
forbidding, he had assumed his German look, as Marthe put it. Marc
preferred to think of him as a Goth from the delta of the Danube.

'You're not sure?' asked Marc.

'I think we're making a big mistake,' whispered Louis, leaning against
the door. 'I think we should have called the cops.'

'No, we can't,' said Marc, also in a whisper.

'Because?'

'Because of the doll,' said Marc, still keeping his voice low. 'You
explained it all very well in the cafe. To the cops he's a murderer, but to
Marthe, he's her little boy.'

'And to us? We could be in deep shit.'

'Yes. Come on, ring the bell, we're not going to stand here all day.'

Marthe opened the door cautiously and considered Louis with the same stubborn expression as the previous night. For the first time in her life, she was only half trusting him.

'No need to put on that German look,' she said with a shrug. 'You can see he hasn't gobbled me up. Come on in.'

Going ahead of them into the small room, she sat down on the bed, alongside a thin young man hanging his head, whose hand she patted.

'This is the man I told you about, Clément,' she said. 'And he's brought a friend along.'

The man looked up suspiciously, and Louis had a shock. Almost everything about that face was unattractive: its long shape, vague structure, large forehead, white skin marbled with blue veins in places, and thin lips; even his ears, which did not curl at the edges, were unappealing. The eyes improved the general impression a little: they were large and dark, but totally expressionless; he had a shock of fair curly hair. Louis was fascinated as he watched Marthe uninhibitedly stroking the head of this rather off-putting person.

'This is the man I told you about,' Marthe repeated, still rubbing his head.

Clément nodded a sort of unspoken greeting towards Louis. Then he repeated it for Marc.

Louis realised that Clément did show signs of mental impairment.

'That's all we need,' he murmured, putting the suitcase on a chair.

Marthe approached him, crossing the three metres that separated them with caution, glancing towards the bed as if her movement might endanger her protégé.

'What are you staring at him like that for?' she hissed angrily under her breath. 'He's not a wild beast.'

'Not an angel either,' Louis snarled back.

'I never said he was a film star. No need to look at him like that.'

'I was looking at him because of who he *is*,' said Louis, almost inaudibly. 'And because of the guy they're talking about in the papers, the one who waited under the windows of those women. Because you're *right*, Marthe, that's him, no question. From the descriptions, his odd-looking head, the get-up, it all matches.'

'Don't talk about him like that.' Marthe spoke threateningly. 'What's come over you?'

'What's come over me is that he really has nothing going for him.'

'He's got *me*. And if you won't help him, that'll have to do. You can go.'

Marc watched the battle of wills between Louis and Marthe, somewhat disconcerted by Louis's hostile attitude. Normally, the German was expansive and calm and didn't make snap judgements. He distrusted perfection, respected shortcomings, was at home with doubt and muddle. He didn't insult people unless it was really worth doing so. His scornful dismissal of the poor guy sitting on the eiderdown was disturbing. But then again, Louis didn't like killers, and he did like women. Obviously, he had no faith at all in this man's innocence.

Clément, hands clasping his knees, hadn't taken his eyes off Marthe and seemed to be struggling to understand what was going on around him. Marc thought he looked simple-minded, and that made him sad. Marthe had certainly chosen an odd kind of doll.

Marc drank some water from the tap, wiped his mouth on his sleeve and tapped Louis on the shoulder.

'We haven't even heard what he has to say,' he said gently, pointing his chin towards Clément.

Louis took a breath and realised with surprise that Marc was perfectly unperturbed while he was almost beside himself, whereas usually it was the other way round.

'It's like I was saying before we got here,' he said, calming down. 'This guy seems to confuse us all. Marthe, can you get me a beer and we'll try to have a talk?'

He threw a cautious glance towards the catatonic-seeming individual who hadn't budged from the bed, and who was continuing to grip his knees and stare at Louis with those blank dark eyes in that pale, pale face.

Marthe, still angry, pushed a wooden chair towards Louis. Marc picked up a big cushion and sat down cross-legged on the floor. Louis looked at him enviously, then sat on the chair with his long legs stretched stiffly in front of him. He took a deep breath before beginning.

'So your name is Clément. Clément what?'

The young man sat up straighter.

'Vauquer,' he replied, with the conscientious expression of someone who wants to reply satisfactorily.

He glanced across at Marthe who gave him a gesture of approval.

'Why did you come to find Marthe?'

The man frowned and muttered for a few moments to himself as if he were chewing his words. Then he turned back to Louis.

'(a) Because, which I mean to say, I didn't know anyone, and (b) because I was personally, as for me, in a horrible machination. And the machination is (c), and it was in the newspapers. Which I mean to say, I heard next morning.'

Louis, taken aback, looked at Marthe.

'Does he always talk like that?' he whispered.

'It's because he's in awe of you,' she said irritably. 'He's trying to talk proper, and he can't manage it. You've got to be more straightforward.'

'You don't live in Paris?' Louis began again.

'I live in Nevers. But I know Paris personally, as for me, from being a child. With Marthe.'

'But you didn't come to Paris to see Marthe?'

Clément Vauquer shook his head.

'No, I came after the phone call.'

'What do you do, in Nevers?'

'I play tunes on the accordion, on the streets in the day, and in cafes in the evening.'

'You're a musician.'

'No, I just play the accordion.'

'Don't you believe him?' Marthe interrupted.

'Wait, Marthe, just let me handle it. It's not that easy, believe me. And sit down instead of standing up ready to pounce, you're making us all nervous.'

Now Louis had rediscovered his slow and calm way of speaking. He was concentrating on the skinny young man. Marc, sipping from a can of beer, watched. Clément's voice had been a surprise: sweet and musical, pleasant on the ear, despite the muddled words.

'And?' said Louis.

'And what?' asked Clément.

'What was this phone call about?'

'I got it in the cafe where I go to work and especially Wednesdays. The boss said, telephone wants Clément Vauquer, so, who it was, was me.'

'Yes,' said Louis.

'The telephone asks do I want a job with the accordion in Paris. New restaurant, every evening, good pay. Man had heard me play, and he had this work, as for me, personally.'

'And then?'

'The boss told me, you should say yes. So I said yes.'

'What's the cafe called, the cafe in Nevers?'

'A l'Oeil du Lynx, that's it, its name.'

'So, you said yes. And then?'

'They explained, they said which day I must arrive, a hotel where I must live, an envelope they will give me. The name of the restaurant where I will work. And I followed all the explanations right, so (a) I arrive on Thursday, (b) I go to the hotel, and (c) they give me an envelope with money in, advance money.'

'What was the hotel called?'

Clément Vauquer moved his jaws for a few moments.

'A name with *boules* in it. Hotel des Trois Boules? Or maybe more. By metro Saint-Ambroise. I could find it again. My personal name, Clément Vauquer, it's on the register, with a telephone in the room, and a toilet, and everything. He called to say he had a delay.'

'What do you mean?'

'He had a *delay*. I was meant to start work on a Saturday, but the restaurant wasn't ready, building works, three weeks late. This man said I could do something else while I was waiting, that's how I was personally, I mean to say, looking after the women.'

'Tell me as clearly as you can,' said Louis, leaning forward. 'Were the women your idea, then?'

'My idea?'

'Talk more clearly,' snapped Marthe, looking at Louis. 'You can see it's hard for him. His story's complicated, put yourself in his place.'

'The idea of finding these women, was it you that had it?' Louis went on.

'Finding the women, but what for?' asked Clément. He sat with his mouth open, hands still clasped on his knees, perplexed.

'What did you want to do to the women?'

'I wanted to give them a plant, in a pot, and watch their . . .'

The young man frowned and moved his lips without speaking.

'. . . their morals,' he went on. 'That was what the telephone said. I had to watch their morals, so the restaurant would be respectable, with their morals, when they worked there, because they were going to be the waitresses.'

'So what you're saying,' said Louis, still speaking calmly, 'is that this man asked you to keep an eye on his future waitresses, and report back to him.'

Clément smiled. 'Yes, that's it. I had their two names and addresses, personally, for me. I had to begin with the first one, and go on to the second. Then there would be the third.'

'Try to remember exactly what the man said on the phone.'

There followed a very long silence. Clément Vauquer moved his jaw from side to side and pressed a finger against his nose. It seemed to Marc as if he was trying to force ideas out of his head by pressing his nose. And oddly enough, the system seemed to work.

'I will repeat with his voice,' Clément said, frowning and still touching his nose. 'His voice is deeper. I will say it like I remember personally. "The first girl, her name is something or other, she looks like a serious girl, but you never know. She lives in the Square d'Aquitaine, this number, and you must go and check up. You don't need to hide, and it isn't hard work. Stand in the street, and see if she brings visitors home, men visitors, or if she goes to cafes to smoke, or drink, or if she goes to bed late or what, from the light in the window, or if she gets up early or late or what. You do this for five days, Friday, Saturday, Sunday, Monday, Tuesday. Then you go and buy a plant in a plastic pot, and take it to her, say it is from the restaurant, so you can see inside, what her place is like. I will call you Wednesday to hear, and then you do the same with this second girl that I will tell you about."'

Clément gave a loud sigh and looked at Marthe.

'He said it better than that,' he said, 'but that is what he meant. It was my job, before the restaurant was going to open. But he said it better than that. So (a) I went to the Square d'Aquitaine, and did the job. And (b) the girl was very respectable, personally, I mean to say, so Wednesday, I took her this plant, a pretty fern, and I rang the bell. They smell nice, ferns do. She was very surprised, but she took the fern, but she didn't let me in, she was very respectable, so I didn't get to see her flat. I was worried. Then (b) . . .'

Here the man stopped.

'Have I already done (b), Marthe?' he whispered.

'You've got as far as (c),' Marthe told him.

'So (c),' said Clément, immediately turning back to Louis, 'I had to watch the *second* girl, from the Monday after. She was not such a respectable girl, her house was on the rue de la Tour-des-Dames. She didn't look like she would make a good waitress. She didn't have a man in the house, no, but there was one outside, they went away in a blue car and she came back very late. Not so respectable. And (d) I did take her a plant but it wasn't such a big fern, because of the man in the blue car, I didn't like him. She kept the plant just like the other one. And she was surprised, just the same. And I couldn't see inside, just the same. And then I had finished my work. On the telephone, the restaurant man said, "Well done, you," and told me to stay there, not to go away, he would soon tell me where to go for the third one, but especially, not to go away. Especially.'

'And after that you stayed in your hotel room?'

'No, I went out, the next day but one. I went to the cafe for coffee.'

Here he stopped again, opened his mouth and looked at Marthe.

'It's fine,' said Marthe. 'Just carry on.'

'So,' Clément said, 'there were people and newspapers, and they read the paper out. They said the name of the street and the name of the woman, this same woman, she was *dead*.'

Suddenly looking anxious, he stood up and walked round the small room between the bed and the sink.

'And that's it,' he said breathlessly, 'the end of the story.'

'But when you were in the cafe, what did you think?'

'Shit, shit, shit! That's enough,' Clément burst out. 'I can't tell you any more story, I can't, I don't have proper words. I already said it all, personally, I mean to say, to Marthe. *She* can tell you, I don't want to talk any more, I've had enough of these women. Talking about them all the time, makes me want one.'

Marthe went over and put her arm round him.

'He's right,' she told Louis. 'You'll wear his poor brain out with all your questions. Tell you what,' she said to Clément, 'you're going to have a shower now, my boy, a nice long shower, five minutes, I'll call out stop when it's time. And you can wash your hair too.'

Clément nodded.

'While we're at it,' said Louis, picking up the suitcase, 'tell him to change into these clothes. And pass me his, so we can hide them properly.'

Marthe handed Clément the black clothes, and pushed him towards the tiny bathroom. She looked at Louis with suspicion.

'Give you his clothes, so you can keep them yourself? And what next, I mean to say? You'll give them to the police?'

'You're starting to talk like him,' said Louis.

'Why, what did I say?'

'I mean to say.'

'So? I haven't done you any harm, have I?'

'No, it just means you've got him under your skin, you're hooked, if you want my opinion.'

'Well, he's my little boy, isn't he?'

'Yes, which I mean to say, Marthe, he is indeed your little boy.'

'Stop taking the piss like that!'

'I'm not taking the piss, I'm trying to tell you, you'd kill all your friends for the sake of this guy you haven't seen for what? Sixteen years?'

Marthe collapsed on to the bed.

'It's just that I'm the only person who can help him,' she said in a low voice, 'that's what's killing me, Ludwig. I'm the only one who believes him, but he's telling the *truth*, because Clément is the only person in the *world* who would have agreed to do that *fucking* stupid job, looking out for those women without asking questions, without suspecting anything, without wondering why, and without reading the newspapers. He even went and gave them those pot plants covered with his fingerprints. He's cornered, Ludwig. He's too flummoxed now, and this other man is too clever.'

'You really think he's flummoxed?'

'What do you think? That he's having us on?'

'Why not?'

'No, Ludwig, no. He was already like this when he was little. God knows, I did my best, but you can see for yourself. Damaged by his family, you can't do much about it now.'

'Where did he get his weird way of talking?'

Marthe sighed.

'He thinks it makes him sound as if he can talk properly. He must have picked up all these expressions somewhere, and he just drops them into the way he talks. But to him it sounds as if he's being more serious, do you understand? So . . . what . . . what do you think of him?'

'Not a lot that's good, Marthe.'

'I thought so. He makes a bad impression.'

'It's not just that, Marthe. He's on edge, he's possibly violent. He gets disturbed when women are mentioned. It turns him on.'

'Me too,' commented Marc.

Louis turned towards Marc, who was still sitting cross-legged on the floor and smiling up at him.

'We hadn't heard anything from you,' said Marthe. 'That's unusual.'

'I was listening,' said Marc, nodding towards the bathroom. 'He's got a nice voice.'

'What's that you were saying about women?' asked Louis, taking another beer.

'Well, it turns me on too, to talk about women,' said Marc, enunciating each syllable clearly. 'And if *anything*'s normal, that ought to be. It's not fair of Louis to pounce on that and accuse this guy, who's already got the odds stacked against him. And if he's fond of Marthe, well, that's perfectly understandable too.'

Marc winked at Marthe. Louis sat thinking, slumped on his chair, his long legs stretched out.

'Maybe he's taking you in as well,' he said, staring at the wall. 'Because he's got a nice voice. He's a musician. And if there was a good band playing, you'd march off to war like a fucking idiot.'

Marc shrugged.

'I just think this guy is a one-off,' he said. 'Simple-minded enough to do what someone tells him without asking questions, blind enough not to see the pit that's being dug under his feet, perfect material for someone manipulative. And you can't really overlook that.'

Just then, Clément emerged from the bathroom, his hair dripping wet, and wearing the black jeans and T-shirt belonging to Marc, holding the silver-buckled belt in one hand.

'Do I have to put this on personally?' he asked.

'Yeah,' said Louis. 'Personally.'

Clément began threading the belt through the loops on the jeans; it was a long-winded operation.

'You didn't answer the question I asked you just now. When you were in the cafe and you heard about the murder, what did you think?'

Clément gave a groan, and sat on the bed, barefoot, holding his socks. He pressed the side of his nose before beginning to put the first sock on.

'(a) That I *knew* this woman who was dead, that I gave the fern to. (b) I'd brought her bad luck, on account of watching her, and then they were talking about me in the paper. Which I mean to say, it was about the coincidence, so I thought I was in a trap, which on account I wanted to find Marthe.'

Holding a sock in one hand, Clément thrust his face closer to Louis.

'A machinery,' he said.

'A machination,' Marthe added.

'Which I mean to say, no way to escape,' Clément went on firmly, 'because I was chosen, and brought from Nevers by the telephone.'

'And why would *you* have been chosen, and not anyone else?'

'Because I'm more stupid than anyone else!'

There was a silence. The young man pulled on the other sock. He was very punctilious about doing everything.

'How do you know that?' asked Louis.

'Well, because that's what everyone has always told me,' said Clément, with a shrug. 'I'm stupid, because personally, I mean to say, I don't always understand things, or the papers, I can't read them. Only Marthe never said that to me, but Marthe is a kind person, personally.'

'Quite right,' said Marc.

Clément smiled at Mark. He had a tight-lipped smile, no teeth showing.

'Do you know *how* those women were killed?' Louis insisted.

'I don't want to talk about it, it upsets me.'

Marc was no doubt about to say 'me too', but was quelled by a look from Louis.

'Right, Marc, we'll leave it there,' he said, standing up.

Marthe looked at him anxiously.

'No,' said Louis irritably. 'I just don't know. But for now, whatever your kid's done, we're all of us boxed into a corner. So, can you cut his hair short, get the curls off, and dye it some other colour? Nothing too obvious please, just dark brown. Not red, anyway. He'll have to let his beard grow too, and that'll have to be dyed later, that's if they haven't caught him first.'

Marthe gave a start, but Louis put his hand gently over her mouth.

'No, old friend, let me finish, and do exactly what I ask you. Don't let him leave here on any account, even if he complains he wants to have a coffee in a cafe.'

'I can read stories to him.'

'Yeah, right,' said Louis, still sounding exasperated. 'And lock the door behind you if you have to go out. And his rucksack, all his gear, give it to me. We'll have to get rid of it.'

'How do I know you're not going to keep it?'

'You don't. Do you own a gun, any weapon?'

'No, I wouldn't want to.'

Marthe gathered Clément's things and put them into the rucksack.

'What about the accordion?' she asked. 'You're surely not going to take that away from him?'

'Did he have it with him when he was standing in the street outside those women's homes?'

Marthe looked enquiringly at Clément, but he had stopped listening to anything that was being said and was smoothing the red eiderdown with his hand.

'My boy,' Marthe said loudly, 'you didn't take the accordion with you, did you, when you were watching the women?'

'No, Marthe, course not! It's too heavy, and it's no use for watching people.'

'See,' said Marthe, turning to Louis, 'and they didn't say anything about it in the papers either.'

'OK then, but he mustn't play it, not a note, see that he doesn't. Nobody must guess you've got anyone in here with you. When it's dark, we'll come and fetch him to take him somewhere else.'

'Somewhere else?'

'Yes, old lady. A place where there'll be no women to kill and where he can be watched night and day.'

'You mean prison!' cried Marthe.

'Don't keep shouting!' said Louis, losing his temper for the third time that day. 'And just trust me for once. The question we're facing is whether your little boy is a monster or just simple-minded. And it's the only way to get him out of the fix. And for now, since I don't know the answer, I'm not going to hand him over to the cops, OK?'

'OK, but where are you going to take him?'

'To the dosshouse. Marc's place.'

'I beg your pardon?' said Marc.

'We don't have any choice, Marc. And I can't think of anywhere else. We have to get this none-too-bright kid somewhere safe from the cops, and at the same time safe from himself. So your dosshouse, because there are no women there, which is a big plus.'

'Right,' said Marc. 'I hadn't really thought of it like that.'

'And there'll always be someone around to keep an eye on him. Lucien, Mathias, you, or your uncle.'

'And what makes you think they'll agree?'

'Vandoosler senior will agree. He likes dodgy situations.'

'That's true enough,' Marc conceded.

Louis made a few more anxious recommendations to Marthe, glanced for a last time at Clément who was still stroking the eiderdown, looking depressed, hitched the rucksack on to his shoulder, and pulled Marc out into the street.

'Let's get something to eat,' said Marc. 'It's nearly four o'clock.'

IX

'FIND US A QUIET TABLE,' SAID LOUIS AS THEY WENT INTO A CAFE ON THE PLACE de la Bastille. 'We don't need to broadcast our wretched machinations. I'm going to make a phone call, so order us something to eat.'

Louis joined Marc a few minutes later.

'Got an appointment with the police chief in the 9th arrondissement,' he announced as he sat down. 'The sector for the second murder, the one in the rue de la Tour-des-Dames.'

'And you're going to tell him what?'

'I'm not going to *tell* him anything, I'm going to listen. I want to know what the cops think about these two murders, what lines they're following, and how far they've got. They may have an identikit picture by now. I'd like to see it.'

'Do you think he's going to tell you all that, your chief of police?'

'Yeah, I think so. We worked together when I was in the Ministry of the Interior.'

'What excuse will you give?'

Louis hesitated.

'I'll say these murders remind me of something, but I'm not sure what. Some rubbish like that. Not important.'

Marc pulled a face.

'No, it's fine, you'll see. This cop owes me, I got his son out of a fix, about eight years ago.'

'What kind of fix?'

'He was involved with this gang of skinhead dealers, crack cocaine, bad stuff. I got him out before the drug squad pounced.'

'And on what grounds would you do something like that?'

'On the grounds that he was the son of a cop who could be useful to me one day.'

'Bravo.'

Louis shrugged his shoulders.

'The boy wasn't dangerous. He didn't have the profile.'

'People say that.'

'I know what I'm doing,' said Louis more sharply, looking up at Marc.

'OK, OK,' said Marc, 'let's eat.'

'I never saw him hanging round the same kind of people again, and please don't come the social worker with me. What's important now is the shit Marthe has got herself into. We need information from a police source. That's essential if we're going to know what to do. I imagine that the cops, like the press, are looking for a serial killer.'

'And you're not?'

'No, I'm not.'

'Well, it doesn't look like a contract killing or a gang or anything. He seems to pick women at random.'

Louis waved a hand in the air, wolfing his chips. He didn't usually eat quickly, but he was in a hurry.

'No, of course not,' he said. 'I think, like you and like everyone else, that this is some maniac, obsessive, sexual psychopath, call him what you like. But not a serial killer.'

'You mean he won't kill anyone else?'

'On the contrary, he will.'

'Shit. We're talking at cross purposes.'

'It's a matter of counting. I'll explain later,' said Louis, gulping down the last of his beer. 'I'm off. Can you please take Marthe's doll's belongings back to the dosshouse? I can't cart them round to the police station with me. Just wait for me there to get in touch.'

'Don't come before eight, I'll be at work.'

'Really?' said Louis, sitting down again. 'I heard you'd found work. Middle Ages?'

'No, not Middle Ages. Or middle management. Housework.'

'Housework? What do you mean?'

'I'm talking French, Louis, which I mean to say. Housework. For three weeks now, I've been a cleaning lady two-thirds of the time. Vacuuming, dusting, washing, polishing. And I take ironing to do at home. And now it's you that looks like the social worker. Go and see your senior policeman, I've got floors to clean.'

X

COMMISSAIRE DIVISIONNAIRE LOISEL CALLED LOUIS INTO HIS OFFICE WITHOUT making him wait. He seemed genuinely glad to see him. Loisel was about the same age as himself, fifty-ish, slim, fair-haired, and a smoker of tiny cigarettes as thin as straws. To the police and in the Ministry, Louis Kehlweiler was generally known as 'the German', as Loisel now greeted him. There was nothing Louis could do about this, and nor did he really care. Half-German, half-French, born during the war, he didn't know where his roots were and would have preferred to be called 'the Rhine', if anything, but that was a presumptuous dream which he didn't confide to anyone. He answered either to Louis or Ludwig. Only Marc Vandoosler, by some stroke of genius, sometimes called him 'son of the Rhine'.

'Long time no see,' said Loisel. 'Greetings, my German friend.'

'How's the son?' asked Louis, taking a seat.

Loisel raised his hands in a gesture of reassurance, and Louis responded with a nod.

'And yourself?' the commissaire went on.

'I got the push from the Ministry four years ago.'

'It was always on the cards. And since then, nothing? No work for clients?'

'I earn a living doing translations.'

'But there was that Breton business, wasn't there? And I heard something about neo-fascists in Dreux, and some old man locked in the attic?'

'You're well informed. Yes, I have been involved in a few cases on the side. It's harder than you might think to keep right out if it, when you've got filing cabinets bulging with sensitive material. And your files harass you! They keep shouting out their memories, bombard your ears. Instead of some affair passing you by, it sets up an echo howling through the cabinets. Making such a row that you can't sleep in peace, if you really want to know.'

'And this time?'

'There I was peacefully translating a book about Bismarck, and some guy comes along and murders two women in Paris.'

'The scissors killer, you mean?'

'Yes.'

'And that set up an echo somewhere in your files?' asked Loisel, suddenly showing interest.

'It didn't leave me indifferent. It reminded me of something, but I can't tell you exactly what.'

What rubbish I'm talking, Louis thought.

'You're having me on,' said Loisel. 'It reminds you of something, but you don't *want* to tell me what.'

'No, no, really. It's an echo that hasn't got a name or a face attached, and that's why I've come to see you. I need some more details. That's if you don't mind us having a chat about it, of course.'

'No-o,' said Loisel with some hesitation.

'If it comes to anything, I'll tell you about what's bothering me.'

'All right. I know you're on the level, my German friend. There's no harm our discussing it a bit. You're hardly likely to go running to the newspapers.'

'They already know most of what there is to know.'

'Most of it, yes. Have you been to see my colleague in the 19th arrondissement? About the first murder?'

'No, I came straight here.'

'Why?'

'Because I don't like the chief in the 19th. If you want my opinion, he's a waste of space.'

'Ah, you think so?'

'Yup.'

The divisionnaire lit another of his skinny cigarettes.

'Quite agree,' he said firmly.

Louis realised that they had just done a deal, since nothing cements a partnership more than agreement that a third party is a waste of space.

Loisel ambled over to a metal filing cabinet, dragging his feet. He had always done this, surprisingly for a man who liked to project an image of virility. He pulled out a voluminous file and let it fall theatrically on the desk.

'Here it is,' he sighed. 'The nastiest psycho murders we've had in the capital for years. Needless to say, the Ministry of the Interior's breathing down our necks. So if you can help me and I can help you, with a bit of honest give and take ... And if you were to lay hands on this character ...'

'Goes without saying,' said Louis, who was thinking that this character was at that very moment curled up on Marthe's eiderdown, while Marthe read him a story to distract him from his unfathomable thoughts.

'So what do you want to know?' asked Loisel, leafing through some of the papers.

'These murders, were there any details that didn't get reported in the press?'

'Not really. Look, here are the photos, that'll tell you more than anything else. As they say, one picture ... These are the official photographs of the first murder, 21 June, Square d'Aquitaine. The chief of the 19th wouldn't even pass the info on to me. Dog in the manger or what? Can you beat it? We had to get the Ministry to weigh in and force his hand.'

Louis pointed to one of the photographs.

'Yes, that's the woman in the Square d'Aquitaine. Not particularly pretty, but you can't tell, because she was strangled. He got into her flat somehow or other, about seven in the evening. He stuffed a gag in her mouth, then banged her head against the wall apparently.'

'The papers said he strangled her.'

'Yes, but he knocked her out first. It's not that easy to strangle someone just like that, if you get my drift. Then he dragged her to the carpet in the middle of the room. You can see the tracks of her shoes on the pile. That's where he strangled her, and then stabbed her about a dozen times, just about everywhere on the torso with a small blade, probably scissors. He's the stuff of nightmares, this guy.'

'No sexual assault?'

'Nothing at all.'

'Does that bother you?'

'In cases like this, you'd certainly expect it. But see for yourself. Her clothing is in order, the body is in a decent position. No trace of sexual contact.'

'And this woman, remind me of her name?'

'Nadia Jolivet.'

'And do we know anything about Nadia Jolivet?'

'The chief in the 19th investigated her, couldn't find anything out of the ordinary. Here, read it: age thirty, secretary in a commercial firm, had a fiancé. A normal life. When the second murder was committed about ten days later, my colleague stopped looking into Nadia Jolivet's background. I'd have done the same, as soon as we heard about the bastard who was hanging about outside their houses. And as for my victim here . . .'

Loisel reached into the dossier and pulled out another set of photos which he spread on the desk.

'Here we are, Simone Lecourt. Same thing exactly. Knocked out, dragged into the middle of the room, gag in her mouth. And butchered by the killer.'

Loisel shook his head, stubbing out his cigarette.

'Sickening,' he commented.

'Did the gag give any clue?'

'No.'

'No links between the two women?'

'No. It's true we didn't explore that too deeply, because we've almost got our man, but as far as we can see, the two women had never met. They don't have anything in common except that they're thirty-ish, unmarried, and were in employment. Both of them were reasonably attractive, but didn't look at all alike, physically, one was dark, one fair-haired, one thin, the other quite well built. If this is some nutter going after women who remind him of his mother, he doesn't re-member her very well.'

Loisel smiled and lit another cigarette.

'But we'll get him,' he said, 'it's only a matter of days. You've seen the papers. The witnesses have all described a man hanging around these addresses for several days before the murders. He sounds as if he's a bit simple, which makes me think it'll be quite easy to catch him. Look, we have seven reliable witnesses. Seven! The man was so visible, standing around in doorways, that the whole of France could have identified him. And we have a statement from Nadia's colleague at work, who says she saw this same guy follow her home from the office two days running. And Simone's boyfriend noticed him when he brought her back late one night. So you see, it'll be a piece of cake.'

'Because you've got some fingerprints?'

'Yes, all ten prints on some plant pots he brought the victims! See what a complete idiot we're dealing with? Both victims, presented with a fern in a flowerpot, the same prints on both. We presume that's how he got inside the flats. A guy bringing flowers, the girl's going to be far less suspicious. Still, a fern – he might have chosen something a bit prettier. An imbecile, that's what he is, but a dangerous imbecile.'

'I suppose a fern smells nice. Did he leave his prints anywhere else? Or just on the flowerpots?'

'Nowhere else.'

'How do you explain that? He brings the pot in his bare hands, but doesn't leave prints anywhere else. And if he took the trouble to put gloves on before committing the murders, you'd think he would take the trouble to get rid of the fern.'

'Yeah, I know, that struck us too.'

'I would think so.'

'He could have knocked her out, strangled and stabbed her without leaving fingerprints. There were carpets in both flats – not parquet floors or lino in either case. Or he could just be someone totally stupid, like I said, who didn't think at all. It happens.'

'Why not?' said Louis, his thoughts returning immediately to the small man with blank eyes whom Marthe was protecting as if he were made of porcelain. At that moment, they would probably have finished the story, and Marthe would be cutting his hair in the tiny bathroom and preparing to dye it with some concoction of her own invention.

'So what does this guy look like?' asked Louis suddenly.

Loisel went over to the filing cabinet and pulled out another dossier.

'This has just come in,' he said, 'fresh off the computer. Seven reliable witnesses, like I said. Take a look at this face, and tell me if you don't think he looks like a complete cretin.'

Loisel slid the identikit portrait across the desk and Louis had a shock. It was a frighteningly good likeness.

XI

CLÉMENT VAUQUER HAD FALLEN ASLEEP AFTER LOUIS LEFT, WITHOUT EVEN EATING. Since then he had lain curled up on the red eiderdown, while Marthe tiptoed as quietly as possible round her room: Marthe was not blessed with the gift for silence. Now and then she went over to the bed and contemplated her little Clément. He was sleeping with his mouth open and had dribbled on to the pillow. Never mind, she'd change the pillow slip. She could understand why Louis found him off-putting, his appearance was certainly unattractive. The others would think the same, probably, no – certainly. The thing was, she had never been able to finish his education, that's what had spoilt everything. He wasn't the way he seemed. The artificial way of talking, it was just embarrassment, and the way he pursed his lips was just to defend himself. His eyes had always been like that, such a dark brown that you couldn't see the pupils. Dark brown eyes are beautiful, they can be the stuff of dreams. If they would only leave her Clément with her a little longer, she could change him. Feed him up, let him see the sun a bit, his skin would improve, his face would look less pinched. She'd read him stories, teach him again how to talk properly instead of the weird language he had strung together, God knows how. She'd teach him not to keep saying 'person-ally', 'which I mean to say', as if he had no existence and had to restate the contrary with every sentence. Yes, she had a pretty good idea of how she could repair her little protégé. He had got himself entangled in a terrible mess, but he would come through, she'd fix him up, so it was very lucky that he had found his way to her. She'd make him look good. Nobody had bothered with him for sixteen years. She'd make him look good and Louis would be flabbergasted by her achievement.

It reminded her of a book she'd seen as a child, *The Girl Who Wasn't Beautiful*. The little girl in the story starts off very plain, but in the end with help from everything around her, for some unknown reason, raindrops, squirrels, birds and all the forest creatures, she gets to be pretty and charming and queen of the woods. Another book she had liked was *The Adventurous Little Fisher-Duckling*: this duckling, wearing check shorts, did one stupid thing after another, but it all came out right in the end, by some miracle. Marthe sighed. No point daydreaming, my girl. You're too old for fairy stories, ducklings and little girls who blossom into beauties. The truth was that Louis had felt immediate antipathy for her little Clément, and things had got off to a bad start, so even if all the woodland creatures in the world came running to help (which was unlikely), what good would it do?

Marthe roamed the room, muttering to herself. No, no squirrels would be able to fix this. But for now, it would probably be a good thing to spruce her boy up, and cut his hair as Louis had suggested. The German was in a bad mood, yes, but he wasn't about to hand him over to the cops. Not straight away, at least. She had a little time to work on her boy.

Gently shaking Clément by the shoulder, she said: 'Wake up, son, I've got to do something about your hair.'

She sat him down on a stool in the bathroom and tied a towel round his neck. The young man allowed himself to be propelled about, without a word.

'Got to cut your hair short,' she announced.

'People will see my ears,' Clément said.

'I'll leave a bit to cover the top of your ears.'

'Why are my ears such a funny shape?'

'No idea, son, but don't worry. Look at Ludwig's ears, they're no better. He's got very big ears, they spoil his looks.'

'Ludwig's the one asked me all those questions?'

'That's right.'

'He made me feel tired personally,' said Clément plaintively.

'That's his job, making people feel tired. You can't always choose. His job is to track down bad men, all kinds of bad men, so to do that he has to wear people down, exhaust them. It's like if you want to shake a tree to get the nuts down. If you don't shake it, you don't get the nuts.'

Clément nodded. This reminded him of the way Marthe used to teach him things when he was little.

'Don't move or I'll go wrong. These are kitchen scissors – not sure how they'll work for cutting hair.'

Clément lifted his head suddenly.

'You won't hurt me with the scissors, will you, Marthe?'

'Of course not. Keep still.'

'What was that about ears?'

'If you start really looking at everyone's ears, just look at them and nothing else, in the metro for instance, well, then you see that they're all terrible, horrible things, make you feel sick. Let's stop talking about ears, it makes me feel ill.'

'Me too. Especially women's.'

'Well, for me it's especially men's. So you see, son, that's nature. That's how it's organised.'

'Yes,' Marthe said to herself, as she chopped off his curls. She would take his education in hand again, if she had the time.

'Next I'm going to dye your hair brown like your eyes, and I'll pop a bit of make-up on you, some fake tan to give you the right colouring. Trust me. You'll see, you'll look great, and the cops will never recognise you. Then we'll have some pork chops for our supper – that'll be nice, won't it?'

XII

MARC VANDOOSLER HAD FINISHED HIS HOUSEWORK FOR MADAME MALLET RATHER late, and the others had already started their supper when he arrived in the refectory. It was the godfather's turn to cook and he had made a gratin dauphinois. It was one of his specialities.

'Eat up, it's getting cold,' said Vandoosler senior. 'By the way, the German came round at lunchtime and pinched some of your clothes. I thought you ought to know.'

'Yeah, I know,' Marc said, 'we met in the street.'

He helped himself to food.

'It was for hiding someone the cops are after,' he said.

'Typical Kehlweiler,' said his uncle grumpily. 'So what did he do, this guy?'

Marc looked round at Mathias, Lucien and his godfather, who were all stuffing themselves with gratin dauphinois and didn't know.

'Not a lot,' he said gloomily. 'He's just the maniac who stabbed those two women in Paris, the scissors killer.'

Three heads jerked up together. Lucien snorted. Mathias said nothing.

'And I have to tell you,' Marc went on, in the same gloomy tones, 'that he's coming to stay the night here. He's been invited.'

'You're kidding, aren't you?' said Vandoosler senior with a laugh.

'I'll fill you in, in just a minute.'

Marc got up to check that the three windows in the large room were shut.

'Crisis meeting of general staff,' muttered Lucien.

'Oh, shut up,' said Mathias.

'The scissors killer,' Marc said, sitting down again, 'the guy the newspapers are all talking about, has taken refuge with our dear old Marthe, who used to look after him when he was a poor little street kid. And Marthe is hanging on to her toy doll like a lioness, and swears black and blue that he's innocent. She's asked Louis to take charge. But if Louis gives the doll up to the cops, they'll take Marthe as well. Old story, baby and bathwater, work it out for yourselves. And Louis is going to bring this guy round here tonight, because he's afraid he might attack Marthe, whereas here there aren't any women, not one, no thanks to anyone, by the way. Just four solitary, virile men on whom Louis is counting. We have to watch him day and night. That's all.'

'General mobilisation,' commented Lucien, taking some more from the dish. 'Have to see the troops are properly fed first.'

'Maybe this seems like a joke to you,' said Marc sharply, looking at him, 'but if you'd seen poor old Marthe's face, she's aged ten years, and if you saw this guy's face, he looks like he's not all there, and if you'd seen photos of the two women who've been murdered, you wouldn't make jokes about it.'

'I know – do you think I'm stupid?'

'I'm sorry. I've been cleaning all Madame Mallet's windows and I'm worn out. Now I've given you the lowdown, I'm having a pause, I'm having something to eat, and I'll go into detail over coffee.'

Marc didn't often drink coffee because it made him jittery and everyone agreed he didn't need that, because he already looked as if he drank ten coffees a day. In another register, coffee did nothing to reduce Lucien Devernois's non-stop talking, but since Lucien enjoyed making a noise, he wouldn't have missed his shot of caffeine for anything. As for Mathias Delamarre, whose calm demeanour sometimes took the form of an impressive mutism, his large frame was immune to this kind of detail. So the godfather filled three cups, while Marc tried to unfold his ironing board. Mathias gave him a hand. Marc plugged in the iron, pulled over a large laundry basket full of clothes and conscientiously put a T-shirt on the board.

'Cotton-viscose mix,' he remarked. 'Low heat.'

Then he nodded, as if to convince himself of this principle, which was something of a novelty for him, before he explained the details of the case of Marthe's 'doll'. From time to time, he paused to spray the linen with a vaporiser, since he had declared he couldn't handle a steam iron. Mathias considered Marc was making a good fist of it. For the past three weeks, since he had been bringing ironing home, it had become fairly usual for the four men to linger downstairs around the steaming linen, as Marc attacked his pile of laundry. He had made his calculations. If he did four hours' housework a day, plus two hours of ironing at home, he could make seven thousand francs a month. That allowed him time to work on his medieval history research in the mornings, and for the time being, Marc was managing to calculate the rents of thirteenth-century landlords before midday, and devote the afternoon to the vacuum cleaner. It had been one night, as he had watched Lucien polish their refectory table with a soft cloth and had heard him expound on his love of polishing things, that Marc Vandoosler, who knew nothing at all about housework, had decided to become a professional cleaner, after twelve years being an unemployed medieval historian. He had asked Marthe to give him a basic skills course, and within a fortnight he had four employers lined up.

Lucien, who was a born pessimist, had viewed with anxiety his friend's change of professional tack. It wasn't so much that the Middle Ages were going to lose a good researcher that bothered him. (Lucien, being a contemporary historian who specialised on the 1914 War, had no time at all for the Middle Ages). No, it was because he feared Marc wouldn't be able to take to his new career and would come a cropper in the gap between the idea and its execution. But on the contrary, Marc had persisted, and by now it was clear he even took a genuine interest in comparing household products, for instance cleaner-plus-polish versus straightforward cleaning fluid – he said the former created a build-up.

Marc had finished giving the details of their exchanges with Marthe and her murderer, and the other lodgers, each in his own way, were now feeling the strain at the thought of having to shelter and guard this man.

'Where'll we put him?' asked Mathias, the practical one.

'There,' said Mark, pointing to the small lobby off the refectory. 'Where do you think?'

'We could put him outside in the toolshed,' suggested Lucien, 'if we bolt the door. It's not cold.'

'Yeah, right,' said Marc, 'and that way everyone in the street would see us coming and going, taking him stuff to eat, and the cops would be round in a couple of days. And what about the toilet? You volunteering to empty a slop bucket?'

'No,' said Lucien. 'It's just that I'm not keen to have this psychopath here at all. We're not used to having to doss down with murderers.'

'You really don't get it, do you?' said Marc, raising his voice. 'This is all about Marthe. Do you want to see her go to jail?'

'The iron!' shouted Mathias.

Marc gave a cry and picked up the iron.

'See what you nearly made me do, you numbskull. Nearly burnt Madame Toussaint's skirt. I already told you that Marthe totally believes Clément's story, she is convinced he's innocent, and we have no choice but to believe what Marthe believes, until we can get her to believe what we believe.'

'Clear as mud,' sighed Lucien.

'So, to sum up,' said Marc, unplugging the iron. 'We put him up in this little downstairs room. The shutters can be closed from the out-side. For tonight's shift on guard, I'm proposing Mathias.'

'Why Mathias?' asked the godfather.

'Because I'm worn out, Lucien is hostile to the entire operation, so he's not reliable, and Mathias is solid, trustworthy and brave. The only one of us who's all those things. So it would be best in the first place if he's there to face up to whatever happens. Tomorrow we'll start taking turns.'

'You didn't ask me for my opinion,' commented Mathias, 'but that's OK, I'll sleep by the fire. If he –'

Marc held up a warning hand.

'Here they are,' he said. 'They're at the gate. Lucien, those scissors hanging up there, take them down, hide them away somewhere, no point leaving temptation around.'

'But they're my scissors for chopping up chives,' cried Lucien, 'they're fine where they are.'

'Just take them down!' shouted Marc.

'I hope you realise,' said Lucien, slowly unhooking the scissors, 'that you are a compulsive coward, Marc, and you'd have been worse than useless in the trenches. As I have several times observed to you.'

With a face like fury, the younger Vandoosler advanced on Lucien and grabbed him by the shirt.

'Just get it into your head, once and for all,' he snarled through gritted teeth, 'that in the days of your fucking trench warfare, I would have got myself a cushy number behind the lines, writing poetry, with four women sharing my bed. And as for your scissors for chives, I do not want to see them stabbing some girl in the stomach tonight. That's all.'

'All right, all right,' said Lucien, stretching out his arms. 'If you're going to take it like that . . .'

He opened the sideboard and dropped the scissors on a pile of tea towels.

'Troops are edgy tonight,' he murmured. 'Must be the heat.'

Vandoosler senior opened the door to Kehlweiler, accompanying Marthe's protégé.

'Come in,' he said to Louis. 'They're shouting at each other tonight. The arrival of the young man is rocking the boat a bit.'

Vauquer came in with his head lowered, and at first no one took the trouble to greet him or introduce themselves. Louis made him sit at the table, guiding him with a hand at his back, and Vandoosler went to warm up some coffee.

Marc was the only one who moved towards Clément, with an interested look on his face, and ran his hand several times over his now short dark hair.

'That's good,' he said, 'very good, the way Marthe's done it. Show me the back.'

The young man bent his head forward, then up again.

'Perfect,' Marc pronounced. 'And she's given you a bit of make-up too. That's good. Really fine piece of work.'

'Just as well,' said Louis. 'If you'd seen their identikit portrait . . .'

'Looks like him?'

'Very. Until he's grown his beard for ten days, the kid had better not leave here. And we should find him some glasses.'

'I have some,' said Vandoosler senior. 'Sunglasses, quite big, it's summer so that would fit, and it won't harm his eyes.'

They waited in silence for the older man to climb up to his fourth floor. Clément Vauquer stirred his coffee noisily, but said not a word. Marc sensed that he was close to tears, that he was afraid at finding himself without Marthe, and surrounded by strangers.

The godfather brought in the glasses, and Marc carefully manoeuvred them on to Clément's nose.

'Open your eyes,' he said. 'They're not slipping?'

'Slipping?' asked Clément hesitatingly.

'The glasses.'

He shook his head. He looked exhausted.

'Drink up your coffee and I'll show you your room,' Marc went on.

And he drew Clément by the arm towards the little room, closing the door behind them.

'Here we are. This is where you'll live for now. Don't try to open the shutters, they're barred from the outside. We don't want people to see you. And don't try to run away either. Do you want something to read?'

'No.'

'Would you like a radio?'

'No.'

'OK, go to sleep then.'

'I'll try.'

'Listen,' said Marc, dropping his voice.

But as Clément wasn't listening, Marc grabbed his shoulder.

'Listen!' he repeated.

This time he got Clément to look him in the eye.

'Marthe will come to see you tomorrow. I promise. Now you'll be able to sleep, won't you?'

'Personally?'

Marc wasn't sure if the question referred to Marthe or to getting to sleep.

'Yes, personally,' he said firmly, hoping for the best.

Clément seemed comforted, and curled up on the little bed. Marc went back into the large room, troubled. He really didn't know what to make of this man in the end. Automatically, he headed for his own room to find him some shorts and a T-shirt to sleep in. When he opened the door to give them to him, Clément was already fast asleep, fully dressed. Marc dropped the clothes on the chair and closed the door gently.

'Right,' he said, sitting down at the big table. 'He's asleep. Personally.'

'Apparently it's my fault he's so tired, I've worn him out with my questions,' commented Louis. 'Marthe accuses me of scrubbing out his brain with soap. I'll have to start again tomorrow.'

'What more do you hope to find out?' asked Marc. 'We've been round the houses with him.

'Not if Marthe's right.'

Marc stood up, plugged his iron in again, and picked a flowered dress out of the basket.

'What do you mean?' he asked, as he smoothed out the garment on the ironing board.

'If Marthe is right, and Clément is being used as a scapegoat, he was chosen very carefully. Chosen because he's simple-minded, no doubt about it, but not only for that. Because you can find plenty of simple-minded people right here in Paris, and it's going to a lot of trouble, isn't it, to search him out in Nevers and then pay for his hotel room. That sort of complication only makes sense if the killer wanted *Clément* and nobody else – out of all the simple-minded guys in the country. It means this Other Person is making use of his handicap, but he's also working out some sort of personal vendetta. He must know Clément Vauquer and hate him. All this is if Marthe is right, of course.'

'Talking of Marthe, she must come and see him tomorrow.'

'That's not wise,' said Louis.

'I promised him, and we'll have to live with it. Otherwise he'll get out, one way or another. He won't be able to stand it.'

'*He* won't be able to stand it?' exclaimed Louis. 'Shit, he's nearly thirty years old, he's not a baby.'

'I'm telling you, he won't be able to stand it.'

'What about the girls he killed, or well, might have, he was able to stand that all right, wasn't he, our little doll?'

'You've just been saying, this very minute,' said Marc, folding the dress, 'that we are starting from where Marthe is, and the idea she's got fixed in her head. At least for twenty-four hours, at least so that we can ask him some questions along those lines. And you can't even hold to the plan for two minutes.'

'You're right,' said Louis, giving in. 'We should hold the line for twenty-four hours. I'll be back tomorrow around two.'

'Not before?'

'No, in the morning I want to go round to the police station in the 9th, and see those photos again. Who's on guard tonight?'

'Me,' said Mathias.

'Excellent choice,' approved Louis. 'See you tomorrow.'

'I'll come out with you,' said Marc.

'Tell me,' said Louis, hesitating. 'I see you're ironing a dress. Is there a woman in the house?'

'Would that be so odd?' asked Lucien stiffly.

'No, no,' Louis said quickly. 'It's just, you know, him, Vauquer . . .'

'I thought we were presuming he was innocent,' said Lucien. 'So, no worries, OK?'

XIII

ONCE OUTSIDE, THE TWO MEN WALKED UP THE STREET IN SILENCE.

'So,' asked Louis, 'is it yes or no?'

'It's no,' Marc replied brusquely. 'There isn't a woman in the house, not the shadow of a woman, it's the Sahara Desert if you must know. Doesn't entitle you to spit on the sand, though.'

'And the dresses?'

'Madame Toussaint's laundry. I do ironing at home, like I told you.'

'Ah yes, your work.'

'Exactly, my work. Does that bother you?'

'What's the matter with you at the moment?' asked Louis, stopping short. 'You spend your whole time yelling.'

'If you're talking about the dosshouse, it's normal, we yell all the time. Lucien loves it. And it provokes Mathias out of his calm a bit, so everyone benefits, and it distracts us from our worries, our money problems, and the fact that we have these dresses about the place with no women inside them.'

Louis nodded.

'Anyway,' Marc went on, 'do you think there's a hope in hell that Marthe's doll is *not* involved?'

'I'd put it higher than that. Hang on a minute, while I go over to the drinking fountain, won't be a tick. I must just get Bufo wet.'

Marc stiffened.

'You've got your toad there?' he said in a panicky voice.

'Yes. I had to go and get him just now. He was bored stiff sitting in my pencil basket, hardly surprising if you think about it. I have to give him some air. I'm not asking you to hold him.'

Marc, hostile and disgusted, watched as Louis sprinkled water on his large grey toad, made a few soothing remarks to it, and stuffed it back in his capacious right-hand pocket.

'Yuk!' was his only comment.

'Want to get a beer?'

The two men sat down in a near-deserted cafe. Marc took care to sit on Louis's left because of the toad. It was half past eleven at night, but the air wasn't cold.

'I *do* think,' Louis began, 'that Marthe's doll is genuinely simple-minded.'

'My thoughts too,' said Marc, raising a hand to call the waiter's attention.

'And in that case, he wouldn't be capable of inventing this story about the restaurant owner, even to save his own skin.'

'Yeah, right. The guy must exist.'

'What guy?'

'Well,' said Marc, still waving his hand in the air, 'the one who's manipulating the doll. The Other. The killer. He must exist.'

'Your arm isn't working,' Louis observed.

'I know,' said Marc, letting it fall. 'Never have any luck getting waiters to see me.'

'Lack of natural authority,' suggested Louis, raising his arm in turn.

He immediately ordered two beers from the waiter and turned back to Marc.

'See if I care,' said Marc. 'I'm not impressed. We were saying, this guy must exist ...'

'Probably. We can't be sure. But if he does exist, we know a couple of things about him. He knows Clément Vauquer, he hates his guts, and he's not a serial killer.'

'I still don't get the last bit.'

Louis pulled a face and drank some beer.

'Because this guy counts. He *counts* things. The first woman, the second, the third. Remember what Vauquer said. On the phone, the guy talked like that: "The first girl", "the second girl". He counts and if you count, you know where you want to end up, with a total. Or else there's no point counting. Someone who sets out on an indefinite massacre doesn't bother counting. You don't count to infinity – why bother? I think the killer has given himself a fixed number of women to kill and that his list has an end. He's not a serial killer, he's the killer of a *series*. Do you see the difference? The killer of a series.'

'Ye-es,' said Marc without conviction. 'You're giving a lot of importance to details.'

'Figures are never details. Plus a serial killer would never have hired the services of a scapegoat. Let's assume the man who did this wanted to use Vauquer for a limited number of victims. Vauquer is the fall guy for a well-planned operation, but not for an endless killing spree. If there is some individual behind this, he's as dangerous as can be, and perfectly in control of his system. He *chose* the fall guy, he *chose* the women. And not by chance, certainly not by chance. If this series has any value to him, it must have a meaning. To him, that is.'

'What kind of value?'

'Symbolic value, or representative. He may be setting out to kill seven women to represent all the women in the world for instance. So you understand, those seven women can't be chosen by chance, they have to make up a set, have a meaning, fit into a pattern.'

Louis tapped his fingers on his glass of beer.

'I *think* that's how it works,' he went on, 'and if you think about it, you'll see, it's really a simple and commonplace mechanism. But in any case, better be on your guard. We absolutely have to keep Clément under lock and key, *especially* if he's innocent. And then if there is a third murder, we'll know it's not our simple-minded boy who did it. That would be solid evidence.'

'Do you really think there'll be a third murder?'

'Yes I do, *mon vieux*. The Other is just at the start. Our problem is we don't know how many names are on his list, or its meaning.'

Louis went home on foot, chatting to his toad.

XIV

BY ELEVEN NEXT MORNING, KEHLWEILER WAS ARRIVING AT THE POLICE STATION in the 9th arrondissement. On his way, he had bought that day's papers and offered up a prayer that the three evangelists, as Vandoosler senior insisted on calling them, had kept close guard. The identikit of the supposed murderer was all over the front pages, and its likeness to Clément leapt out at him.

Anxious and treading heavily, Louis walked into the station. This time, he was kept waiting. Loisel was no doubt not too pleased to see him come back so soon, asking about the same affair. Louis Kehlweiler had the not very reassuring reputation of a well-trained ferret, determined to explore all the rabbit holes he could find. Because of the unpleasant fallout that might result from looking into things too closely, people didn't much like finding him sniffing around a case without being asked. Perhaps Loisel was already regretting having been so open and frank the day before. After all, Kehlweiler wasn't working at the Ministry any more. Kehlweiler was nobody now.

Louis was thinking of possible ways of keeping his hand in when Loisel opened his door and beckoned him forward.

'Ah, it's the German again. So there's something on your mind?'

'Just a detail I'd like to check, and an idea I'd like to share with you. After which, I'll be off to ask questions in the 19th arrondissement.'

'Don't bother,' said Loisel with a smirk. 'I've been put in charge of both inquiries now. I'm the overall coordinator.'

'Excellent news! So I'm glad I was able to be of service.'

'Meaning what?'

'It was bothering me that the other case was being handled by your colleague,' said Louis evasively. 'So last night, I allowed myself to make one or two discreet calls to the Ministry, mentioning your name. Glad it worked out.'

Loisel stood up and shook Louis's hand.

'Don't mention it, *mon vieux*. And not a word to anyone, you'd blow my contacts.'

Loisel made a silent sign of understanding, and sat back down looking pleased. Louis felt no shame. Telling lies to the police was routine, for him as well as for them. And all this was on Marthe's behalf.

'What was it you wanted to check, my German friend?' asked Loisel, now once more the friendly cooperative man of the day before.

'The photographs of the crime scene and the victims, with a close-up on the upper part of the body, please.'

Loisel trudged over to the filing cabinet with his usual slouching gait, his feet slapping on the lino. The noisy footsteps returned and Loisel put the photos on the desk. Louis looked at them carefully, with a concentrated expression.

'There,' he said, pointing to the right of the head. 'On the carpet, do you see something?'

'Yes, some blood. I know about that anyway, because this is the victim on my patch.'

'This is a shagpile carpet, isn't it?'

'Yes, it was some kind of goatskin.'

'Don't you think that there, near the head, there are signs of fingers pulling the strands of the carpet in all directions?'

Loisel frowned and went over to the window, photo in hand.

'You mean the carpet seems to be tangled?'

'Yes, that's it, as if it had been interfered with?'

'Well, possibly, but a carpet like that, a long-haired goat rug, it's going to look untidy whatever. I don't see what you're getting at.'

'Now look at the other photo,' said Louis, coming over to join him at the window. 'The first murder. Look at the same place, near her left ear.'

'It's an ordinary fitted carpet, what do you want me to see?'

'Traces of scratching or rubbing, as if the guy had dragged his hand along the carpet in just the same place.'

Loisel shook his head.

'No, *mon vieux*, frankly, I can't see anything.'

'OK. Maybe I'm seeing things.'

Louis put his jacket on, picked up his newspapers and headed for the door.

'Tell me, before I go, Loisel, what are you waiting for now? A third murder?'

Loisel nodded.

'Certainly, unless we catch this guy first.'

'Why certainly?'

'Because he's got no reason to stop, that's why. With sex maniacs, once they get started, you can't stop 'em. Where? When? We haven't any leads. Our only chance of saving the third woman, is *that*,' he said, pointing to the identikit in the paper. 'Two million people in Paris, surely there's one who can tell us where he is. With his loony-looking face, he's hardly likely to go unnoticed. Even if he dyes his hair red, he'd still be recognisable. But it would surprise me if he thinks of that.'

'Yes,' said Louis, glad that he had advised against red. 'And what if he goes into hiding when he sees the paper?'

'If he's hiding, there will always be people somewhere around. Though I can't imagine who'd be perverse enough to help shelter a bastard like that.'

'Yeah, right.'

'Apart from his mother, of course,' sighed Loisel. 'Mothers aren't like other people.'

'No, right.'

'But his mother must have been pretty weird herself, if he's ended up doing this. Well, I'm not going to shed tears over him, am I? That's all we need. With any luck, he'll be right here in this office tonight. So for the third victim, I'm not too worried, you see. OK, goodbye and thanks again for . . .'

Loisel made a sign indicating a telephone call.

'Think nothing of it,' said Louis gravely.

In the street, Louis breathed deeply. He imagined for a few minutes that Loisel might be having him followed, and that he could unsuspectingly have limped straight over to the dosshouse in the rue Chasle. He imagined the meeting between Loisel and Vauquer under the roof of an ex-cop and three rather dodgy evangelists, and thought that this would not be a very smart career move. Although, as he suddenly recollected, his official career had ended. He checked that none of Loisel's men appeared to be tailing him. Only once in his life had he ever been taken in by someone on his tracks.

He thought about the photographs again, as he made his way slowly to the bus stop. This was not the moment to waste time by crossing Paris on foot, and his knee was hurting. He had indeed seen some traces of something on the carpet alongside the heads of the victims. But what? It was scarcely visible in the first case, much clearer in the second. Had the murderer been searching for something near the victims' heads?

On the bus, reading their newspapers, the passengers were all looking at Clément Vauquer's face, searching their memories. Well, they would have a job to sniff him out in the little room in the evangelists' house. For the moment, only six people knew his name. No, eight, because of the two prostitutes in the rue Delambre. Louis gritted his teeth.

XV

LEANING AGAINST THE WALL OF HER BUILDING IN THE RUE DELAMBRE, GISÈLE scanned the newspaper, her heavy eyebrows knitted in consternation.

'Hellfire!' she muttered. ''I'm not dreaming things. It *is* him. I'm sorry, but it *is* him.'

Gisèle staggered back on her high heels at the shock. She needed time to think. Marthe's little street kid hadn't been wasting time. It certainly made you wonder.

A client was approaching, with careful steps. She recognised him, someone she saw about once a month. As he drew closer, she shook her head.

'Not that I can afford to put anyone off,' she said, 'but I just can't see you now. You'll have to come back another time.'

'Why? Are you waiting for someone else?'

'I can't, I tell you,' said Gisèle more loudly.

'Why can't you?'

'Because I need to think,' Gisèle shouted.

Instead of responding, the man, surprisingly, went away at once. Funny thing, Gisèle reflected. Men don't like women who think. And they're not wrong, because when I'm thinking, don't come round bothering me.

Lina, the younger woman, having heard Gisèle cry out, had come to the end of the street.

'You having any trouble, Gisèle?'

'No, nothing serious. Kind of you, but if I need you, I'll call.'

'Gisèle, um, there is something. I've been thinking about it since this morning.'

'Well, don't think too much, it puts the punters off.'

'You seen a paper today?'

'The paper? Yeah, seen it. And?'

'That guy they're looking for, about those two girls got killed. Did you look?'

'Yeah.'

'And it didn't remind of you anyone?'

'Nope,' said Gisèle confidently.

'Gisèle, you *must* remember . . . it's the same guy from the other day, the accordionist who was looking for Marthe. I could swear it's him.'

'Don't swear. Not a good idea.'

Gisèle unfolded her paper again with impatient gestures and looked at the identikit portrait.

'No, no, Lina, that's not him. Sorry, but it's not him at all. This one looks a bit funny, give you that, but otherwise, no. Sorry, that's not him.'

Worried by Gisèle's confidence, Lina looked at the picture again. She wasn't crazy, no. It was the same guy, it was. Yes, but Gisèle was always right, and Gisèle had taught her all she knew.

'Well,' said Gisèle, 'you going to stand here all night looking at this picture?'

'But what if it is him, Gisèle?'

'It's not him, get that into your head,' she said, wagging her finger, 'and there's an end to it. Because that boy we saw the other day, he's like a son to Marthe, and you can't think that a son of Marthe's, Marthe who's a fixture round here, that *any* son of hers is going to go slashing girls, not after the education he got from her. Right?'

'Right,' said Lina.

'So you see, you're barking up the wrong tree.'

As Lina remained silent, Gisèle started again, in a more serious voice.

'Lina, you're not thinking of reporting an innocent guy to the cops, are you?'

Lina looked at her anxiously.

'Because if so, your beat, after that you can kiss it goodbye. But if you want to throw it all away, because you can't tell a duck from a chicken, it's your choice, you're a big girl.'

'Yeah, I see, Gisèle. But can you swear to me it's not the same guy?'

'I never swear.'

'But it's not him?'

'No, it is not him. And give me your paper, then you won't go getting any more barmy ideas.'

Gisèle watched as Lina walked away. The girl wouldn't talk. But then, with young people, could you be sure? She'd better keep a close eye on her.

XVI

AS HE HURRIED TOWARDS THE HOUSE IN THE RUE CHASLE, LOUIS WONDERED whether there was by chance any of the previous night's gratin dauphinois left over. Vandoosler gave the impression of knowing what he was doing in the kitchen, and it was years since Louis had eaten this favourite dish of his. Because it's the kind of food you only make if there are several people to eat it. When you live alone, you can't expect to eat a collective dish.

True, the three men who shared their lodgings with the old uncle Vandoosler, all of them nearing forty, were not what you might call shining examples of existential achievement. This had often made him smile. But perhaps he was wrong in the end. Because his own life as an investigator, now reduced to being a solitary translator of books about Bismarck and tidying his shoe cupboard, was not exactly a model either. At least they could share their rent, and they each had one floor of the house, they weren't lonely, and in the evening they got to eat gratin dauphinois. Not so stupid, when you thought about it. And no one had said it would last forever. Louis tended to think that the first one to leave the house because of a woman would be Mathias. But then it could be the old man, equally well.

It was past one when he knocked at their door. Lucien ushered him in hurriedly. It had been his turn for guard duty, and he was hastening to finish the washing-up before going out to give a lecture.

'Has everyone eaten already?' Louis asked.

'I have to lecture at two, we always eat early when I have afternoon classes.'

'Is Marc in?'

'I'll call him.'

Lucien picked up a broom and knocked twice on the ceiling.

'What are you doing?' asked Louis, rather taken aback.

'It's our system of internal communication. One knock for Mathias, two for Marc, three for me, four for the old man, and seven is general mobilisation if we're required for front-line action. We can't keep running up and down the stairs all day long.'

'Ah,' said Louis, 'I didn't know about it.'

At the same time, he examined the ceiling, where a whole stretch of the plaster was marked with little dents.

'Yeah, it does damage the decor a bit,' Lucien remarked. 'No system's perfect.'

'And Vauquer, how's that going? No problems?'

'No, nothing to report. You saw the picture in the paper? Scarily like him, wouldn't you say? We had him eat with us at lunchtime with the shutters closed. In this heat, it won't look so odd to the neighbours. Now he's resting. His personal siesta, he called it.'

'Weird how much that guy can sleep.'

'In my opinion, he's stressed,' said Lucien, taking off his apron.

They heard Marc coming down the stairs.

'I'll leave you,' said Lucien, knotting his tie. 'I'm off to teach the young about the major cataclysms of the twentieth century. So much dust in the brain of a child,' he muttered.

He hurried out of the room, greeting Marc as he went.

Louis sat down shaking his head. In this house, he lost his bearings about what constituted normality.

'He's asleep,' said Marc in a low voice, pointing to the door of the lobby.

'Yes, I know,' said Louis, whispering in turn. 'You haven't got any left from last night, have you?'

'Any of what?' asked Marc in surprise.

'Of the gratin.'

'Ah, the supper dish. Yes, quite a bit – would you like me to warm it up for you?'

'Yes please,' said Louis with a sigh of contentment.

'Coffee with it? I'm going to have some.'

'Yes please,' Louis repeated.

He looked around. It was true that the big room with its three tall round-arched windows had something of the feeling of a monastery. Even more so today, with the gloom of drawn shutters and their whispered conversation.

'Right, it's warming up,' said Marc. 'Have you seen the papers?'

'Yes.'

'Poor old Marthe will be worrying her head off about her doll. I'll go and fetch her when I've finished my cleaning job. We can bring the accordion over too.'

'He mustn't play it here, Marc.'

'No, I know. It's just for his morale.'

'Wake him up, we don't have time to lose.'

Marc tiptoed into the little room, but Clément wasn't asleep. Lying on the bed, arms stretched wide, he was looking at the closed window.

'Can you come out here?' said Marc. 'We need to talk some more.'

Clément sat down opposite Louis, his legs tucked under his chair with his feet twisted round the bars. Marc served them coffee and passed a plate of gratin to Louis.

'This time, Clément,' Louis began, 'you need to help us. With this,' he said, pointing to his forehead. 'Did you see the picture they've made of you in the papers? All Paris is looking for you. Except for six people: one who loves you and another five who are trying to believe you. Do you understand what I'm saying?'

Clément nodded.

'If you *don't* understand something I say, Clément, just let me know. Don't worry, there's nothing to be ashamed of, as Marthe would tell you. The earth is full of very clever people who are also total bastards. So if you don't understand, put your hand up like this.'

Clément nodded and Louis took advantage of the pause to eat a forkful of gratin.

'Listen,' said Louis with his mouth full, 'there is (a) this man who hired you to do some work. But (b) this was a big machinery.'

'Machination,' said Clément.

'Machination,' Louis repeated, thinking that Clément learned quicker than he had expected. 'And (c) it could be you that gets accused, instead of this man. This man, he's the one on the telephone in Nevers, and the same one who phoned you at the hotel. Think. Did you recognise his voice?'

Clément pressed his nose with his finger, and lowered his head. Louis went on eating.

'No, not so to speak personally.'

'Was it the voice of a stranger then?'

'I don't know. I didn't recognise it myself, but if it was a stranger, that I don't know.'

'OK, let's drop that. Now (c) . . .'

'You've already done (c),' Marc whispered, 'you're going to confuse him.'

'Shit,' said Louis. 'Right (d). It's possible that this person is acquainted with you, but they've taken a mortal dislike to you.'

Clément hesitated, then raised his hand.

'(d),' Louis went on patiently, 'it's possible this guy is doing all this on purpose to hurt you because he hates you.'

'Yes,' said Clément. 'I understand.'

'So (e), who might there be who hates you?'

'Nobody,' said Clément at once, pressing his nose again. 'I thought about it all night, all by myself.'

'Ah, you thought about it?'

'I thought about the voice on the telephone and who would want to hurt me.'

'But you say there's nobody who has a grudge against you?

Clément's hand went up.

'I mean nobody who hates you.'

'No. Or . . . well, apart from my father.'

Louis stood up and went to rinse his plate in the sink.

'Your father? That's not such a bad idea. So where's your father?'

'He's been dead for years.'

'Right,' said Louis, sitting back down. 'What about your mother?'

'She's in Spain, she's abroad.'

'Did your father tell you that?'

'Yes, she left us when I was just born. But she loves me, she's not like my father. She's in Spain. The voice on the phone, though, that was a man.'

'Yes. I know that, Clément.'

Discouraged, Louis glanced at Marc.

'Let's try something else,' he suggested. 'Tell me where you've been living since you left Marthe in Paris when you were thirteen.'

'My father sent me to special school, in Nevers.'

'No problems with the school?'

'No, no problem. I didn't go to it much.'

'Do you remember what the school's name was?' asked Louis, taking out a pen.

'Yes, the Nevers School.'

'Oh, all right. Was it there you learned to play the accordion?'

'No, after that. I was sixteen years old, personally when I left the school.'

'And you went where?'

'I went to work being a gardener, in the Institut Merlin, five years I was there.'

'And that's in Nevers too?'

'Outside Nevers.'

'The Institut Merlin you say? An institute. What kind of institute?'

Clément raised his arms indicating ignorance.

'For lessons,' he said. 'An institute for lessons for grown-ups, not children. And it's got a big park round it, and I was personally second gardener there.'

'And no problems there either?'

'No, no problems.'

'Think carefully. Were the people nice to you?'

'Yeah, nice.'

'No fights?'

Clément shook his head slowly.

'No,' he said. 'I hate fights, me personally. I was happy there, very happy. Monsieur Henri, he taught me to play the accordion.'

'Who was that . . .?'

'He was a teacher, he taught . . .' Here Clément pressed his nose again. '. . . economics,' he said. 'And I went to lessons too, when it was raining.'

'What kind of lessons?'

'All sorts. They had lessons all the time. I went in through the back door.'

Clément looked intently at Louis.

'I couldn't understand all the big words,' he said.

'But there, you didn't have any enemies?'

'No, no, not at all.'

'And after the institute?'

'It wasn't the same. I asked round the other gardens in Nevers but they all had their gardeners. So I played the accordion. That's what I've been doing now, since I was twenty-one.'

'In the street?'

'Anywhere people give me money. They know me personally round Nevers. I play in cafes, or people hire me on Saturdays. I have money for my room and everything that a person needs to live.'

'Any fights?'

'No, no fights. I don't like fights, I never fight, me myself. I live peacefully and my accordion too. It's OK. But I preferred being a gardener at Merlin.'

'So why did you leave there?'

'Oh, well, because of the rape, this girl, in the grounds.'

Louis gave a start.

'A *rape*? You raped a girl?'

'No. Not me.'

'There was a fight?'

'No, not a fight, not even a fight. I got the hose of cold water, and I sprayed it all over those men, like for dogs, to separate them. I separated them all right. The water was freezing cold.'

'Are you sure that's what you did?'

'Yes, of course, they were horrid men, they were raping this girl, and the other ones holding her down. I did it with my hose, the garden hose. Cold water.'

'So tell me, the men after that, they were . . . er . . . happy about it?'

'No, course not! Freezing cold water, and they didn't have trousers on, it went on their legs and their bums. It's very cold, you know, water like that on your skin. That got them jumping off the girl. There was one who wanted to kill me. Two even.'

There was a heavy silence, which Louis prolonged as he scratched his head. A ray of sunshine shone through the shutters on to the wooden table. Louis ran his finger along it. Marc looked at him. He was tight-lipped, his features were drawn, but his green eyes were clear and focused. Marc knew, as Louis did, that they had just reached land. Perhaps just a muddy estuary with waves lapping at the edge, but the land was in sight. Even Clément seemed to realise that something had happened. He looked at them in turn and suddenly yawned.

'You're not tired, are you?' asked Louis anxiously, getting out his pen and notebook.

'No, it's OK,' Clément replied gravely, as if girding up his loins for a forced march of twenty kilometres before nightfall.

'Well now, you're going to have to last out, personally,' said Louis in the same manner.

'Yes,' said Clément, sitting up straight.

XVII

CLÉMENT SPOKE FOR OVER AN HOUR, SOMETIMES WITH COMPARATIVE FLUENCY. He had already had to repeat his story more than once to the police at the time, and entire blocks of ready-made sentences had stuck in his memory, which made it easier. Sometimes the dialogue juddered, like a car stalling on the road, either because Louis didn't understand what Clément was saying or because Clément put his hand up to tell Louis he had got lost. So the conversation sometimes went backwards, as each of them picked up equally patiently on points that had been missed. The reconstitution of the story was a long business, but in the end Louis, by then handling it alone, since Marc had had to leave for work, felt he had a clear enough idea of what had happened, although there were some blanks in it that Clément couldn't fill in. Louis was still without certain simple elements such as dates, places and names.

Louis looked at his notes.

He couldn't work out quite when this had happened: sometime between April and June, but it was certainly a warm month, just before Clément was asked to leave the Institut Merlin. So it must have been in spring, about eight years ago. Clément had been sleeping with his window open in his room over the garage, when he heard cries, coming from some distance away in the grounds. He had jumped up and run towards the cries, which were becoming all but inaudible, and found three men attacking a woman. Two of them were holding her down, and the third was on top of her. It was a clear night, but the men were hooded. As for the woman, he recognised her, she was a teacher at the institute. Clément couldn't remember her name. He thought at once of water, and ran to the hydrant for this section of the grounds. By the time he had grabbed the hose and run back, he thought a different man was now lying on top of the woman. He had switched on the tap full force, and directed it at the three men. The water was freezing cold, as Clément insisted many times, and he had also explained gloatingly that his hosepipe had a very powerful jet, intended for the lawns in the institute's grounds, which would really hurt if it hit you at short range The effect on these men who were half undressed was spectacular. They had abandoned the woman, who had immediately crawled into a corner and curled up in a ball. They were shouting and swearing, as they tried to pull up their sodden trousers. Clément pointed out to Louis that it is difficult to pull on tight trousers that are dripping with water. Clément had hosed them down furiously. One of the men had advanced towards him, snarling with anger, and said he was going to beat him up and kill him, but Clément had directed the jet straight at his hooded jacket, forcing it off, and this man, clinging on to his trousers at half mast, had struggled to run away after the others, while turning round and hurling threats at him. Then Clément had turned off the hose and gone over to the woman, who was lying on the floor groaning, and 'all dirty', as Clément put it. She had been beaten, her head was bleeding and she was shivering. He had taken off his T-shirt to cover her up, but had no idea what to do next. That was the point when he had panicked. Turning the hose on those three bastards had been the easy bit. But faced with the woman, he was at a total loss. Then at that moment, the director of the institute – Clément knew *his* name all right, it was Merlin, like the institute – had come running along. When he arrived, seeing Clément alone with the injured woman, he had thought at first that it was Clément who had raped her, and that was what the police had thought too, since Clément was the only witness. Squelching across the muddy grass, the director had lifted up the young woman and told Clément to help him carry her to his private house. Without making a noise, as he did not want a crowd of students to come running. From there, they had phoned the police and an ambulance, which had taken the young woman to hospital. The cops had then carted Clément off, and it was two hours before they let him go home. He was forbidden to leave the town.

But – and at this point, Clément became very distressed – the woman had died in the night, in hospital. And in the morning, one of the institute's students was found drowned in the Loire. They had called Clément in again for questioning. Yes, it was the one whose hoodie he had managed to get off. At the time, he had known this student's name very well, a big guy who was always harassing him, Hervé something Pousselet, Rousselet, something like that. The cops had concluded that this Hervé, realising he'd been recognised, had managed to murder the victim in the hospital, meaning to come for Clément afterwards, but finally had been unable to go through with it and had thrown himself into the river.

After that, Merlin, the institute's director, had told Clément it would be best for the institute if the whole drama was forgotten, and that he would be well advised to find another job. He had written him a long reference, saying that he was a good gardener.

'I was unhappy when I left,' Clément said. 'So was the director. We got on all right.'

'What about the other two rapists? Did you have any idea about their identity?'

Clément put his hand up.

'Did you know who they were?'

'I couldn't recognise them, because of the hoods. The smallest one, the one who escaped first, because he had his trousers on . . .'

Clément shook his head slowly.

'I have no idea personally,' he said regretfully. 'He was old though, old, at least fifty.'

'So he'd be about sixty now,' said Louis, still taking notes. 'What makes you think he was old?'

'His shirt. It was an old man's shirt, with a vest underneath.'

'How did you know he had a vest on, if it was the middle of the night?'

'With the water,' said Clément, looking at Louis as if he thought he was stupid. 'It makes it so you can see through.'

'Oh, OK, sorry. And the other one?'

'The other one had his pants down,' said Clément with a malicious smile. 'I hated him. And under his hood, when I was spraying water straight at his belly, he shouted something like: "You'll spray later, just you see." I didn't understand.'

'Perhaps he meant "You'll pay later".'

'What would I have to pay?'

'No, it means he had it in for you.'

Clément raised his hand again.

'It means he knew who you were, and he hated you.'

'I hated him too!'

'So you knew who he was, even with the hood?'

'Oh yes, I knew him all right,' Clément said viciously. 'He had his usual dirty old shirt, and it was his voice, his nasty, shitty voice.'

At that moment, Clément's ill-favoured little face, leaning towards Louis was distorted with disgust. It made him look less prepossessing than ever. Louis started back a little. Clément grabbed hold of his shoulder.

'The other man was the Secateur,' he said.

Clément stood up and put both hands flat on the table.

'The Secateur,' he said. 'And *nobody* believed me, myself. They said there was no eminence.'

'Evidence,' said Louis.

'And they didn't do anything, after all the branches he cut, and the woman . . .'

Louis had stood up in turn and was trying to calm Clément down. His skin had turned a blotchy red. In the end, Louis managed to force him to sit down which wasn't very difficult, and held him against the back of the chair.

'So who is this man?' asked Louis firmly.

The commanding voice and the two hands on his shoulders seemed to settle Clément. He moved his jaw wordlessly.

'The head gardener,' he said, 'the tree monster. Maurice and me, we called him the Secateur.'

'Who's Maurice?'

'The other boy with me, he worked in the greenhouses.'

'A friend?'

'Yes, of course.'

'And what did this Secateur do then?'

'He did this,' said Clément, escaping from Louis's grasp and standing up.

With the fingers of his right hand, he imitated a cutting movement, and clicked his tongue: 'Tsk, tsk, tsk.'

'He was cutting plants with his secateurs,' said Louis.

'Yes,' said Clément, pacing round the table, 'he was all the time with this big cutter thing. Tsk, tsk, tsk. That was all he liked doing, in his life. Tsk, tsk. If there wasn't a plant to cut, he did it just in the air, he cut the air. Tsk, tsk.'

Clément stood quite still, holding out his hand and looked at Louis, screwing up his unreadable eyes.

'Maurice and me, we found tree trunks all chopped about with his secateurs. That wasn't good for the trees. Tsk, tsk. He was spoiling them. Apple trees, little ones, he tore the bark off them.'

'Are you quite sure about this?' Louis asked, stopping Clément as he began to walk round the table again.

'He had these secateurs. Tsk, tsk. And he always had them in his personal hand. But I didn't have any eminence about the trees, or about the woman. But the voice, when he yelled at me, yeah, I'm sure it was him.'

Louis thought for a bit and started to pace around the table himself.

'Have you seen him since then?'

'No, personally, not.'

'Would you recognise him?'

'Yeah, yes, sure.'

'You say you recognised his voice. And what about the voice on the phone, in Nevers, the call from Paris. Could that be his voice?'

Clément stopped and pressed the side of his nose.

'Come on, you've got ears, and you know what his voice is like. So was it him on the phone?'

'The telephone makes it all different,' said Clément sulkily. 'The voice isn't in the air, it's in plastic. You can't tell who it is.'

'But *could* it have been him?'

'I dunno. I wasn't thinking about him when the telephone voice was talking, I was thinking about this man with the restaurant.'

'And anyway, it was eight years or so since you'd heard him, I suppose. Do you know his proper name, this Secateur?'

'No-o, I've forgotten.'

Louis sighed, with some exasperation. Apart from the name of the director and one of the rapists, the one who had died, Clément couldn't seem to recall any proper names. But still, to be fair, he had provided a whole story, quite a coherent one, dating back several years. It shouldn't be too hard to reconstruct it, if Clément was telling the truth, as Louis now believed.

He folded away his notes carefully, putting them in his pocket. He tried to imagine what it would feel like for a brutal rapist to find himself drenched in icy water from a powerful hose. Pain, humiliation, fury. His virility destroyed by being soaked: he'd have no reason to be well disposed to his opponent. In such a man's mind, even if he was not entirely primitive, hate and a desire for vengeance might last a long time. It had been years since Louis had come across a motive so unsuitable, but at the same time so compelling.

He turned his head and smiled at Clément.

'You can go and have a rest now if you want.'

'I'm not tired,' Clément said unexpectedly.

Louis realised, as he was on the point of leaving, that in Marc's absence there was nobody left to act as Clément's guard. And while they were still not sure about anything, they couldn't take the least risk of him running away. He thought of going upstairs to see if Vandoosler senior was there, but did not dare leave Clément alone for three minutes. His gaze fell on the broomstick that Lucien had left leaning against the wall after calling Marc. He hesitated. Using this method seemed to him somehow contagious, as if he were giving up a section of his mental integrity. But in this house there wasn't much choice.

Louis seized the broom and banged four times on the ceiling, then he listened carefully and heard a door bang. The old cop was coming down. You couldn't argue with that, the system did work.

Louis stopped Vandoosler on the stairs.

'Can I leave you in charge of Clément till the others get back?'

'Of course. Are you getting anywhere?'

'Possibly. Tell Marc that tomorrow I'm going to Nevers. I'll call tomorrow evening. Can I still get a phone message to you from the cafe on the corner?'

'Yes, till 11 p.m.'

Louis checked that he had the number and shook hands with the former policeman.

'Till tomorrow. Keep an eye on him.'

XVIII

LOUIS WAS UP EARLY (FOR HIM) AT SEVEN O'CLOCK, AND BY HALF PAST TEN HIS car was reaching the outskirts of Nevers, in Burgundy. The light was beautiful and the weather warm, and he felt a certain lightening of the spirit as he drove past the sign telling him he was entering the Nièvre département. Years before, he had undertaken several missions in the region and it was a pleasure to see the Loire again, which surprised him. He had forgotten the irregular shimmer of islands in midstream, and the flocks of birds flying over the surface, but it all came back in a second. The water was low and the sandbanks were exposed. Even in this summer season, he knew the river could be dangerous. Every year, swimmers were sucked into its whirlpools, thinking they could swim across with a few dozen strokes.

Driving slowly, as was his habit, and with the river to his right, Louis considered the rapist who had drowned himself the day after the crime. Yes, it was perfectly possible to drown yourself in the Loire, even when the river was running low. But it was equally possible to drown someone else. Clément had not expressed any doubt about the official version of the deaths of the young woman and her attacker, though perhaps he wasn't capable of doing so. But that might not be the only way to read what had happened. Louis had told Marc the previous evening the whole ghastly story of the gang rape, and Marc had seemed impressed by the character described as 'the Secateur'. Truth to tell, so had Louis.

In Nevers, he had to find his way to the police headquarters. He parked in the town centre, made a pit stop in a cafe for a drink and visit to the toilets, and adjusted his tie, looking in the mirror over the bar, before confronting the cops. Something Kehlweiler was proud of was that after twenty-five years of investigations of all kinds, he knew one policeman in every city, as sailors are supposed to have a girl in every port. In fact, there were some exceptions to the rule, especially since his early retirement. He couldn't keep up these days with all the transfers, departures and promotions, and his system was no longer a hundred per cent reliable. But it was still more or less working. He took out an index card from his pocket, on which he had noted down the names of the cops in Nevers. He didn't know the police chief, but he had once worked on a delicate case with Inspector Jacques Pouchet, who was now a captain. Louis turned the card over. At the time, he hadn't made very extensive notes. All he had was *Jacques Pouchet, inspector, Nevers, soft right in politics – good professional results – likes me well enough, is a bit wary, but didn't obstruct me – owes me a beer on account of a bet on the colour of the Nièvre breed of chickens.* A bet is a useful way in, it means you're the kind of person who remembers meeting someone, it can prompt friendly contact and might be effective.

Louis pocketed the card, wondering what on earth he had made up about the Nièvre chickens, since he knew not the first thing about them. He crossed over towards the station.

Pouchet was in his office, he was told. Louis showed his ID, and scribbled a friendly note which he gave the secretary, and waited. Pouchet received him three minutes later.

'Ah, so it's the German. Haven't seen you in years,' he said, opening his door. 'And what brings you here? Not going to stir it up for us, are you?' he added, with a touch of apprehension.

'Don't worry,' said Louis, who was always rather pleased to see that his reputation still preceded him. 'I'm not on Ministry business. This is a cold case, no politics involved.'

'That's OK then,' said Pouchet, offering him a cigarette. 'On the level?'

'Absolutely. It's about a gang rape that happened some years ago at the Institut Merlin –'

'Oh, is that all?' Pouchet interrupted him.

'I'd say it was quite enough to be going on with.'

'I remember it well. Hang about, I'll be back.'

Louis sat smoking as he waited. Pouchet was clearly relieved that Kelhweiler wasn't there for any more worrying purpose, so he would show him the file without any anxiety.

'You want the whole story?' asked Pouchet, as he returned with a file under his arm.

'Could we go to a cafe perhaps?' asked Louis. 'You owe me a beer. We had a bet on the colour of chickens from the Nièvre, and you lost.'

Pouchet gave him a worried look, then burst out laughing.

'Yes, of course, my German friend, you're absolutely right!'

So it was an affable inspector that Louis took to the cafe at the end of the street. The mention of chickens had put Pouchet in a good mood, but Louis wondered whether in the end he really remembered the bet as well as all that, since he hadn't mentioned any colour, any more than he had himself.

Louis went to the cafe toilet, checked no one else was around and brought his toad out of his pocket. He sprinkled him with water from the washbasin and popped him back *in situ*. With this heat, you couldn't be too careful.

'Well?' asked Louis, coming to sit down.

'It was a gang rape, like you said, and it took place inside the grounds of the Institut Merlin . . .'

'What sort of institute would that be?'

'It was a kind of private school, a crammer, teaching business studies and economics. Two years post-baccalaureate studies, with a diploma of business accountancy at the end of it. Fee-paying of course, and high fees too. Good reputation, old established school, it used to do well.'

'Used to?'

'Ah well, after the rape business, and the two deaths, as you can imagine, things went belly up. It couldn't open the next autumn, not enough enrolments. It simply went bust. Must be about six years ago, Merlin decided to sell the property to the town council. It's a retirement home now. High fees still.'

'Oh, blast it! So all the staff will have dispersed, teachers, other people . . . and there's no way of getting in touch with any of them?'

'If you were expecting to be able to see them all together today, no, no way.'

'Right, I see,' said Louis, frustrated. 'Still, tell me the story. I've heard one version and I need to know if it's right.'

'Well, there was this young teacher of English, name of Nicole Verdot. She lived in during the week, like some of the other staff and all the pupils. The boarding system was thought more effective in terms of results, it seems. What would you think about that?'

'I wouldn't know,' said Louis, who didn't want to say anything that might disturb his fragile entente with this policeman.

'One thing about it is the kids didn't hang about in the streets after lessons, they were kept on a tight rein.'

'If being on a tight rein meant raping a woman after lessons, I don't see the advantage.'

'You could be right, it hadn't struck me. Anyway, what was she doing outside, the young teacher, at nearly midnight? We never discovered that. Going for a walk, meeting someone? It was a warm night, this was in May, the night of the 9th . . . and then . . .'

Pouchet raised his hands and let them fall heavily on the Formica tabletop.

'... And then these three men fell on her like mad dogs. The youngest gardener turned up, but a bit too late, unfortunately. It's a funny thing, this guy thought of something pretty clever, he fixed up a hosepipe and sprayed them with water. That's how he got them to run away, by turning the hose on them.'

'Why did you say "it's a funny thing"?'

'Oh, because this gardener, we had to question him for a long time, since he was the only witness, well, he didn't have too much up here, if you see what I mean,' said Pouchet, tapping his forehead. 'Very odd-looking he was. Christ, it was hard getting him to answer questions. But his story checked out, from start to finish: we found footprints of the three men in the muddy grass, and also the gardener's, and we found one hoodie jacket on the ground, the famous hoodie he managed to get off.'

'And he recognised the men?'

'Just the one, Hervé Rousselet, a student who was repeating the first year, aged twenty, a rich kid, but a real tearaway. He'd been getting into trouble in Nevers all his teens. The gardener *claimed* to have recognised one of the others, his boss, the head gardener. But there I think he was having us on, because he wanted to get his boss in trouble, he seemed to hate him, called him "the Secateur". We called that guy in too and interrogated him, but we got nowhere. The young woman had also recognised just one of the attackers. She kept repeating "I saw him, I saw him", but she couldn't get the name, poor woman, she was in such deep shock. They sedated her in the hospital and then ...'

Once more, Pouchet let his hands fall on to the table in despair.

'... then the student guy killed her in the night. To stop her talking of course.'

'She wasn't under guard?'

'Yes she was, *mon vieux*, what do you think? The murderer got in through the window, first floor, but the duty constable was outside in the corridor. Between ourselves, we really fucked up. You're not going to tell anyone about that, are you?'

'No. How was she killed?'

'Suffocated with the pillow, and then strangled for good measure.'

'Jesus,' said Louis.

'But this Rousselet character, it didn't help him for long. He drowned himself in the Loire. He was found the next day. And that tied it all up. Sad, a really sad case. As for the other guys, never managed to lay hands on them.'

Pouchet observed Louis.

'Are you on their track by any chance?'

'Could be.'

'Well, I'd be pleased if you got lucky. Need anything else?'

'Tell me about the young gardener.'

'What can I say? Clément Vauquer, I've got his name here, and like I said, the boy didn't seem very bright. Felt sorry for him, but he was a bit odd. Brave though, because he tried to help the woman, one against three men who might have gone for him. I can think of plenty of people who'd have run away. But no, he didn't run. Brave, yeah, I have to say. But all it brought *him*, was he ended up on the street without a job.'

'Do you know what became of him?'

'I think he used to busk in the cafes round here, A l'Oeil du Lynx for instance. I could find out if you like.'

Louis made a mental note that the Nevers cops had evidently not made any connection between their local accordionist and the identikit picture published the previous day. That wouldn't last. Sooner or later, someone in Nevers would identify him. It was a matter of hours, as Loisel might say.

'And the Secateur? Did he stick around too?'

'Never saw him again. But I didn't bother to look. Do you want his real name?'

Louis nodded and Pouchet consulted the file.

'Thévenin, Jean Thévenin, forty-seven at the time. You ought to go and ask Merlin, the ex-director. He might have kept him on for a bit, to look after the gardens until it was sold.'

'Do you know where I'd find him?'

'I think he left the area. But I could find that out back at the office – my secretary knows one of the ex-teachers.'

Pouchet paid for the beers with a wink, because of the bet.

The secretary told Louis that Paul Merlin had indeed left the area. He had stayed for a while in Nevers after the sale, then taken an administrative post in Paris.

Pouchet took Louis off to have lunch with a couple of colleagues. Louis took Bufo into the toilets again to sprinkle him. He was concerned about the drive back in the heat. But Marc would never have agreed to look after the toad, of course. Marc was looking after Marthe's doll, which was already asking a lot of him. Louis was also feeling worried about their protégé. He wondered how much longer they would be able to conceal him from the manhunt under way across the whole country. And how long it would take him to decide whether Clément was a dangerous madman or a brave boy, as Pouchet had said. Well, at any rate the story about the rape in the gardens was true, Clément hadn't been inventing anything. So there were at least two men out there who had cause to detest him, two rapists. One of them was no doubt this Jean Thévenin, aka the Secateur. Louis thought once more about the wounds inflicted on the two women in Paris and shuddered. He hated this image of the secateurs. As for the other one, the third man, nobody knew anything about him.

Louis took his leave of the Nevers police rather late in the afternoon. The most delicate task was yet to complete. He put a hand on Pouchet's shoulder and the captain looked at him in astonishment.

'Just suppose,' said Louis quietly, 'that you were to hear something about that young gardener before very long.'

'The one with the hosepipe? I'm going to hear something about him?'

'Yes, Pouchet, just suppose, and mixed up in something very bad.'

Pouchet looked baffled and made to speak but Louis stopped him with a gesture.

'And suppose that the Paris police and I don't see things the same way, and suppose for a moment that I'm the one who's right. And that I need some time, say a few days. Then suppose you're in a position to give me those few days, by forgetting you've seen me. Not an action, just a simple omission, of no consequence.'

Pouchet stared hard at Louis, looking undecided and anxious.

'And suppose,' said the captain, 'that I want to know why I should do that?'

'Fair enough. Let's suppose that young Vauquer, the one who acted well on that occasion, deserves a chance, and that you're prepared to trust me on that? And suppose that I don't want to make trouble for you.'

Pouchet rubbed his lips with his thumb, perplexed, then held out his hand without looking Louis in the eye.

'Suppose I agree,' he said.

The two men walked in silence to the door. Louis held out his hand again.

'What would be good,' said Pouchet unexpectedly, 'would be to have another bet. That way we can think about a future beer.'

'Any ideas?' Louis asked.

'Look,' said Pouchet, pointing to a poster for an agricultural show pinned up in the restaurant window. 'I've always wondered: is a mule a cross between a female donkey and a male horse, or a mare and a male donkey?'

'Is there a difference?'

'Yes, apparently, but what it is I have no idea, I promise. So which one will you bet on, Kehlweiler?'

'Female donkey, male horse.'

'OK, I'll take the mare and donkey. First one to find out the truth calls the other.'

The two men bade farewell once more and Louis returned to his car.

Seated at the wheel, he took out his card and added under Pouchet's name: *Good man, better than good. Judged him a bit hastily last time. Got file on rape of Nicole Verdot – prepared to cover for me. Second bet on origin of mule – I've said female donkey male horse. Winner pays for beer.*

Then he took a rag out of the glove compartment, dampened it with water from the gutter, placed Bufo on the passenger seat and covered him with the rag. Now his amphibian would not bother him.

'See, Bufo,' he said to the toad as he started the engine, 'there are two guys out there somewhere who have no fine feelings. Neither one of them would think of putting a nice cool cloth on your head.'

Louis pulled away from the kerb slowly.

'And you know what I'm going to do, old man? I'm going to get my hands on those two guys.'

XIX

LOUIS OVERSLEPT AND WOKE UP DRENCHED IN SWEAT. THE PARIS HEAT WAS stronger than ever. While he filtered his morning coffee, he called the cafe in the rue Chasle, whose name, oddly enough, was the Ane Rouge, the Red Donkey. It reminded Louis of the bet he had agreed the previous day with Jacques Pouchet, and he wondered how he was going to discover the truth about the mule, a matter to which he was actually profoundly indifferent. But this was no ordinary bet, it had a secret lining. Under cover of the bet, their agreement and Pouchet's silence were crucial. If Loisel found out that Louis knew the identity of the identikit man, Clément Vauquer would be blown out of the water.

The cafe owner told him to hold on, while she fetched Vandoosler senior to the phone. The ex-cop spent hours playing cards in the back room with his local cronies from the quarter, and also with a woman for whom he apparently had a weakness. Idly picking up his dictionary while he waited, without much hope, Louis looked up 'mule' and at once found that it was a 'cross between a jackass and a mare'. For the ignorant, a statement in brackets explained that 'the cross between a stallion and a jenny-ass is known as a hinny'. In his surprise, Louis put the phone down on the desk. It felt odd to be discovering something that everyone else in the world apparently knew. Except Pouchet, who was as ignorant as himself, which did not console him. If this was what he had come to, perhaps he would find other big gaps in his knowledge, the real meaning of words like chair or bottle for instance which he might have been using wrongly for fifty years. Louis felt for the card on which he had written down the bet. He could no longer remember which combination he had chosen.

Female horse and male donkey, right. That produced a hinny. Shit. He poured himself a large cup of coffee and then heard a squawking noise from the telephone.

'So sorry,' he said to Vandoosler, 'I had a reproductive problem this end. Can you please answer me with monosyllables? How did last night go? . . . And Vauquer? . . . Good. And Marthe has seen him? And she was happy? . . . Good, thank you. Nothing more in the papers? . . . Good. Tell Marc the story about the rape is quite true . . . Yes, not now. I'm going to look for the director of the institute.'

Louis hung up, put the dictionary away and called Nevers police headquarters. Pouchet wasn't there, and his secretary took the call. 'Tell him,' Louis said, 'that we should still go on supposing I'm right, except about the mule, where I'm wrong, and that I therefore owe him a beer.' The secretary got him to repeat the message twice, wrote it down, and hung up without comment. Louis took a shower, put Bufo in the bathroom because of the heat, and went to the local post office. He found Paul Merlin's address in the telephone directory. It was Saturday, so there was a good chance of finding him at home. Louis looked up at the big clock. Ten past twelve. Ridiculous time. He would be putting Merlin out no doubt, he'd be having lunch with the family. And his shabby clothes were not appropriate either. Merlin lived in the 7th arrondissement, rue de l'Université, the west end of Paris: obviously he must have made a packet from selling the institute, and wouldn't be living in a garret. He had better dress more respectably, in case this director was a stickler for appearances, something not uncommon among educationists.

So Louis waited until two thirty before presenting himself at 7 rue de l'Université, a bijou house of two storeys with an eighteenth-century courtyard. He checked his white shirt, lightweight summer suit and bronze tie, by glancing at the mirror in a nearby bank. His hair was a bit long, so he tucked it behind his ears. His ears were too big, but there was nothing he could do about that.

He rang the bell and got Merlin himself on the intercom. He had to spend some time negotiating into the receiver, but Louis was persuasive and Merlin finally agreed to let him in.

He had been putting away some files and looked rather out of temper as Louis appeared.

'Forgive me for troubling you like this,' said Louis affably, 'but I couldn't wait. The matter's rather urgent.'

'And it's about my institute, the one I had in Nevers?' said Merlin as they shook hands.

Louis realised with a shock that Merlin looked amazingly like his pet toad Bufo, which immediately attracted him to the man. But unlike Bufo, Merlin wore clothes, conventional, well-cared-for clothes, and didn't live in a pencil basket. His office was large and luxuriously furnished, and Louis was glad he had made an effort with his appearance. On the other hand, like Bufo, this man was an odd shape and his head drooped forward. Like Bufo, he had a dull greyish complexion, soft lips, heavy jowls and drooping eyelids, and above all that worried expression that amphibians have, as if detached from the futile business of this world.

'Yes,' Louis went on. 'It's about an incident at the institute, some years ago, on the 9th of May, a young woman –'

Merlin lifted a heavy hand.

'The disaster you mean? You know it meant the end of the institute? An establishment dating from 1864?'

'Yes, I know, the police in Nevers told me.'

'Who are you working for?' asked Merlin, giving him a suspicious look.

'The Ministry of the Interior,' said Louis, offering him one of his old business cards.

'All right, I'm listening,' said Merlin.

Louis searched for the right words. From the small courtyard came the ear-splitting sound of a plane or a chainsaw, and it seemed to trouble Merlin too.

'Apart from the student Rousselet, two other men took part in this rape. I'm looking for them. In particular, Jean Thévenin, the head gardener.'

'The one they called the Secateur, you mean? Unfortunately, the police were unable to prove he had been there at all, and he denied it.'

'Unfortunately?'

'I didn't like the man.'

'Clément Vauquer, the gardener's boy, was sure that the Secateur was one of the rapists.'

'Ah, Vauquer,' said Merlin with a sigh. 'Yes, he said that. But of course, who would believe Vauquer? He was, how shall I put it, simple-minded? No, perhaps that's a bit harsh, but limited. Very limited. Has *Vauquer* told you about all this? Have you seen him?'

Merlin's voice sounded concerned and wary. Louis stiffened.

'No, never,' he said. 'It's all from the archives at police headquarters in Nevers.'

'So, may I ask what interest you have in this ancient history? It was all a long time ago.'

The same distrust in his voice, the same concern. Louis decided to get to the point more quickly.

'I'm involved in the search for the scissors killer.'

'Ah,' Merlin said, opening his toad-mouth.

He stood up without a word, went over to the well-organised bookshelves and fetched a folder: he undid the strap and took out a newspaper cutting of the recent identikit picture resembling Vauquer, which he placed in front of Louis.

'To tell you the truth, that's why I was concerned, I thought *he* must be the Paris killer,' he said.

There was a silence during which the two men watched each other. A bird of prey doesn't necessarily win against an amphibian. The toad is good at manoeuvring backwards into his lair, leaving the kite frustrated and without its prey.

'So you recognised him from that, did you . . . Vauquer?' Louis asked.

'Well, obviously,' said Merlin, shrugging. 'He worked for me for five years.'

'And you haven't told the police?'

'No, I haven't.'

'Why not?'

'There are always plenty of people who'll do that. I'd rather it was someone else, not me, that gave him away.'

'Why?' asked Louis again.

Merlin moved his fleshy lips.

'I was fond of the kid,' he admitted, with some reluctance.

'He doesn't look very reassuring,' said Louis, staring at the newpaper cutting.

'No, that's right,' said Merlin. 'His face puts people off, he looks like he's only half there. But faces, well, what do they tell you? As I said, I liked him. Now that we both know what we're talking about, what are the police saying now? Are they sure he's the man they want?'

'Yes, certain. The evidence looks overwhelming, he won't be able to get away with it. But they haven't got a name yet.'

'But *you* know it,' said Merlin, pointing with his long finger. 'So why haven't you said anything either?'

'Someone will do it,' said Louis with a shrug. 'It's a matter of hours. They may even have got him by now.'

'But you don't think he's guilty, is that it?' asked Merlin. 'You're looking as if you have doubts.'

'I doubt everything, it's a professional reflex. I think the evidence against him is just too obvious, too overwhelming. Standing for days watching those women, in full view of everyone, leaving fingerprints. It all seems too good to be true. And as we know, when something is too good to be true, it prompts doubts.'

'I can see you don't know Vauquer, he wasn't what you might call subtle, no, a very simple man. What bothers you about it?'

'The rape at the institute. He didn't attack the girl – on the contrary, he defended her.'

'Yes, I still believe that myself.'

'So massacring women now? That doesn't fit.'

'Unless that trauma back then, and losing his job, worked on him, made him vulnerable,' said Merlin thoughtfully, looking at the picture. 'As I said, I liked the lad, and he defended the girl, as you said. On rainy days, he would take shelter in a classroom and listen to the lectures, French, economics. After five years with us, he ended up speaking a weird kind of language, half learned.'

Merlin smiled.

'He used to come into my office to clip the ivy round the window and take care of the indoor plants. When I had a bit of spare time, I would sometimes play games with him, dominoes, dice, cards, easy things – he liked that. Monsieur Henri too, the economics teacher, he spent time with him. He taught him to play the accordion by ear. And you might not believe this, but he was talented, really talented as a musician. Well, I suppose we were trying to offer him some protection.'

Merlin gestured to the paper.

'And then it all seems to have gone wrong.'

'I don't agree,' said Louis. 'I think perhaps someone else is using Vauquer, and taking revenge on him.'

'One of the rapists you mean?'

'Yes, possibly. And you might be able to help me.'

'Do you really think so? Is there a chance you're right about this?'

'More than a chance.'

After this, Merlin sat back in his armchair and said nothing for a while. The sound of the machine in the yard was still deafening to their ears. Merlin fiddled with a couple of coins in his hand, rubbing them this way and that. He moved his lips, sighed, and his eyelids drooped heavily. Louis thought he was doing more, this engaging amphibian. He was trying to overcome some kind of emotion before speaking again. Three minutes went by. Louis was content simply to stretch out his long legs under the desk and wait. Suddenly Merlin got up and went over to the window.

'Will you stop that racket!' he yelled, leaning out. 'Stop it, will you? I've got someone up here.'

Then he shut the window and remained standing.

They heard the machine whine and fall silent.

'It's my stepfather,' Merlin explained with an exasperated sigh. 'He spends all day with his wretched tools, even Sundays. In the institute, I gave him a barn for all his carpentry, and that was fine. But for the last five years, it's been hell.'

Louis nodded, understanding.

'But what can you do?' Merlin went on as if speaking to himself. 'He's my stepfather after all, I can't chuck him out on the street at seventy years old.'

Looking weary, Merlin came back to his chair and plunged into thought again for a few moments.

'I would give anything,' he then said sternly, 'to see those two men under lock and key.'

Louis waited.

'You see,' the ex-director went on, emotion cracking his voice, 'those three men ruined my life. And Vauquer almost saved me. I was in love with the woman in the case, Nicole Verdot, I wanted to marry her. I was hopeful she might agree, but I was going to wait until the summer holidays to ask her. And then this happened. A young woman and three absolute bastards. Rousselet killed himself, and I can't feel sorry about that. As for the other two, I'd give anything to catch them.'

He sat up and put his arms on the table, leaning forward.

'Well, what about the Secateur?' asked Louis. 'Any idea where he is?'

'No, alas. I sacked him too of course, after the crime. There was certainly a cloud of suspicion hanging over him, even if the police failed to find any evidence. If Vauquer was quite appealing in his way, Thévenin was the opposite. The Secateur, as the boys called him, was horrible. Filthy dirty, always eyeing up the girl students. Mind you, he wasn't the only one. People in expensive suits could be the same way. Starting with my stepfather,' and here Merlin gestured towards the window dismissively with his chin. 'He was always watching the girls too, trying to see more of them. Not threatening, you understand, but annoying and irritating. Always a problem if you have a residential institution for young people: seventy-five girls and eighty-odd boys well, believe me, you've got potential for trouble. This Thévenin, I'd hired him against my better judgement because he was recommended by a family friend. He was good at his job, produced splendid vegetables. According to Vauquer, he was also stripping bark off the trees, but I don't know if that was true.'

'And you didn't see him back at Nevers after that?'

'No, sorry, I didn't. But I might be able to help, I could ask around. Obviously I still know a lot of people in Nevers, someone might tell me.'

'Thanks, that would be helpful,' said Louis.

'But the other man, I just don't know. I suppose he could be an outsider, some acquaintance of the Secateur or Rousselet, I don't know. Only the Secateur would know for sure.'

'That's why I want to lay hands on him,' said Louis, standing up.

Merlin got up too and saw him to the door. The sound of machinery in the courtyard started up again. Merlin looked resigned, very like Bufo when there was a heatwave, as he shook hands with Louis.

'I'll make enquiries,' he said. 'And let you know. But please keep my personal story to yourself.'

Louis crossed the cobbled courtyard slowly enough to look through the window of a studio and see the man using the noisy equipment. White-haired and bare-chested, the seventy-year-old looked hale and hearty. He put down his machine to wave cheerily at Louis. Louis could see on the bench beside him a large number of wooden statues and a great deal of disorder. As he shut the door to the street, he heard a shout from the first floor, as Merlin cried: 'Give it a rest, can't you, for God's sake!'

XX

AS THE DAY ENDED, LOUIS CALLED ON MARTHE, REASSURED HER ABOUT THE well-being of her doll, and urged her once more to be careful.

Towards ten that evening, he arrived to see Clément Vauquer and told him in detail about his visit to the former director of the Institut Merlin.

'He was fond of you,' he said to Clément, who oddly enough showed no sign that evening of wanting to go to bed, and was looking rather restless.

'I liked him too,' said Clément, pressing his nose agitatedly.

'Who's on guard tonight?' Louis whispered to Marc.

'Lucien.'

'Tell him to be on the alert. Your guest seems disturbed.'

'Don't worry. How are you going to track down the Secateur?'

Louis gave a rueful grin.

'It's not going to be easy,' he muttered. 'Going through all the Thévenins in France would be too hard. I looked the name up this morning, there are lots of them. We don't have time for that. It's urgent, Marc, really urgent, you understand? Keeping Clément safe from the police, and other women safe from the killer . . . We can't hang about. I think we should try the cops. They might have a file on him. Nathan might be able to tell me.'

'What if he doesn't have a record?'

'Well, I have some hopes of Merlin, who's going to try and find out. He's really hostile to this man, so he's prepared to make an effort.'

'And if *he* doesn't find him?'

'We'll just have to try the phone book.'

'And if this Thévenin doesn't have a telephone? I'm not in the book either, and I exist.'

'Oh, give it a rest, Marc, will you? Let's imagine we've got a chance. He must be somewhere, this Secateur, so we'll find him.'

Louis ran his hand through his hair in discouragement.

'He's in Montparnasse Cemetery,' came Clément's musical voice.

Louis turned slowly to look at Clément, who was folding and unfolding a piece of silver paper.

'What did you say?' asked Louis aggressively.

'The Secateur,' said Clément, with the crooked smile he wore whenever he mentioned the man. 'He's personally in Montparnasse Cemetery, as for where he is.'

Louis caught Clément by the arm and glared fiercely at him, his green eyes like gimlets. Clément was able to stare back without apparent difficulty, and as far as Marc knew, he was the first person who had ever done this. Even he, who knew Louis well, tended to look away when Louis had this keen probing stare in his eyes.

'Did you *kill* him?' Louis asked, gripping the young man's scrawny arm.

'Kill who?'

'The Secateur.'

'No!' said Clément.

'Let me deal with this,' said Marc, elbowing Louis aside.

Marc took a chair and sat between their simple-minded protégé and Louis. This was no less than the fourth time in three days that Louis had lost his cool and Marc had found it, which was an unusual state of affairs. Vauquer certainly managed to reverse everything surrounding him.

'Tell me,' said Marc gently. 'Is the Secateur dead?'

'No – why would he be?'

'Well then, what's he doing in the cemetery?'

'He does the garden.'

Louis caught Clément's arm again, but less roughly.

'Clément, are you sure? The Secateur does the maintenance at the Montparnasse Cemetery?'

Clément raised his hand.

'I mean he's gardening? In the cemetery?' said Louis.

'Yes. What else can he do? He's a gardener.'

'How long have you known about this?'

'Always. When he left our garden in Nevers, this was nearly the same time as me, he went gardening in Nevers cemetery first, then he went to Montparnasse. The gardeners in Nevers told me about him, they said he doesn't always go home, he sleeps there – in among the graves!'

The young man twisted his lips again, whether in hate or disgust, it was hard to tell.

'The gardeners in Nevers, they know everything,' Clément concluded.

In this firm pronouncement, Louis recognised for the first time Marthe's way of speaking and thought it rather touching. Marthe had indeed left her imprint on the boy.

'So why didn't you tell me?' asked Louis, looking rather shamefaced.

'Did you ask me?'

'No,' Louis admitted.

'So that's all right then,' said Clément, in relief.

Louis went over to the kitchen sink, took a long drink of water, avoided wiping his mouth on his sleeve since he was wearing his best suit, and ran his wet hands through his hair.

'Off we go then,' he said.

'To the cemetery?' asked Marc.

'Yes. Tell Lucien to come down and take over.'

Marc banged the ceiling with the broom three times to fetch his co-lodger. Clément, who had worked out the system in the three days he had been there, watched with a smile.

'That's what I used to do for apples,' he said, looking amused. 'Made them fall down.'

'Yeah, and this is going to fall down one day,' said Marc, 'you'll see.'

A minute later, Lucien came hurrying dowstairs and into the refectory, holding a book.

'My tour of duty?' he asked.

'Yes, keep an eye on him, he was rather agitated just now.'

Lucien gave a little military salute and flicked back a long lock of hair from his forehead.

'Don't worry,' he said. 'Are you going far?'

'To the cemetery,' said Marc, putting on a black cotton jacket.

'What fun. Give Clemenceau my kind regards if you see him. On your way, soldier.'

And Lucien, without taking any more notice of them, sat down on the bench, smiled at Clément and opened his book: *1914–1918: A Culture of Heroes.*

XXI

LOUIS HAD AGREED TO TAKE A BUS TO MONTPARNASSE CEMETERY. THE TWO MEN were now walking quickly through the darkness.

'He's very odd, don't you think?' said Louis.

'He couldn't have guessed you were looking for the Secateur,' said Marc. 'You've got to try to understand him.'

'No, no, I mean your friend Lucien. He's very odd. Well, as far as I'm concerned.'

Marc stiffened. He allowed himself unlimited licence to criticise Lucien or Mathias and to yell insults at either of them, but he wouldn't have anyone else touch a hair of their heads, even Lucien's.

'He's not odd at all,' Marc snapped.

'If you say so. But I don't know how you can stand him for months on end.'

'Perfectly well,' said Marc curtly.

'OK, OK, don't blow your top, he isn't your brother, after all.'

'How do you know?'

'Marc, cool it, forget I said anything. I was just wondering if he could be counted on. It makes me a bit anxious to have him looking after Clément, he doesn't seem to have taken in the seriousness of the situation.'

'Listen,' said Marc, stopping short and staring up as Louis's tall shadow loomed over him. 'Lucien is perfectly aware of the situation, and if you want to know, he is more intelligent than you and me put together. So you needn't worry.'

'If you say so.'

Calming down, Marc was now examining the long wall bordering Montparnasse Cemetery.

'How do we get in?' asked Louis.

'Over the top.'

'You're good at climbing, Marc, but I've got this bad leg. Where can we get through?'

Marc looked around.

'There are some big dustbins over there, you could get over using them.'

'Right, good idea.'

'In fact using dustbins to climb walls is one of Lucien's ideas.'

The two men waited until a group of passers-by were out of sight, then dragged a large bin into the rue Froidevaux.

'But how will we know he's there?' asked Marc. 'The cemetery is huge. There are two sections.'

'If he's there, he'll be showing a light, I should imagine. And we'll look for that.'

'Why not wait until tomorrow?'

'Because it's urgent, because he's said to sleep here, and because it would be good if we can catch him at night, and on his own. People are more vulnerable at night.'

'Not all of them.'

'Put a sock in it, Marc.'

'All right. I'll help you up on to the bin. Then I'll get on the wall and heave you up.'

'Right, let's go.'

Marc found it hard all the same to haul Kehlweiler over. He weighed eighty-six kilos and measured one metre ninety. Rather excessive, in Marc's opinion.

'Don't have a torch, do you?' asked Louis rather breathlessly, once they were both down on the ground.

He was bothered about his best suit, afraid he might have ruined it.

'Yes, but we don't need one for now. You can see quite well, there aren't any trees here.'

'Yes, this part's the Jewish cemetery. Let's move slowly towards the trees over there.'

Marc walked along silently. Louis's presence behind him was reassuring. It wasn't so much the place that bothered him – though he wasn't wild about it – so much as the possibility of this man, 'the Secateur', lurking somewhere in the shadows with his tool. Clément had a way of talking about him that made you shudder. He felt Louis's arm grab his shoulder.

'There!' whispered Louis, over to the left.

About thirty metres ahead, a small light was flickering near a tree, and it was possible to make out a figure seated on the ground.

'You approach from the right, and I'll go this way,' Louis ordered.

Marc left him and went round the back of the trees. Half a minute later, the two men found themselves one each side of 'the Secateur'. He didn't notice them until the last moment and then gave a violent start, dropping the tin plate from which he was eating. He picked it up unsteadily, staring at the two men before him, and tried to stagger to his feet.

'No, Thévenin, stay down there,' said Louis, pressing his large hand on the man's shoulder.

'What the fuck is this about?' asked the man. They could hear his marked Nièvre accent.

'You are Thévenin, yes?'

'So what if I am?'

'And you sleep in your workplace?'

'So what if I do? Doesn't hurt anyone.'

Louis switched on the torch, and ran the beam across the man's face.

'What the fuck are you up to?' yelled Thévenin.

'Just want to see what you look like.'

He looked at the man closely, then pulled a face.

'We're going to have a little chat,' he said.

'No, we're not. I don't know you.'

'Never mind. We're here on behalf of someone else.'

'Oh yeah?'

'Yes. And if you won't talk today, you will tomorrow. Or later. Doesn't matter, this person's not in a hurry.'

'Who's that, then?' asked Thévenin in a whining and suspicious voice.

'The woman you raped in Nevers with your two pals, Nicole Verdot.'

Thévenin made to stand up and Louis pushed him down again.

'Just keep still,' he said calmly.

'It was nothing to do with me.'

'Yes it was.'

'I wasn't even there.'

'Yes you were.'

'For Christ's sake,' Thévenin shouted. 'Are you crazy or what? Are you from her family? I tell you I never touched that girl.'

'Yes you did. You were recognised, I could even tell you what you were wearing, and your voice was recognised, same whiny voice as today.'

'Who's been feeding you all this shit?' cried Thévenin, gaining in confidence. 'Oh, I get it! It was the *kid*. I bet it was the kid! The village idiot!'

Thévenin burst out laughing, and picked up the bottle he had rested against the tree trunk. He took a long gulp of wine.

'It's him, isn't it?' he went on, waving the bottle under Louis's nose. 'That halfwit? Know how much you can trust *him*, do you, your witness?'

He laughed again, pulled over an old rucksack and rummaged inside it feverishly.

'There he is!' he cried, shaking a newspaper under their eyes, with the identikit picture showing. 'That's him! A murderer! That's your so-called witness!'

'I know about all that,' said Louis. 'Can I look inside here?' he asked, grabbing the bag.

'What the fuck . . . !' said Thévenin.

'We're getting tired of hearing "what the fuck" from you, Thévenin. Marc, can you shine the torch here?'

Louis emptied out the contents of the bag on to the gravel: cigarettes, a comb, a dirty T-shirt, two tins of food, a sausage, a knife, three porn magazines, two sets of keys, a quarter baguette, a corkscrew and a cloth cap. It was all rather smelly.

'And the secateurs,' asked Louis. 'Lost them, have you?'

Thévenin shrugged.

'Don't have 'em no more.'

'But you were attached to them, didn't budge without them. They called you "the Secateur".'

'That was the village idiot used to call me that. Half-witted imbecile. Couldn't tell the difference between a dahlia and a pumpkin.'

Louis conscientiously returned the dirty objects to the bag. He didn't like searching through other people's belongings, whoever they were. Thévenin took another swig from the bottle. Before he put the porn magazines back, Louis leafed quickly through them.

'Like those, do you?' laughed Thévenin.

'No, just checking if you'd cut them up.'

'Why would I do that?'

'Stand up. You've got a toolshed here, haven't you? Show us where it is.'

'Why should I?'

'Because you don't have any choice. Because of the woman in Nevers.'

'Fuck it, haven't I *told* you? I never laid a finger on her.'

'Come along. And Marc, can you hang on to him?'

'Wait, my wine!' cried Thévenin.

'You'll get back to it. Come on.'

Thévenin led them unsteadily to the other end of the cemetery.

'I can't see why you like it so much here at night,' said Louis.

'It's quiet.'

'Open up,' Louis said as they came face-to-face with a small wooden cabin.

Thévenin, with Marc gripping one arm, unlocked the door, and Louis shone the torch into the cramped interior where some basic gardening implements were stored. He spent about ten minutes carefully searching the cabin, glancing from time to time at Thévenin, who would break out laughing.

'Now take us to the main gate and let us out,' he said, closing the door.

'If I feel like.'

'Yes, if you feel like, but you will. Hurry up.'

At the gates, Louis turned to Thévenin and took a firm hold of the front of his shirt.

'Now then, Secateur, stop laughing and listen carefully. I'll be back, you can count on it. Don't try to get away from here, that would be a serious mistake. And don't you dare lay a finger on any woman, you hear? One false move, one victim, and believe me, you'll end up with your companions here in the ground. I won't let you get away with anything, wherever you go. So just remember that.'

Louis took Marc's arm and closed the gate behind them.

When they were back on the boulevard Raspail, feeling almost astonished to be in the city lights, Marc asked, 'Why didn't you push him further while you had the chance?'

'What chance? No secateurs in his bag or in the shed, no scissors anywhere, no sharp instruments. And the magazines were undamaged.'

'What about his home, wherever he lives, why didn't you ask him to take us there?'

'How could I, Marc? The guy was drunk, but he's not stupid. He'd be perfectly capable of going to the cops and lodging a complaint. And from the Secateur to Clément is one step, and from us to Clément just one too. If the Secateur goes moaning to the cops, and tells his story, they'll be round picking up Vauquer at your place next day. We haven't got much room to maneouvre.'

'How would the Secateur be able to say it was you? He doesn't even know your name.'

'No, he doesn't. But *Loisel* knows very well that this case is interesting me, and he'll work it out. And he'd think I'd gone a bit too far without telling him. The problem is that we're not just dealing with idiots here.'

'Yeah, I see what you mean,' said Marc. 'We're cornered.'

'Well, up to a point. There are ways through, but we have to be very careful. What I hope is I've put the wind up him for a bit. And I won't let go of him.'

'You really believe that? I wouldn't think any threat would stop a killer like the one we're after.'

'I just don't know, Marc. There aren't any buses now, let's get a taxi, I'm worn out.'

Marc stopped a cab.

'Want to come and have a beer back at the house?' he asked. 'It might do you good.'

Louis hesitated, then opted for the beer.

XXII

THE LIGHTS WERE STILL ON IN THE REFECTORY IN THE HOUSE IN THE RUE CHASLE. Louis glanced at his watch: 1 a.m.

'Your Lucien's working late then,' he said, pushing the gate open.

'Yes,' said Marc levelly. 'He works very hard.'

'How do you organise it to keep watch over Clément at night?'

'We slide the bench in front of his door, and sleep on it with cushions. Not very comfortable. But it means he can't come out without our knowing. Mathias actually sleeps *under* the bench, with no cushions, but then Mathias is a bit special.'

Louis didn't dare comment. He had blotted his copybook enough already by making remarks about Lucien.

Lucien was still sitting at the table. He wasn't working. Head on his arms, he was fast asleep, leaning on *1914–1918: A Culture of Heroes*. Marc went quietly over to open the door to Clément's little room. He looked in, then wheeled round to stare at Louis.

'What?' asked Louis, suddenly alarmed.

Marc shook his head slowly, open-mouthed, unable to speak. Louis rushed to the door.

'Gone!' said Marc.

The two men stared at each other, stunned. Marc had tears in his eyes. He fell on Lucien and shook him violently.

'Marthe's doll!' he cried. 'What have you done with him, you bloody idiot?'

Lucien woke up, his forehead furrowed.

'With who?' he said hoarsely.

'Clément of course!' said Marc, still shaking him. 'Where is he, for God's sake?'

'Ah, Clément. Don't worry, he just went out.'

'Out! Out where?'

'Just for a little walk. He couldn't stand being locked up all the time, poor kid. Normal.'

'But how could he go for "a little walk"?' Marc cried, falling on Lucien again.

Lucien looked at Marc quite calmly.

'Marc, my friend,' he said steadily, sniffing, 'he went because I granted him permission.'

Lucien looked at his watch.

'I gave him an exit leave of two hours. He'll be back soon. In forty-five minutes to be precise. Let me get you a beer.'

Lucien went to look in the fridge and brought back three beers. Louis had sat down on the bench, looking massive and threatening.

'Lucien,' he said in a neutral voice, 'did you do this on purpose?'

'Yes.'

'You did this on purpose to get up my nose?'

Lucien met Louis's gaze.

'Maybe,' he said. 'But mainly so that he could get some fresh air. There's no risk, his beard is growing, he's got short dark hair, he's got glasses on, he's wearing some of Marc's clothes. What's the problem?'

'So he can get some fresh air, you say?'

'Yes, absolutely, fresh air,' said Lucien, without dropping his gaze. 'For him to walk about, feel free. Three days now, you've kept that guy shut up inside four walls, with the shutters closed, treating him like some poor sap who won't even notice what's happening, as if he has no feelings at all. You get him up, you tell him, "eat this, Clément", you ask him questions, "answer me please, Clément", and when *you've* had enough, you shove him back into his bedroom, "OK now, Clément, leave us in peace, go to sleep!" So what did I do? What did I do?' he repeated, leaning across towards Louis.

'You made a fucking big mistake,' said Louis.

As if he hadn't heard, Lucien went on: 'I gave him his little wings, a scrap of human dignity, that's what I did.'

'And I hope you know where his little wings have taken him.'

'Straight to jail!' cried Marc, turning on Lucien. 'You've sent him straight to jail.'

'No, I haven't,' said Lucien. 'Nobody's going to recognise him. He looks like a cool dude from round Les Halles, the way he's dressed now.'

'What if someone *does* recognise him, you moron?'

'There is no true liberty without risk,' said Lucien casually. 'As a historian you ought to know that.'

'And what if he *loses* his liberty, you fool?'

Lucien looked in turn at Marc and Louis, and put a beer in front of each of them.

'He will not lose his liberty,' he said, enunciating each word clearly. 'If the cops catch him, they will have to let him go. Because he isn't the killer.'

'Oh really,' said Marc. 'And the cops know that, do they? That's new.'

'It is new, yes,' said Lucien, opening his beer sharply. 'But the cops don't know that yet, I'm the only one who knows.'

'But I'm prepared to share it with you,' he added, after a short silence.

Then he smiled.

Louis opened his beer and took a few mouthfuls, without taking his eyes off Lucien.

'This had better be good,' he said unbendingly.

'That's not the point. The point is whether it's *true*. Isn't that right, Marc? And it is true.'

Lucien left the table and went to sit on a small three-legged stool near the fireplace. He did not look at Louis.

'The first murder,' he began, 'took place in the 19th arrondissement, in the Square d'Aquitaine. The second was in the rue de la Tour-des-Dames in a completely different district, the 9th. And the third murder, unless we can prevent it, will take place in the rue de l'Étoile, which is in the 17th.'

Louis blinked. He failed to understand.

'Or possibly,' Lucien went on, 'in the rue Berger. But I favour the rue de l'Étoile, the street of the Star, it's just a short street. If the cops want to get somewhere, they could call on all the young women living alone in that street, to warn them to be on the alert and not open their door to anyone. But,' he said, glancing at Marc and Louis, 'I doubt the police will listen to what I'm saying.'

'Have you gone completely nuts?' asked Louis through his teeth.

'Aquitaine? La Tour? The *Tower*? Remind you of anything?' asked Lucien, and repeated the words again. 'Don't these names mean anything to you?'

'Ye-es,' said Marc hesitantly.

'Aha,' said Lucien hopefully. 'What?

'A poem.'

'Which one?'

'That one by Nerval.'

Lucien jumped up and took a book from the sideboard. He turned to a page with the corner turned down, and read out loud, stressing certain words:

Je suis le Ténébreux, – le Veuf, – l'Inconsolé,
*Le prince d'**Aquitaine à la Tour** abolie:*
*Ma seule **Étoile** est morte, – et mon luth constellé*
*Porte le **Soleil noir** de la Mélancolie.*

I am the Dark One, – the Widower, – the Unconsoled,
*The prince of **Aquitaine** whose **Tower** is ruined:*
*My only **Star** is dead, – and my constellated lute*
*Bears the **Black Sun** of Melancholy.*

Lucien put the book down, with flushed cheeks and a few drops of sweat appeared on his brow: Marc knew this for a sign he was getting carried away. He was on his guard because, while Lucien's flights of fancy were sometimes catastrophic, there was always the possibility that they were strokes of pure genius.

'The killer is following the poem, line by line,' Lucien said, banging his fist on the table. 'It can't just be a coincidence that the street names Aquitaine and La Tour were chosen. Impossible. It's got to be the poem! A love poem, one of the most famous poems in the French language, a cryptic poem about myths and fantasies, a mad poem. And to someone who has got hold of it, a deluded path to crime.'

Lucien broke off, relaxed his fist and drank some beer.

'And tonight,' he said, breathing out hard, 'I tested Clément: I read him that verse. And I promise you he had never heard it before in his life. Clément isn't the killer. And that's why I let him go out.'

'Oh, for God's sake!' said Louis, standing up abruptly. White with fury, he made for the door, but turned towards Lucien.

'Lucien,' he said in a shaky voice, 'if you had ever learned anything apart from your fucking Great War and your fucking poetry, you'd know that nobody kills someone because of some words in a *poem*. Nobody goes round killing women to decorate lines of verse, like hanging glass balls on a Christmas tree. Nobody! No one has ever done it and never will. And that's not a theory, that's reality. That's life, and that's what murder is like. Real murders. Not ones you've made up in your fancy-schmancy brain, like the intellectual wanker you are. The ones we're dealing with are real murders, not some elaborate game. So let me tell you this, Lucien Devernois, if your miserable, fucking, intellectual fantasies have sent little Clément to jail for life, I will personally make you eat a copy of your book every Saturday at one in the morning, to remember this moment.'

And he went out, slamming the door.

In the street, he forced himself to take a few deep breaths. He could have strangled Lucien for inventing this learned nonsense. Nerval indeed! A poem! Gritting his teeth, Louis walked down the rue Chasle to the little wall where Vandoosler senior liked to sit when there was a bit of sunshine. He sat down and waited for Clément's supposed return. If Clément respected the two hours furlough granted by the idiot Lucien, he should be back in about a quarter of an hour.

Louis counted off the minutes of this anxious quarter-hour. It was at this point that he understood how important were the slender hopes they had given old Marthe, and how much he wanted to be able to return her doll to her safe from the police. Gripping his thighs, he looked up and down the street. And precisely fifteen minutes later, he saw the slight, furtive figure of the obedient Clément come trotting along. Louis sat back in the shadows. When the young man went past him, his heart was pounding, as if for a lover. Nobody was following him. Louis watched as he entered the house and closed the front door. Safe.

He plunged his face into his hands in sudden relief.

XXIII

LOUIS COLLAPSED ON TO HIS BED AT 2.30 A.M., DRENCHED IN SWEAT, AND DECIDED he wouldn't get up in the morning. It was Sunday anyway.

He woke at ten minutes to midday, feeling better disposed towards life. He reached out his arm to the radio to listen to the news, and stood up heavily.

He was in the shower when he heard a word that alerted him. Turning the tap off and dripping with water, he listened.

. . . must have taken place late last night. A thirty-three-year-old woman . . .

Louis rushed out of the bathroom and stood by the radio.

. . . according to first reports, Paulette Bourgeay was surprised by her killer while alone at home in the rue de l'Étoile, 17th arrondissement. The victim, who was discovered this morning, had probably opened the door to the murderer, sometime between eleven thirty and one thirty. The young woman had been strangled and stabbed in several places. The wounds correspond to those found on the previous two victims killed in Paris in the last month, in the Square d'Aquitaine and the rue de la Tour-des-Dames. The police are still hunting for the man whose identikit portrait was published in the press and who might be able to help them with their inquiries . . .

Louis turned down the sound, letting the news carry on quietly. He paced round the room, for several minutes, fist pressed to his mouth in anguish, then he snatched up a towel, dried himself, picked up his clothes and began to dress on autopilot.

Oh God, no, a third woman. He thought quickly about the times. Between eleven thirty and one thirty. They had left the Secateur in the cemetery at about a quarter to midnight. So he would have had time. And as for Clément, he had been out for two whole hours, thanks to Lucien, who had given him his little wings, and had returned only at a quarter to two. He would have had plenty of time to get across Paris and back.

He frowned. Where had the third murder been? Then he stopped still, holding his shirt. Rue de l'Étoile. Street of the Star. Had he heard right, or was he imagining things because of Lucien's demented babble?

Turning the sound back up, he searched for a continuous news station. Presently he heard the item again:

. . . *mutilated body of a young woman found in a flat in the rue de l'Étoile in Paris, at about eight this morning . . .*

Louis turned the radio off, and lay down on his bed without his shirt on for several minutes. Then he slowly finished dressing and picked up the phone. What had he said to Lucien last night? He'd called him something like a fucking wanker, and a shitty little intellectual and various other choice insults. Their next meeting would be tricky.

But for now, Lucien was the one who was right. Yet, as he dialled the number at the cafe, Louis shook his head. All the same, something was surely wrong.

The cafe owner called Vandoosler senior over. He put down his cards and went to find Marc from the house. Five minutes later, Marc came on the line.

'Marc. It's me. Please just give one-word answers, as usual. You've heard? The third murder?'

'Yes,' said Marc heavily.

'I know Clément got back all right last night. How did he seem? Disturbed?'

'Normal.'

'He knows about the murder?'

'Yes.'

'And what has he said?'

'Nothing.'

'And, er, Lucien, have you seen him this morning?'

'No, I was asleep when he left. He'll be back for lunch.'

'Perhaps he hasn't heard the news?'

'Yes, he has. He left a note, I've got it here, I'll read it to you: "*Nine thirty ack emma. Calling all units. Enemy action reported last night nor-nor-west sector, fully successful, due to strategic failures by high command and consequent lack of deployment of troops. Fresh attacks predicted imminently. Counter-attack must be prepared with maximum efficiency. Signed Private Devernois.*" Don't fly off the handle,' Marc added.

'No,' said Louis, 'but please ask him to come and see me after lunch.'

'At home or in the bunker?'

The bunker was what Louis called the tiny office where he kept his most sensitive files.

'The bunker. If he refuses, which he well might, let me know.'

Louis went out in search of lunch, thoughts running round his head. Three victims already. The killer had a fixed number in mind, of that he felt sure. Louis held to this theory because the killer was counting, and the count had to have a purpose and therefore come to an end. But when? Three women? Or five? Or ten? And if the murderer had picked out a set of five or ten women, he must also have given the sequence a meaning. Otherwise, what was the point of making the sample?

Louis stopped on the pavement and thought, fist up against his mouth, ruminating with the slightest of threads to guide him, and finding it hard to put anything in words.

He couldn't be going to choose ten women simply at random, a sequence of ten. No, the group must have some coherent meaning, forming a world, a model, signifying all women. There had to be a meaning.

But no connection had been found between the first two women. No meaning. And yes, it was true, the poem Lucien had quoted did offer a perfect link, a meaning, a world, a destiny, within which the killer could locate his victims and enjoy his murders. But what Louis could not accept was that the killer chose a poem to determine his choice. To kill because of a poem? . . . No, it was too elitist to be true, too precious, too refined, too chic, not related to reality. And not insane enough, not passionate enough. What Louis was searching for was some kind of crazy superstitious system. Whereas, he felt sure, picking a poem was one of those stupid things an intellectual might do.

He sat at his desk in the bunker, waiting for Lucien. He didn't actually think Lucien would come. He wouldn't have come himself, to be honest, if he'd been insulted that way. True, in the dosshouse, they seemed to take insults differently from most people, which left a glimmer of hope. But what worked for the three evangelists among themselves would certainly not work the same way for him.

As he doodled figures of eight on a piece of blank paper, Louis went on cudgelling his brains, trying to tease out the idea of a ritual series. Could Nerval's poem carry some overall meaning that the killer attached to the series? No, of course not, the idea was grotesque, rubbish. Yes, the complexity of those lines might be fascinating to someone obsessed with signs and symbols, but no, it couldn't be enough to have made the killer choose it.

No, no, no . . . unless it was the poem that had chosen the murderer, and not the other way round. If so, it changed everything. Louis stood up to stretch his legs. He noted on a piece of paper: *It would have to be the poem that chose the murderer*. In that case it could be possible. Anything else was fantasy, but that might make sense. The poem choosing the killer, waylaying him on his path, blocking his route, so that the killer thought fate was showing him the way? And he would follow it.

'Oh shit!' Louis said out loud.

He was going mad. Since when did poems waylay their victims? He put his pencil down on the table. And Lucien rang the doorbell.

The two men nodded curtly to each other, and Louis moved some papers off a chair. Fresh-faced and alert, Lucien did not look either aggressive or even put out.

'You wanted to see me?' said Lucien, tossing back the wayward lock of hair. 'Did you see the news? Rue de l'Étoile! Spot on. Of course the guy didn't have any choice. He's started, so he has to go on. A system is always limiting, it's like in the army, you're not allowed to deviate.'

If Lucien was going to take it like this, apparently not even remembering their quarrel of the previous night, the only thing to do was to follow suit. Louis relaxed.

'What was your reasoning?' Louis asked.

'It's like I said last night. There's only one key that will open the casket, I mean the killer's box, his lunatic closed system.'

'How did you know it was a lunatic closed system?'

'Well, you said it yourself to Marc, didn't you? That it would be a finite number of victims, not a serial killer.'

'Yes, I did. Coffee?'

'Yes please. And if it's a finite number, there's got to be a key.'

'Yeah, OK,' said Louis.

'And the key's the poem. It's as obvious as the nose on your face.'

Louis served the coffee and sat down across the desk from Lucien, stretching out his legs.

'Nothing else?'

'No, nothing else.'

Louis looked a bit disappointed. He dipped a lump of sugar in his coffee and crunched it.

'And what you think,' he went on, 'is that the killer is a fan of this nineteenth-century poet, Gérard de Nerval?'

'That's putting it a bit strongly. Anyone fairly educated might know the poem. It's very famous, kids learn it at school. There's been more written about it actually than about the Great War.'

'Oh no,' Louis said, shaking his head. 'It just can't be right. Nobody would choose a poem to attach corpses to, it doesn't make sense. Our man isn't some kind of aesthete, he's a killer. Whether he's educated or ignorant, doesn't make any difference. He wouldn't have gone out and *chosen* a poem, just like that. It's not a solid enough basis for what he has to do.'

'You already told me that, in your inimitably courteous way last night,' said Lucien shortly, with a sniff. 'But Nerval is the key to this sequence, however absurd you may think it.'

'What I'm saying is that this key is not absurd *enough*. It's too pretty, too perfect, it fits too well. It sounds false.'

Lucien stretched out his legs in turn and half closed his eyes.

'I see what you mean,' he said after a pause. 'The key is very fancy, isn't it? Artificial, a bit over the top, perhaps.'

'In other words, Lucien, it's just a fucking red herring.'

'Maybe. But the bothersome thing is that this false key opens up real murders.'

'Or else it's simply a massive coincidence. We need to forget all the stuff about the poem.'

Lucien sprang up.

'No way!' he said in horror, as he paced round the small office. 'On the contrary, we should tell the cops about it and get them to keep a watch on the next street. And it's in your interest, Louis, because if another woman is killed, it's you who will have to eat the book, binding and all, out of guilt, you understand?'

'What do you mean, the *next* street?'

'Ah now, that's a bit tricky. I think though that the next murder will be related to the *Soleil noir*, the "black sun" in the poem. It's got to be.'

'Explain yourself,' said Louis in a deliberately gloomy voice.

'OK, the first lines contain the words Aquitaine and La Tour. All that's past, so we won't go back there. Line 3 begins: my only Star is dead, *ma seule Étoile est morte*, yeah, that one's over too. What comes next? *et mon luth constellé/Porte le Soleil noir de la Mélancolie*. And my constellated lute/Bears the black sun of melancholy. There aren't any streets with "lute" in the name in Paris, so we get to the black sun, which will be the next symbol picked by the killer. *Le Soleil noir de la Mélancolie*. He has to go with it, he doesn't have any choice.'

'So your conclusion is?' asked Louis, sounding tired.

'A rather uncertain and wobbly solution,' said Lucien regretfully. 'There isn't a rue du Soleil Noir either, in Paris anyway.'

'A shop perhaps, a cafe, a bookshop?'

'No, it's got to be a street. If the killer starts making compromises over the sequence, it will lose its meaning. He can't do that. He started with street names. He's got to stick with them to the end.'

'On that point, I'm with you.'

'So, a street. There aren't a thousand possibilities. I see three, after looking at the Paris map. There *is* a rue du Soleil; there's a rue du Soleil d'Or, or golden sun; and finally, there's a rue de la Lune – the moon might be considered a sort of black sun.'

Louis frowned.

'Yeah, I know,' Lucien said, 'it's not all that satisfactory, but there isn't anything else. I'd go for the rue de la Lune myself, but really one should keep a watch on all three streets. We can't take any chances.'

Lucien sought Louis's eyes.

'You will do this, won't you?'

'It's not up to me.'

'But you will talk to the police, won't you?' Lucien insisted.

'Yes, all right, I'll talk to them,' said Louis curtly, 'but I'd be very surprised if they go along with it.'

'You'll help them to?'

'No.'

'You don't give a damn about the black sun, do you?'

'I don't believe in it, no.'

Lucien looked him and nodded.

'You realise a woman's life is at stake?'

'I realise that better than anyone.'

'But you feel it less than me!' retorted Lucien. 'Just give me a hand, I can't watch three streets all on my own.'

'The cops will help, if they see fit.'

'You'll tell them properly? Not with a smirk, suggesting it's just an off-the-wall idea?'

'No, I promise. I'll let them draw their own conclusions, I won't put in my two francs' worth.'

Lucien looked at him suspiciously and went to the door. 'So when will you go?'

'Now.'

'Would you be able to tell them the title of the poem?'

'No.'

'It's called "El Desdichado". It means "The Disinherited".'

'OK, you can count on me.'

Lucien turned back, his hand on the doorknob.

'It had a different title in an earlier version – want to know that?'

Louis shrugged politely.

'It was in French, not Spanish: "Le Destin". Destiny,' said Lucien, speaking clearly.

Then he went out, slamming the door. Louis stood for a few minutes thoughtfully, in the state of mind of an unbeliever concerned about a friend who has suddenly turned mystic.

Then he wondered since when Lucien, who never seemed to show interest in anything except the Great War, knew such a lot about Gérard de Nerval.

XXIV

IT WAS SUNDAY, BUT OBVIOUSLY WITH A NEW MURDER TO DEAL WITH, LOISEL would be in his office all day. That gave Louis time to visit his two potential killers, the Secateur and the simpleton, both of whom he had allowed to go roaming at night because of his old friend Marthe, and whom he would let go again if he found no other way out. Louis felt sick at the thought of the third murdered woman. He didn't know what she had looked like and was not keen to find out. He counted on his fingers. The first woman had been killed on 21 June, the second ten days later, and the third only six days after that. The killer was working at an accelerated pace. A further murder might be planned for Friday or even earlier. At any rate, they certainly had no time to lose.

Louis checked the time, three o'clock. He couldn't afford his usual luxury of going on foot, he'd have to take his car. He triple-locked the bunker door and went as fast as possible down his two flights of stairs. In the dark hall of the building, pushing open the heavy door to the street, he found himself muttering a line of poetry: *Dans la nuit du Tombeau / Toi qui m'as consolé*. He realised what he was doing as he walked along the warm pavement. It must be part of the Nerval poem, he was sure of it! In the night of the Tomb / Thou who consoled me. Yes. But Lucien hadn't recited those lines, they came from another stanza, the second probably. He smiled as he thought of the obscure tricks memory could play on you. He wasn't aware of having opened a book by Nerval for at least twenty-five years, but in the tumult he was going through, his memory had churned up a fragment from the poem, perhaps from schooldays, like a flower surviving a shipwreck. A sad flower, to be sure. Louis suddenly realised that he wasn't capable of reciting the four lines Lucien had given him, but he would have to keep his promise. So he made a long detour to find a bookshop open on a Sunday, then drove to the Montparnasse Cemetery.

In the daytime, the place looked different, though no less melancholy. He spotted the Secateur, who was dozing in the shade, propped up against a mausoleum, in the farthest point of the triangular section. Reassured, he went to the other part of the cemetery, the larger one, and looked carefully at the trees. It was a while before he spotted incisions on their trunks such as Clément had described. But here and there, on about one in fifteen trees, there were indeed shallow cuts looking like the result of repeated and frenzied slashing, some old and healed over, others more recent, but none of them really new. He returned slowly to the place where the Secateur was slumped, and had to rouse him by poking him hard several times with his shoe before the man woke with a start.

'Good afternoon,' said Louis. 'I told you I'd be back.'

Thévenin, leaning on his elbow, his face flushed and creased, glared at Louis with hostility but did not speak.

'I brought you something to drink.'

The man got clumsily to his feet, smoothed down his clothes hastily, and reached for the bottle.

'You reckon that'll make me talk, do you?' he said, screwing his eyes up against the light.

'Yeah, obviously. Think I'm going to spend money on you out of the goodness of my heart? Sit down.'

As before, Louis pressed the man's shoulder to make him sit back on the ground. Louis could not sit on the ground himself because of his knee, nor did he wish to. He perched himself against a tombstone. Thévenin laughed.

'You're making a mistake,' he said, 'the more I drink, the clearer my head gets.'

'That's the point,' said Louis. Thévenin examined the label on the bottle, with a frown.

'You kidding or what – is this really Médoc?'

He whistled and nodded his head seriously.

'Wow,' he said. 'Médoc, eh?'

'I don't like drinking rubbish myself.'

'Not short of cash then, are you?'

'You didn't tell me the truth last night about the secateurs.'

'Dunno what you mean,' muttered the man, fishing his corkscrew out of the rucksack.

'Those trees over there, they've been cut about. Was that you?'

'No idea.'

Thévenin uncorked the bottle and raised it to his lips.

'So what made those cuts?' Louis persisted.

'Cats. Plenty of 'em in here, they scratch the trees.'

'Were there cats in the Institut Merlin as well?'

'Yeah, plenty of cats there too. You're not having me on, it is Médoc,' he said again, tapping the bottle with a fingernail.

'That may be, but you're having *me* on.'

'I ain't got my secateurs no more, and that's the truth. Not for about a month now.'

'Do you miss them?'

Thévenin seemed to think about this, then took another swig.

'Yeah, suppose I do,' he said, wiping his mouth on his sleeve.

'And you haven't replaced them with something else?'

The man shrugged, without bothering to reply. Louis emptied out the rucksack again, and then patted down the man's pockets.

'Stay there,' he ordered, taking the keys of the toolshed. Louis inspected the shed once more, but nothing was different from the night before. He came back to the Secateur.

'What did you do last night, after I left?' he asked.

The man said nothing, simply arched his back.

Louis repeated the question.

'What the fuck do you think?' said Thévenin. 'Looked at the girls in my mags, finished off my bottle, went to sleep. What else am I going to do?'

Louis caught Thévenin's chin in his left hand and forced him to look into his eyes, remembering that his German father used to do the same to him, saying: 'Your eyes will tell me if you're lying or not.' Louis had long believed that the letters L, for *Luge*, Lies, and W, for *Wahrheit*, Truth, could be read in his pupils, but the Secateur's bloodshot eyes made decoding them difficult.

'What's all this about?' asked Thévenin, his chin still caught in Louis's grasp.

'You don't know?'

'No, I bloody don't,' said the man, grimacing. 'Let me go!'

Louis pushed him away. Thévenin rubbed his face and helped himself to more wine.

'What about you?' he said. 'What kind of monster are you, anyway? Why are you buggering me about? What's your name?'

'Nerval. Mean anything to you?'

'No. Why should it? You're a cop? No, not a cop, something else. Worse than a cop.'

'I'm a poet.'

'Jesus,' said Thévenin, putting the bottle on the ground. 'You don't look like any kind of poet to me, you're having me on.'

'No, I'm not, listen to this.'

Louis took the book from his pocket and read out the first four lines of the poem.

'Doesn't sound a lot of fun,' said the Secateur, scratching himself.

Louis caught the man's chin in his hand once more and, slowly this time, pulled it towards him.

'Nothing?' he said, peering into the shifty red-eyed gaze. 'That doesn't remind you of anything?'

'You must be bloody mad,' muttered Thévenin, shutting his eyes.

XXV

LOUIS PARKED THE CAR NEAR THE RUE CHASLE AND SAT AT THE WHEEL FOR A FEW minutes. The Secateur was eluding him, and he had no way of exerting his grasp. If he piled on the pressure, the man would get scared and run to the police. And they would follow the trail back to Clément before you could turn round.

Someone tapped on the roof of the car. Marc looked in through the open window.

'What are you waiting here for? Roasting yourself to death?'

Louis wiped the sweat from his forehead and opened the door.

'Yeah, you're right, I don't actually know why I'm sitting here, it's unbearably hot.'

Marc nodded. He found Louis strange sometimes. Taking his arm, he guided him towards the house, along the shady side of the street.

'Have you seen Lucien then?'

'Yes, he's a clever lad.'

'Sometimes he is,' Marc agreed. 'And?'

'And his Nerval theory? Complete rubbish,' said Louis calmly.

The two men walked up and down the street a few times, while Louis explained exactly why he thought the Nerval theory a pointless fancy. Then they went into the house, where the refectory shutters were still closed. Vandoosler senior was on guard and Marthe had turned up. She was playing a game of beggar-my-neighbour with her protégé.

'No one saw you come here?' asked Louis, giving her a kiss on her forehead. 'You were careful?'

'Don't worry,' said Marthe with a broad smile. 'It's good to see you.'

'Don't get carried away, old lady. We're not out of the woods yet. And I'm wondering how long we can last.'

He gestured vaguely towards the closed shutters, and Clément, and flopped on to the bench, looking harassed and running his hand through his dark hair, now damp with sweat. He accepted the beer Marc passed him, acknowledging it with a nod.

'You're worried about what happened last night?' asked Marthe.

'Among other things. Did they tell you he went out?' murmured Louis. 'Thanks to Lucien's motherly care.'

Marthe didn't reply. She was shuffling her cards.

'Can you lend him to me for a few minutes?' asked Louis suddenly. 'Don't worry, I'm not going to wear him out with questions.'

'How do I know that?'

'Because he's more likely to wear *us* out.'

Louis grabbed the young man's hand across the table, to get his attention. As he did so, he noticed that Clément had a new-looking watch on his wrist.

'What's that?' he asked, pointing at it.

'A watch,' Clément replied.

'I mean, where did you get it?'

'He gave it me, the one that shouts.'

'You mean Lucien?'

'Yes, it was so I'd come back at the right time.'

'You went out last night, didn't you?'

Clément, as before, was quite calm, faced with Louis's inquisitorial gaze.

'He said I must go out just for two hours, personally. I was very careful.'

'You know what happened last night?'

'A girl,' Clément said. 'Was there a pot plant?' he asked suddenly.

'No, no pot plant. Should there be? Did you take her one?'

'No-oo! Nobody asked me to.'

'OK, so what *did* you do?'

'Went to the pictures.'

'At that time of night?'

Clément twisted his feet round the legs of the chair.

'There's this cinema with naked girls, goes on all night,' he explained, fingering the watch on his wrist.

Louis sighed and put his hands on the table.

'So what?' Marthe called out. 'You don't approve? He's got to have some distractions, poor lad. He's a man, isn't he?'

'All right, all right, Marthe,' said Louis wearily, standing up. 'I'm off,' he added, turning to Marc, who was setting up his ironing board. 'I'm going to see the cops.'

Louis kissed Marthe again without speaking, patted her cheek and went out, still holding his beer.

Marc looked undecided for a moment, then put the iron down and followed him out. He caught up with Louis at the car and leaned in at the window.

'Are the cops after you?' he said 'What are you up to?'

'Nothing. It's this mind-boggling affair. We're up to our necks in a swamp, and I can't find any way to get us out of the shit. I'm just deep in it,' he said, buckling his seat belt. 'Marthe's waiting, you're waiting, the fourth woman is waiting, and I'm in it up to here.'

Marc looked at him in silence.

'Well, we can't stay in the dark for the rest of our lives, can we?' said Louis in a low voice. 'Watching over this simple-minded guy, person-ally, as for him, while the victims mount up.'

'You yourself said there wouldn't be ten thousand victims. You said it wasn't Clément.'

Louis wiped the sweat from his face again and drank a few mouthfuls of warm beer.

'Yeah,' he said, 'and so what if I did? I can't seem to talk any sense. Clément gets on my nerves. Him and the Secateur, they're as bad as each other.'

'You've seen the Secateur again? What was he up to last night?'

'Same as Clément Vauquer – into porn.'

Louis tapped his fingers on the steering wheel.

'I'm wondering who's gone mad,' he said. 'Them or me. I like women, I like their faces, and I like them when they give me permission. Those two, they just get off on *pictures* of anonymous women, and pay money for the treat. I hold that against them. They get on my nerves.'

Louis lingered, his hand still on the hot wheel.

'What about you?' he said. 'Do you pay for porn?'

'I'm not a good example.'

'No?'

'No. I'm demanding, I'm unpredictable. I want them to look at' *me* and to adore me. What would I do with a picture?'

'You're ambitious,' said Louis, discouraged. 'Never mind, I still wonder who's mad.'

He raised his left hand, which for him meant his mind was doubtful and troubled.

'Well, keep an eye on our simple lad,' he said with a half-smile and started the engine.

Marc waved casually as the car disappeared. Then he went back to the house where the ironing and his research on thirteenth-century landholdings awaited him. A house full of men. Marc sighed as he crossed the road in the baking heat. His conversation with Louis had depressed him. He didn't like talking about women when he was on his own, which had been the case now for almost three years, it seemed to him.

XXVI

SINCE HE HAD PASSED HIS DOUBTS AND IN FACT HIS BAD MOOD ON TO MARC'S shoulders, Louis felt considerably better. He walked confidently into the police station, where people were busying themselves: it was hot and noisy. Loisel was moving quickly between the desks in the company of the police chief from the 17th arrondissement, which covered the rue de l'Étoile. Seeing Louis, he made a sign to him.

'Need to see you,' he said, leaving his colleague. 'Follow me. You were right.'

He led Louis into his office, slammed the door, and spread on the already cluttered table about fifteen photos of the murder from the previous night.

'Paulette Bourgeay,' he said, 'age thirty-three, unmarried. Taken by surprise, alone in her flat, like the others.'

'And still no link between these women?'

'They don't seem ever to have met in their lives, not even in the metro. They lived alone, they were fairly young, they didn't have film-star looks or anything.'

'Same system?' asked Louis.

'Yes. A gag in the mouth, strangled, stabbed with something sharp, perhaps scissors, all over the body, really horrible. And here,' said

Loisel, tapping his finger on one photo, 'are the marks on the ground you pointed out. I admit I'd never have noticed them if you hadn't insisted, so I'm grateful. For the moment, it doesn't actually get us anywhere. But I've had enlargements made, and you can see them very well.'

Loisel passed a photo to Louis. Quite clear to see, alongside the victim's head, were marks on the carpet, lines criss-crossing each other as if a hand had been scratching, like a rake.

'Finger marks?' said Louis. 'That's what you think too, do you?'

'Yes. Looks like the guy made several attempts to pick something up. His weapon perhaps.'

'I don't think so,' said Louis.

'No,' said Loisel, 'I don't either, must be something else. We've had that square of carpet taken up and sent to the lab for analysis. But for now, there's nothing conclusive.'

Loisel lit one of his slender cigarettes.

'But *this* time,' he said, 'nobody saw the man lurking in the street the preceding days. No pot plant either. I think you were right. Since the picture appeared in the papers, he's been hiding.'

'You think so?' said Louis distantly.

'Dead sure of it. He's found some accomplices. Or else,' he added, 'he's managed to intimidate some poor saps who are scared of him.'

'Yeah, right,' said Louis. 'That's always possible.'

'Usually in cases like this, we'd look for members of the family. A brother, an uncle, and of course the mother above all, like I said before. But in this case, no point. He doesn't have any family.'

'Oh? How do you know?'

'Because we know his *name*!' said Loisel with a short laugh, cupping his hands together as if he'd caught an insect.

Louis sat back in his chair.

'I'm all ears,' he said.

'His name's Clément Vauquer. Make a note of the name: Clément Vauquer. He's from Nevers.'

'How did you find out?'

'A restaurant owner in Nevers phoned us yesterday.'

Louis breathed again. Pouchet had kept his word.

'It all fits,' said Loisel. 'This chap left Nevers about a month ago, it seems.'

'Why?'

Loisel raised his hands as a sign of ignorance.

'All I can tell you is that this guy drags out a living busking with his accordion. You know the type. He plays quite well, they say, not that I can stand the accordion. Apart from being good at that, he's apparently someone of limited intelligence.'

'And he came to Paris to play his accordion – or to kill people?'

'Ah well, if only we knew, *mon vieux*. But with people like that, you know, not right in the head, could be anything.'

'What else do you know about him?'

'Apparently he stayed at the Hotel des Quatre Boules in the 11th, but the hotel owner isn't totally sure. We're on the lookout. Matter of days, the net's closing in, he won't last long now.'

'Right,' said Louis, 'you've convinced me. But if it's a matter of days, that's still a bit long. You might have another victim before Friday.'

'Yes, I realise that,' said Loisel with a frown. 'I can count. And at the Ministry, they don't want any more victims . . .'

'It's not the Ministry that matters.'

'No?'

'No, it's the next woman.'

'Well, obviously,' said Loisel irritably. 'But we'll get him before that. His hiding place can't hold him forever. There'll be a leak, there's always someone who spills the beans, you can count on that.'

'Yeah,' said Louis, thinking fleetingly of Lucien. 'Now, I have what might be a bit of a lead to propose. Make of it what you will.'

Loisel looked up, intrigued. Louis's leads were never negligible. Louis had taken his book out of his pocket and was leafing though it.

'Here it is,' he said, showing the inspector the first verse of 'El Desdichado'. 'All three street names are here, where those women lived. The next murder might be in a street with a name relating to "black sun", *Soleil noir*. It could be rue du Soleil, or rue du Soleil d'Or, or possibly rue de la Lune.'

Frowning, Loisel looked over the poem, examined the cover of the book, then looked back at the poem and read it again.

'What the devil is this taradiddle about?' he said.

'I'm not going to quarrel with you about that,' said Louis gently.

'Is that what you meant when you came round the other day?'

'Yes,' Louis lied.

'Why didn't you say anything then?'

'Well, precisely because I thought it was some fancy rubbish, the kind of thing an intellectual might dream up.'

'And you've changed your mind?'

Louis sighed.

'No. It's true we do have another murder that fits that scheme, but I haven't changed my mind. Still, I could be wrong. You might see things differently, which is why I'm telling you about it. It just might be a good idea to have someone keep an eye on those three streets, the ones I mentioned.'

'Well, thanks for the help,' said Loisel. 'I'm relieved you've levelled with me, Kehlweiler.'

'Only natural,' said Louis seriously.

'Still,' the commissaire went on, tapping the book cover, 'I don't believe this kind of fancy trick. We don't find murderers going round committing crimes by playing word games with poems, know what I mean?'

'Yes, indeed, I absolutely agree.'

'Pity though, there is something sort of neat about it. Sorry, don't take it personally.'

'Of course not, I just wanted to have my conscience clear,' said Louis, thinking of Clément playing beggar-my-neighbour in the house full of gullible saps. 'You know how it is.'

Loisel shook hands firmly across the table.

XXVII

THERE WAS A MESSAGE ON HIS ANSWERPHONE FROM PAUL MERLIN, THE TOAD-MAN. Louis listened from the kitchen as he cut himself a doorstep of bread which he ate accompanied by everything he could find in the fridge, stale cheese mostly. It was hardly seven o'clock, but he was ravenously hungry. Merlin had some interesting information and wanted to see him as soon as possible. Louis called back, holding the receiver under his chin and agreed to visit him before supper. Then he called the Ane Rouge, and asked for Vandoosler. The old cop was still there playing cards. On Sundays, he spent the entire day in the cafe, unless he was on duty as cook.

'Tell Marc I'll pick him up in my car in twenty minutes,' Louis explained. 'I'll toot when I get there . . . No, not far, just to see Merlin, but I need him. And Vandoos, could you ask him to dress a bit smartly, good shirt, jacket and tie? . . . Yeah . . . I don't know how . . . you'll think of something.'

Louis hung up, and ate the remains of his sandwich standing by his desk. Then he went to visit Bufo in the bathroom, and changed his clothes. He had ruined his best suit climbing the walls of the Montparnasse Cemetery, so he chose something less formal. At seven twenty he picked up Marc, who was waiting in the rue Chasle not looking best pleased.

'Very smart,' said Louis, examining Marc as he got into the car.

'This is my exam suit,' said Marc, frowning, 'and the tie is Lucien's of course. I'm too hot, it's scratchy and I look a fool.'

'You need to look like this when you're visiting in the west end of Paris.'

'I don't know what you want me along for,' Marc grumbled as they drove towards the Invalides, 'but hurry up about it, I'm hungry.'

Louis stopped the car.

'Go and get a sandwich from over there on the corner,' he said.

Five minutes later Marc was back in the car, but looking no happier.

'Don't drop stuff on yourself,' Louis advised.

'Tonight Mathias is on duty and we were going to have a potato omelette.'

'Really sorry,' said Louis sincerely, 'but I need you.'

'Is he interesting, this Merlin?'

'No, not really, but his old man is. You come up with me to see Merlin and once we're talking, you go downstairs on some pretext. His stepfather works down in the courtyard, making a hell of a noise, like I told you. Try to start a chat with him, and see what you can get out of him about Nevers and the institute.'

'And why not the rape, while we're at it?' said Marc, pulling a face.

'Why not?'

Marc turned towards Louis.

'What do you have in mind?'

'I'm thinking of the third man. The attack happened deep into the institute grounds, but not so far from the old man's studio in the barn. And apparently he heard nothing. According to Clément, the third man was older, about sixty, and according to Merlin, his stepfather was always after the girls in the institute.'

'So what do you want me to do?'

'Just register and report. Stay with him till I come out, and that will make it possible for me to look inside his studio.'

Marc sighed and returned to his sandwich.

Merlin received them as courteously as his good manners allowed him, and Louis was pleased to see again his toad-like features. Marc on the other hand was surprised by his appearance.

'I know what you're thinking,' Louis whispered. 'He's a bit like Bufo, isn't he?'

Marc blinked agreement and sat down, trying not to crease his jacket. Merlin was showing slight impatience, and looked enquiringly at Marc.

'One of my collaborators,' said Louis breezily, 'a specialist on sex crimes. I thought he might be able to help us.'

Oh great, Marc thought, clenching his teeth. Merlin was looking at him with a slightly offended air, and Marc forced himself to look calm and responsible, something that didn't come easily.

'I traced him,' Merlin said, turning to Louis. 'I had to spend all day on the phone but I got a result!'

'The Secateur?'

'Yes. It wasn't easy, I assure you, but I've got him now, that's the main thing. He lives out at Montrouge, 29 rue des Fusillés.'

Looking pleased with himself, Merlin went round the desk and flopped into his chair like a toad happily returning to his pond.

'Yes,' said Louis, 'and he works at the Montparnasse Cemetery, I saw him last night.'

'What do you mean? You knew that?'

'I'm terribly sorry.'

'You already knew, and you let me go looking for this man to no purpose?'

'My collaborator found out where he was, after I'd seen you yesterday.'

Oh great, Marc thought again. Merlin threw him a cross look and picked up a few coins from the desk, and fiddled with them, frowning. Then he dropped them into his other hand and fiddled with them again. Marc was interested and forgot the part he was meant to be playing.

'Well, you might have had the courtesy to let me know,' said Merlin, dropping the coins.

'I'm really, really sorry,' Louis said. 'It's just that with this third murder, I didn't think about that. I apologise.'

'Oh well,' said Merlin pocketing his change. 'And what about this third murder? Have the police identified Vauquer yet?'

Just then the sound of the plane came from the yard. Merlin closed his eyes briefly. He looked exactly as troubled and long-suffering as Bufo when Louis took him to a cafe and put him on a pinball machine. Marc took advantage of this interruption to mutter, in character as an important specialist, that he needed to make a call on his mobile phone, and went out. He found it easier to breathe in the yard. Paul Merlin's room smelled of boredom and soap, and he had no wish to be questioned about sex crimes. The windows of the stepfather's studio were wide open. Marc knocked politely when there was a pause in the noise and asked him if he would kindly watch the heavy street door for him, when he left it ajar, as he didn't want to bother Paul Merlin by buzzing the intercom again. The old man, holding a piece of wood between his knees, nodded his agreement.

Once in the street, Marc took off his grey jacket, rubbed his thighs and walked up and down the pavement for a few minutes, a respectable time, he thought for a busy man to make a call on his mobile phone, a device he could not aspire to. He had had time to glimpse in the studio a mass of objects – carpentry tools, boxes, planks, pieces of wood, heaps of shavings, newspapers, photographs, piles of books, a battered kettle, and dozens of statues about the height of a table, lined up on the floor or the shelves. Dozens of small statues, all of women, naked, sitting, kneeling, thinking or praying. He went slowly back through the yard and put his head through the workshop window. The old man made the same sign, signifying OK, and started his plane up again. He was smoothing the torso of one of his statues of women, in a cloud of sawdust. Marc looked at the sculptures surrounding him. Very realistic and detailed, they weren't exactly great works of art. A lot of little women, well made, but too soft and submissive for his taste.

'Is she always the same one?' he called.

'What?' shouted the old man.

'The woman, is she always the same one?'

'All women are always the same.'

'Oh, they are?'

'You interested?' said the old man, still at the top of his voice.

Marc signalled yes, he was, and the old man signalled, fine, come in, and shouted out his name: Pierre Clairmont. Marc shouted his own. He walked awkwardly round the studio, looking at the faces of the statues which were in fact very different from each other and heavily realistic. On the tables were dozens of photographs of women cut out from magazines, enlarged and coloured in. The noise stopped suddenly and Marc turned towards the old man, who put down the plane, in order to scratch at the white hairs on his chest. In the other hand, he was holding the statuette by the thighs.

'You just do women?' Marc asked.

'Is there anything else? But perhaps you have some other ideas. Is there anything else?'

Marc shrugged.

'Anything else?' the old man repeated, still scratching. 'Boats, churches, trees, fruit, fabrics, clouds, deer in the woods? The point is, they all stand in for women, as well you would know, if you had any brains. Symbolic sculpture – what the heck's the point of that? Might as well do women from the start.'

'Well, if you put it that way,' said Marc.

'You know anything about sculpture?'

'Not really.'

The old man shook his head, took out a cigarette from his shirt pocket and lit it.

'I suppose, in your job, you don't have too much to do with poetry.'

'What job do you think that is?' asked Marc, sitting down.

'Cigarette?'

'Yes, thanks.'

'I'd say the police or something like that. Nothing poetic.'

'Oh great,' said Marc to himself once more. His thoughts escaped towards the thirteenth-century leases waiting for him on his desk. What was he doing here anyway in his itchy suit, talking to an old joker who was getting rather aggressive, what was more? Ah yes, Marthe. Marthe and her doll.

'You people are only interested in women when they're dead,' the old man was going on. 'Not very life-loving point of view, is it?'

Yes, I suppose that's right, thought Marc, I do think about people who are dead, millions of them, and they died long ago. The old guy, no longer scratching himself, was lovingly caressing the thigh of his statuette. He moved his thumb up and down over the wood and Marc looked the other way.

'So why,' the old man asked, 'are you digging up that old story from the institute? Got nothing better to do?'

'So you know all about it?'

'Yes, Paul told me yesterday.'

Clairmont spat out some scraps of tobacco to show his disapproval, then returned to his figurine's thigh.

'You don't like going back to that, do you?' asked Marc.

'Paul was very fond of Nicole – that's the woman who died. He took years to get over it. And then one fine day, you bring it all back again.

166

But that's the cops for you, they burst in and disturb your life, everything gets thrown around. They're hard-wired to be like that, aren't they? They have to come and poke their noses in, like a lot of red ants, never mind the harm they do. And for what? You'll never find those other two that did the rape.'

'We don't know that for sure,' said Marc feebly.

'No evidence at the time and none to be found today,' said Clairmont briskly. 'Let sleeping dogs lie is what I say.'

He leaned across the table, hoisting himself up on a stool, reached down among some packing cases and brought up a statuette by the shoulder. He put it down beside Marc on the floor.

'There she is, poor girl,' he said. 'I even had her cast in bronze so that she would survive forever.'

At that moment, Louis came into the studio, introduced himself and shook the man's hand.

'Your colleague,' said Clairmont, 'has no artistic sensibility. I don't know if you're the same, but if so, I'm sorry for you.'

'Vandoosler is an expert,' said Louis with a smile. 'He is a specialist on pathological sexuality, which doesn't make him much of a dreamer. We can't all be such great experts.'

Marc glowered at the German.

'Pathological sexuality, eh?' said Clairmont slowly. 'So that's why the pair of you have come to see me, is it? And what's going on in your tiny expert brains? What do you think? Old Clairmont spends all day long fingering his little women, he's got a screw loose, he's obsessed.'

Marc shook his head, watching the thumb smoothing the statuette's thigh. Louis patted the head of the statuette on the floor.

'She's the one you were talking about?' he asked.

'Yes, she is, right enough,' said the old man, 'that's the one you're interested in, the woman from the institute, Nicole Verdot.'

Louis gently lifted up the little figure of a kneeling woman.

'Does this look like her?'

'Nobody else does sculptures as true to life as I do. Spitting image. Ask anyone in the trade. Even the ears are right.'

Alas, thought Marc.

'Was it done when she was alive?'

'No,' said the old man, lighting another cigarette. 'I did it after her death, from pictures and the newspapers. I always work from photos, but that's her all right. Paul couldn't stand to look at it, because it looked so much like her. He cried like a baby when he saw it. That's why I keep her hidden, he thinks I've thrown this one out.'

'Did he ask you to do it?'

'What, Paul? You must be joking.'

'So why did you do it?'

'To honour her, so that she would live forever.'

'You loved her yourself?'

'Not specially. I love all women.'

'She had quite a big nose,' remarked Louis, putting the statuette gently down again.

'Correct,' agreed the old man with a nod.

Louis glanced round the studio.

'Mind if I take a look?' he asked.

Clairmont nodded, and Louis slowly examined all the work benches. The old man stared at Marc.

'You didn't tell me about your rather special expertise. Have you been in that line a long time?'

'Since four years old,' said Marc. 'I took to study very early.'

Clairmont threw away his cigarette end.

'You probably think *I've* got a bee buzzing round in my bonnet,' he said, patting the head of Nicole Verdot as she knelt humbly before him. 'But if I were you, I'd check out my own psyche first.'

Marc nodded, passively agreeing. He thought about the expression and the noise the bee would make buzzing away in your ear. Yes of course, he too had a bee in his bonnet, undeniably, but not for the reason Clairmont thought. You might say the same for Clément and for Lucien too, with his trench warfare. And for the German with his sordid crimes. But not for Marthe. Marc looked at the old man's hand which had not stopped stroking the unfinished figurine. Yes. Clairmont certainly had a bee in his bonnet, a very common or garden variety.

XXVIII

'FIVE THINGS,' SAID MARC TO LOUIS, HOLDING UP HIS FINGERS, AS THE CAR DREW away from the Merlin house. 'Number one, I have serious reservations about the profession you saddled me with, without consultation.'

'Oh?' said Louis. 'You didn't like it?'

'Not at all, no way,' said Marc. 'Number two, what did the cops say about the Nerval poem? Three, you know the expression "a bee in your bonnet"? Appropriate here. Four, what did you think of those awful statues? And five, I really need a drink. Those two, the toad lookalike and his stepfather, they finished me off.'

'Who's looking after Clément tonight?'

'I am, the uncle's replacing me till I get back.'

'We mustn't put a foot wrong from now on. The cops have got Vauquer's name. Right now, they know who he is, and where he comes from. They're going to go over his record with a toothcomb. And when they find out about the rape in the institute and the murder of the girl, Nicole Verdot, they'll go berserk. I hope Lucien realises that if Clément had been arrested last night, we'd all be in jail with him.'

'We don't always know what Lucien realises. He sometimes sees that a drawing pin has come loose on the kitchen noticeboard, but he wouldn't recognise his twin brother in the street.'

'You mean there's another one like him?' asked Louis, as he parked the car in front of a cafe.

'No, there isn't. Lucien says he's one of a kind, they broke the mould.'

'Thank goodness for that,' said Louis, 'in fact that's the best news I've heard all week.'

'But what about his Nerval theory? Did you tell the police?'

'Cross my heart, yes. I got Loisel to read the whole verse. Conclusion: they couldn't give a damn. Loisel says this is murder we're dealing with, not some kind of literary quiz.'

'And they're not going to watch those streets?'

'Nope, not at all.'

'What about the women then? The next victims?'

Louis spread his arms wide.

'Let's go and have a coffee in the cafe.'

The two men sat at an isolated table in a corner window.

'Raise your efficient arm and order two beers,' said Marc. 'And are you the same, you couldn't give a damn about the street names?'

'Yes. You know quite well what I think.'

'What I mean is, do you *really* not care as much as you're saying? There's no doubt buzzing away in any corner of your mind?'

'I often have something buzzing away there, you know that.'

'That'll be the bee then. The bee in the bonnet. That toad's stepfather said that. What do you think of him?'

Louis pulled a face.

'He likes women to be on their knees, weak, victims, begging and finally transfigured by being submissive. If this wasn't so desperately commonplace, it might fit with the third rapist. He has the cast of mind and the obsession. And he made a sculpture of Nicole Verdot. Bit creepy, wouldn't you say?'

'And the third woman? No leads there?'

'They're not looking for anything, because they think they've identified the killer. All we can say is that she had no connection to the other two. She was just this inoffensive, rather plump young woman, and she was savagely murdered like the others, without there being any sign of rape. No plant pot with fingerprints either.'

'But that doesn't let Marthe's doll off the hook,' Marc sighed. 'He couldn't have found a fern so late at night. What about the marks, the ones on the carpet?'

'Yes, just the same, just as odd. Sort of stripes on the pile, hardly visible. Loisel only noticed them because I'd drawn them to his attention.'

'He has an idea about them?'

'No. Nothing.'

'And you?'

'Me neither. But it must mean something. It's probably quite important. If we could understand what they were, we might be able to get Clément Vauquer off the hook. It's the killer's trademark, a sign he leaves, a signature if you like, his bee's footsteps.'

'His bee?'

'Yes, well, you started it, the bee the killer has in his bonnet.'

Marc nodded.

'Actually it's more like a bloody great bluebottle,' he said.

'Quite,' agreed Louis.

XXIX

LOUIS DROPPED MARC OFF AT THE HOUSE IN THE RUE CHASLE AT ABOUT ELEVEN, after drinking four beers and two cognac chasers. Marc had become chatty and even a bit too cheerful, and Louis warned him again about exercising extreme vigilance that night. He was slightly drunk himself – he had already knocked back a couple of glasses of Sancerre with Paul Merlin – and he climbed wearily up the stairs to his flat.

He went round the room abstractedly, glancing anxiously at the translation of the Bismarck biography which had lain untouched on his desk for almost a week, and took a bottle of water into the bedroom. Listlessly, he shook out the bedding. This was an obligatory evening ritual, since Bufo had adopted the bad habit of taking refuge at night between the mattress and the quilt – an aged German quilt that had belonged to Louis's father, as heavy as lead and perfect for keeping you fixed in bed when you were feeling a bit light-headed after too much beer. It was also perfect for the toad, to whom it no doubt recalled the comforting shelter of rocks. Louis would automatically dislodge him, and Bufo would have to be content with a space at the bottom of the bookshelves, behind the big Larousse dictionary. This was a superstitious principle of Louis's: as long as he sent Bufo off to curl up somewhere else, there was always a hope of not being alone in bed. And hope was half the battle.

'Off you go, Bufo,' he said, as he picked him up gently. 'You're abusing your rights as an amphibian. How do you know I'm not expecting someone? Not a princess who has been transformed into an ugly old toad like you, no, a real beautiful woman who would love me alone. Think that's funny, do you? Well, you're wrong, *mon vieux*. It could happen. A real beautiful woman with two legs, not some poor resigned woman on her knees, like the ones Clairmont carves. And it's just as well you didn't come with me, you would not have liked him one bit. You have too pure a soul, you're like Marc. But I think you might like Merlin better, he's the spitting image of your grandfather, and what's more he serves a cracking Sancerre. But anyway, if this fantastic vision should turn up tonight, try to be a bit more welcoming than you were to Sonia. Remember Sonia? The girl who lived here last year and you made faces at her for five months. Well, she pushed off, Sonia did, she thought you were repulsive. And she ended up thinking the same of me . . .'

Louis put Bufo down behind the Larousse.

'And don't try to read everything, it'll only get you into trouble.'

He turned off the light and collapsed into bed. He tried thinking about the hypothetical being who might join him there, but quickly realised that he wasn't going to get to sleep easily tonight. His heart was thumping and images were racing through his head. Oh shit. He lay on his back, arms by his side, but the faces of the three murdered women rose up to haunt him. The last one, Paulette, reproached him with having done nothing to help her, because he had laughed at the idea of the rue de l'Étoile. He explained calmly that at the time Lucien Devernois was laying out his poetic theory, she was almost certainly already dead. Louis was now too hot and threw off the quilt in irritation. The fourth woman, the one who might be a victim by Friday, now turned up, kneeling down with her hands raised in prayer like the figures at Clairmont's. Her features were vague and touching, and Louis tried to get rid of her. But she reappeared, surrounded by all the wooden faces carved by Clairmont. Louis expelled her from his mind again, and tried unsuccessfully to sleep face down. Then he resigned himself, rather against his will, to trying a method of getting to sleep Marc had told him about, which he called the system of the vicious demons.

The problem is that people can't sleep when they want to, but if they are forbidden to do so, they can't help dropping off. So the method consisted of keeping your eyes wide open and fixing your gaze on some point on the bedroom wall. If by any chance you shut your eyes, hundreds of nasty little demons would pour out of the spot and eat you up. And you are absolutely not allowed to treat this as a joke. According to Marc, you invariably fall asleep after ten minutes max, unless of course you replace the little devils with little fairies, which would stop you falling asleep at all. Louis re-expelled for the third time the images of wooden statues, and with eyes wide open looked hard at the lock on the door to keep the crowd of demons shut up inside. And he did think for a moment that the method was going to work, but then the wooden women put up a fierce fight and scattered the demons from the other side of the door. Infuriated, Louis sat up, switched on his lamp and sipped some water. Three o'clock. He might as well get up and open a beer.

He felt his way to the kitchen and sat down with a bottle. Perhaps the best thing to do was to harness himself to Bismarck, and find out whether the Iron Chancellor did or did not change his mood in May 1874. He switched on the desk lamp and the computer. It was just as the machine began its warming-up hum that one of the wooden statues moved out of line and forced itself on his attention. Frozen, hand poised over the keyboard, his heart pounding, Louis considered the silent face which had come to the forefront of his exhausted mind. It was indeed one of Clairmont's statuettes, one that he'd lifted up that evening in the studio. He looked hard for a few minutes, trying not to forget this face. Only then did he allow himself to move and switched on all the lights. Then he leaned up against the bookshelves, beer in hand. He had seen this face somewhere before, he was sure of it, but this woman was not anyone he knew. He didn't think he had ever spoken to her, or even gone near her, and yet she was undoubtedly familiar to him. Louis paced round the flat, struggling against his desire to sleep, which was now becoming overwhelming. But he was too anxious that the wooden woman would have vanished by morning, so he kept walking round, gripping his beer. It was more than an hour before his stimulated memory at last allowed his disordered recollections to float to the surface, and suddenly presented him with the essential information. Louis glanced at his watch: ten past four.

Smiling to himself, he turned off the computer and got dressed. This woman had died some years before, her name was Claire something, and she lived somewhere in his filing cabinets. She had been murdered. And if he wasn't much mistaken, she was the real first victim of the scissors killer.

He ran a comb through his hair and went out, closing the door quietly.

XXX

LOUIS PARKED HIS CAR OUTSIDE THE ARÈNES DE LUTÈCE, THE ROMAN AMPHITHEATRE
in the 5th arrondissement, and hurried towards his bunker nearby. It
was a warm night with no moon. Everyone seemed to be asleep except
for two shirtless gay guys, lounging by the railings, who made inviting
signs as he went past. Louis declined politely with a gesture, and wondered what they would have thought if they knew he was searching in
the night for a dead woman.

He went upstairs cautiously and undid the three locks on his door
with care. From the next flat, he could hear the snores of his elderly
neighbour who was a light sleeper, and Louis didn't intend to wake
him. He started the coffee and opened up one of his filing cabinets. He
couldn't remember the full name of the woman who had been murdered, but he could perfectly well remember where it was: Nevers.

A few minutes later, Louis was putting on the table a cup of coffee
and a rather meagre file. He took out some press clippings and photos.
No, he hadn't been mistaken, it really was the woman whose face he had
recognised among Pierre Clairmont's sculptures. Drooping eyelids, an
open smile, a mass of curly hair pinned back behind her ears: Claire
Ottissier, aged twenty-six, a social worker for the town council of Nevers.

Louis took a few sips of his coffee. Praise be for the vicious little
demons, he thought. Thanks to their intervention, he had forced the

wooden women to cut short their dance and abruptly reveal their weighty secret. Without them, he would perhaps have continued to obsess all night without coming up with anything important.

Claire Ottissier had been murdered in her flat in Nevers, one evening at about seven o'clock as she returned from work. Getting on for eight years ago, Louis calculated. The killer had knocked her unconscious, strangled her with a stocking and then stabbed her several times with a short blade. The weapon had not been identified. On the bloodstained lino near the victim's head, the police had noticed some mysterious marks, as if the killer had run his fingers through the blood. The *Écho Nivernais*, the local paper, had described the scene at length, adding that *'the investigators are working on these puzzling marks, which will no doubt soon reveal their sinister message'.*

Louis helped himself to a second coffee, put in sugar and stirred. The puzzling marks had, needless to say, never revealed anything at all.

That was why he had been so disturbed by the tangled carpet at the scene of the second victim. He had already noted something like that eight years earlier, and it now seemed to him perfectly clear that Claire had been the first woman to be murdered by the scissors killer, long before the victim in the Square d'Aquitaine. What had happened in the meantime? Had there been other murders which had gone undetected? Outside France perhaps? Was the woman in the Square d'Aquitaine in fact the twentieth victim?

Louis stood up, rinsed out the cup and stood thinking. He was wide awake now and the first light was appearing through the shutters. He hesitated about what he should do vis-à-vis Loisel. It would be an act of kindness to inform him about this first crime by the scissors killer. But to accuse Clairmont without any evidence wouldn't help Clément. Even if it delayed the manhunt. Louis was inclined to let murderers have more rope with which to hang themselves, a very risky method which Loisel wouldn't like at all, and you could understand him.

Undecided, he came back to the table and looked at the last news-paper cuttings from eight years ago. A long article in *La Bourgogne* had gone into detail about the victim's life, her schooling, her merits, her professional career and her marriage plans. Then there was a separate article headed 'PASTRY COOK GIVES CHASE, RISKING HIS OWN LIFE'. Louis jumped. He had no memory at all of this development. One of Claire's neighbours, Jean-Michel Bonnot, a baker and pastry cook, alerted by the sounds coming from his normally quiet neighbour's flat, had knocked and then, finding the door unlocked, had gone inside the apartment. He had surprised the killer kneeling beside the young woman's body. The killer – and it was not clear whether this was a man or a woman, according to the report – had leapt up, pushed him aside roughly and rushed down the stairs. The neighbour had given chase. But since he had paused to tell his wife to attend to the victim, the killer had got ahead. Bonnot had nevertheless pursued his quarry along the embankment of the Loire, but had lost the figure in the old streets. Still in shock, Bonnot had unfortunately been unable to give more than a very vague description of the individual, who had been muffled up with a scarf, a woollen hat and a big coat. '*The investigators nevertheless have high hopes of being able to apprehend the murderer who only nar-rowly escaped the courageous pastry cook.*'

Two other papers carried photos of Bonnot, but without details of his account. The following week, a few lines assured readers that the inquiry was still under way. Then silence. On an index card attached to the last report, Louis had written, '*Unsolved crime, filed.*' Plus the date.

He leaned back in his chair, eyes closed. So they had not been able to lay hands on this man or woman, but someone had seen the killer. Without being able to give a proper description, the baker had never-theless given chase and seen how this person ran, moved. That could be an immensely important element.

He had to see this guy right away. Chin in hand, he gazed at the features of Claire Ottissier. Then he fell asleep, his head on the table.

XXXI

IN THE MORNING, LOUIS, STILL FEELING QUITE DAZED, PARKED IN THE SHADE on the corner of the rue Chasle. It was ten thirty and the sun was already beating down fiercely. This time, Louis had brought along an old vaporiser, in order to spray Bufo from time to time. He grabbed the file on the woman from Nevers, thrust the toad into his jacket pocket, and walked across the bare patch of garden that Marc called 'the fallow strip', in medieval field-system terminology, not without reason. He knocked a few times at the dosshouse door, without getting any answer. He backed up to the gate and whistled. The head of Vandoosler senior popped out from a skylight under the slate roof.

'Oh, it's you, the German,' he called down. 'Come on in, the door's open! Just push it!'

Louis shook his head, and walked back across the fallow strip. Vandoosler called down to him in the hall that St Mark was out cleaning houses, St Luke was busy teaching, and St Matthew was down in the cellar, with you-know-who and you-know-who.

'And what the fuck are they doing down there?'

'Sticking together bits of flint!' the old policeman called, before slamming his door.

With heavy steps and deep in thought, Louis made his way down the narrow spiral staircase that smelled of wet cork. In the cellar, with its vaulted ceiling, between a set of wine racks and a workbench covered with tools and propped up with telephone directories, Mathias was leaning over a long table lit by a powerful lamp: scattered on its surface were hundreds of little fragments of flint. It was the first time Louis had set foot here. And he had no idea that Mathias had made himself this underground cave. Clément, by now with a stubbly beard, was standing alongside him, examining a piece of stone and concentrating hard, poking out his tongue. Marthe, perched on a tall decorator's stool alongside the wine bottles, was muttering to herself, cigar in mouth, as she did a crossword.

'Ah, Ludwig,' she said. 'Just in time. Can you tell me the capital of Chad? Eight letters, fourth letter a.'

'N'Djamena,' said Mathias without looking up.

Taken aback, Louis asked himself if anyone in this strange house had any idea of the gravity of the situation. Mathias held out a hand to shake, greeted him with a cheerful smile and went back to work. If Louis understood right, the point of the operation was to reconstitute a piece of flint that some prehistoric man had devoted himself to shattering into hundreds of pieces, thousands of years ago. Mathias was able to select, try, and place one piece after another with remarkable speed. Clément was attempting to fit together two bits of flint, not very successfully.

'Let me see,' said Mathias.

Clément held out his hand, showing his effort.

'OK,' said Mathias with a nod, 'stick them together, but don't use too much tape.'

The hunter-gatherer looked up at Louis with a grin.

'Vauquer is actually good at this, personally,' he said. 'He's got a good eye for it. Reassembling flints is tricky stuff.'

'How old are these?' asked Louis.

'They date from 12,000 BC.'

Louis nodded. He had the feeling that to bring out the photo of the woman who had been murdered in Nevers might seem inappropriate in Mathias's palaeolithic sanctum. He'd better get Clément out of it.

Louis took the young man upstairs to the ground floor, and sat him down at the big table, the shutters still being closed.

'Are you OK here?' he asked.

'Yesterday, someone knocked at the door and everyone got worried about me, personally,' Clément replied.

'You mean someone came visiting?' asked Louis in alarm.

Clément nodded gravely, looking straight at Louis.

'A very long visit from a strange woman,' he said. 'But they took me down to the cellar with Mathias. And because I was bored and sad, Mathias got me to work with those little bits of stone. They were made by cavemen a long time before I was born. It's important to mend them. Then after the omelette last night, I played beggar-my-neighbour with the old man, because they don't have TV here. The strange woman, she'd gone, personally.'

'Did you think about the other women? The murders?'

'No-o. Or maybe I did. But I don't remember.'

Just then Marc came in with a pile of shirts under his arm, and greeted them with a vague wave.

'Headache,' he said, pushing past. 'The cognac last night, probably. I'm going to make some strong coffee.'

'Good, I was just going to ask for some,' said Louis. 'I got only two hours' sleep last night.'

'You couldn't sleep?' asked Marc, dropping the shirts into the laundry basket. 'You didn't try the little demons?'

'Yes, I did, but they got crushed by all those women made of wood.'

'So it goes,' said Marc, bringing out the cups. 'Stuff happens.'

'And you're not interested in hearing about my night?'

'Up to a point.'

'Well, just listen carefully,' said Louis, opening the file on Claire Ottissier. 'Last night, one of Clairmont's wooden statues was going round in my head like crazy until I stopped and paid it some real attention. It hurt a lot and it stopped me sleeping.'

'Sure it wasn't the cognac?'

'It could be the cognac as well, but no, it was that damned statue, believe me. Remember the one that was by the clock, facing the wall?'

'Yeah, maybe, but I didn't really look at it.'

'Well, I did. And it's *her*,' said Louis, sliding the newspaper cutting across the table. 'Spitting image, as Clairmont would say.'

Marc came over to the table, holding the kettle, and looked at the yellowing paper.

'Doesn't mean anything to me,' he said.

'What about you, Clément?' asked Louis, showing him the photo.

Marc took a couple of pills and filtered the coffee, while Clément looked at the woman in the picture and Louis looked at Clément.

'Have I got to say something about, I mean to say, this woman?' asked Clément.

'Yes, that's it.'

'Like what?'

Louis sighed.

'You don't know her? You've never seen her? Perhaps some evening, eight years ago in Nevers?'

Clément looked at Louis in silence, his mouth open.

'Oh, for heaven's sake, don't bully him,' said Marc, pouring out the coffee.

'Don't you start acting like Marthe now. He's not made of glass.'

'Yes, he is a bit,' said Marc, 'and if you panic him, he'll shiver to bits or run away. Explain what you want clearly, and don't set traps.'

'All right, begin again. This woman, Clément, she used to live in Nevers, she was called Claire, and she was strangled eight years ago, one night, in her flat. The murderer stabbed her a lot of times. And near her head, there were these weird marks, just the same as with the three women killed here in Paris, in the Square d'Aquitaine, the rue de la

Tour-des-Dames and the rue de l'Étoile. So that means this killer started on his series a long time ago. He started with this woman, in Nevers.'

'She's dead?' asked Clément, pointing to the woman's face.

'Yes, absolutely,' said Louis. 'And then the killer disappeared for eight years, maybe abroad, then he came to Paris, and started it again.'

'The Secateur,' said Clément. 'Tsk, tsk.'

'Either the Secateur or the third man,' said Louis. 'The one at the rape, the one whose name we don't know.'

'But why did this guy rape the woman in the park, but not touch the others?' asked Marc, pulling the newspaper across.

'Maybe the third man didn't touch that woman either. Ask Clément. He told us that one man ran away first, because he was still fully dressed, remember?'

'Clairmont?' asked Marc, looking carefully at the cutting.

'Well, he certainly made a sculpture of her, in any case, which is pretty creepy. Like he did of Nicole Verdot.'

'But he didn't vanish for eight years and nor did the Secateur.'

'Tsk, tsk,' said Clément, looking down into his coffee.

'No, I know,' said Louis. 'I asked Merlin about his stepfather and the old boy never left his side, to his regret in fact. But then he could, like the Secateur might, lie low for a number of years, repressing his . . .'

'His buzzing bee,' suggested Marc. 'The deadly creature buzzing in his bonnet.'

'Well, if you must,' said Louis, waving his hand, as if to bat away the insect. 'That's unless the third man is a completely different individual. An accomplice of the Secateur, say. He takes part in the rape, he kills the woman that night, and Rousselet as well, and less than a year later, he kills this young woman, Claire. Then after that, he takes fright and goes as far away as he can, to Australia or somewhere, and nothing more is heard about him and his crimes.'

'Yes,' agreed Mark, 'we don't often get a lot of news from Australia, if you think about it.'

'But he comes back,' Louis went on, 'with the same obsessions in his head. Only this time, he doesn't take any risks. He prepares an exit strategy for himself with great care. And he tries to find the little wretch who turned a hose on him and soaked him with freezing water right in the middle of the rape.'

'That's me, that's what I did,' said Clément, looking up suddenly.

'Yes, Clément,' said Louis gently, 'don't worry, I remember that. So he goes looking for him, he finds him almost in the same place he'd left him, back in Nevers. He gets him to go to Paris, and he makes him the fall guy.'

'Yeah, I get it now,' Marc said, 'you've spent all night on this. But it still doesn't get us anywhere. It adds one more crime, true, but we already knew this guy's bee was buzzing because of some past event.'

'Drop the bee please.'

'And it tells us that that old guy, Clairmont, carves images of *actual* women who've been killed, which is not negligible of course. But it still doesn't give us enough evidence to get Clément out of the frame. The old man could just be a fantasist who reads the local paper. All he got hold of was their photos, not real women.'

'By the way,' said Louis suddenly, 'did someone visit here yesterday?'

'Not to worry, some girl Lucien knows. We took Clément down to the cellar. She didn't hear or see anything, it's OK.'

Louis made a gesture of impatience.

'Can you try and get it into Lucien's head,' he said aggressively, 'that this is no time to fix up dates with women in this house?'

'I have already.'

'That guy is going to land us right in it.'

'Oh, change the disc,' said Marc defensively.

Louis sat down the other side of the table and thought for a few minutes in silence, chin in hands.

'This woman in Nevers,' he said, 'takes us forward three places. Because of her, we have something on the old woodcarver, though without any proof, I agree. But it still means he's involved somehow. Secondly, it makes nonsense of Lucien's poetic theory. The scissors murders started long before the Square d'Aquitaine case, probably in Nevers with this poor girl Claire, and perhaps continued somewhere else – Australia for the sake of argument.'

'If you must.'

'So we would need some lines that came *before* the first verse of his poem, and that makes no sense at all.'

'No, it doesn't,' Marc agreed. 'But you also said this murderer counts his victims. In that case, why did he talk to Clément about the "first" woman and the "second" one? If they weren't?'

Louis pulled a face.

'Well, we'd have to say they were the first that Clément was supposed to be trailing, but not the first in the criminal series.'

'So the series is not finite, in that case?'

'Oh, stuff it, Marc, I don't know. All I do know is that we have to forget all about "El Desdichado" and the black sun and all that. The key must be somewhere else. And my third point is that from this murder years ago in Nevers, we might have some chance of getting a description of the murderer. At least it might indicate if it was Clairmont or the Secateur.'

'Tsk, tsk,' said Clément.

'Or you-know-who's doll,' Louis confided in Marc's ear. 'Or someone completely different. Because we know that the night when Claire Ottissier was killed, the murderer was almost caught by the neighbour who chased him for some time. A "courageous pastry cook" as they call him. You can read the article.'

Marc gave a whistle.

'Yeah, you see?' said Louis. 'I'm off to Nevers again after lunch. Come with me if you can manage it. Let your godfather and Mathias stay with Clément, it's fine, they've got all those stones to fit together.'

'What about my cleaning jobs? Eh? You think I can just drop them?'

'Cancel them, it's only for a day or two.'

'That makes me look unreliable,' Marc grumbled. 'I've only just managed to find these jobs. And why do you want me to come anyway? You can perfectly well chat up this courageous pastry cook on your own.'

'Yes, of course, but I couldn't do a sketch of Clairmont or the Secateur and you could, you're good at drawing.'

'Tsk, tsk,' said Clément.

'Just forget about the Secateur for a bit, will you, Clément?' said Louis, putting a hand on his arm.

Marc was looking sulky and undecided.

'Well, think about it,' said Louis. 'I'll be back at about two. Maybe Madame Toussaint's ironing is less urgent than a murder case.'

Marc glanced at the laundry basket.

'Madame Mallet's ironing,' he corrected him. 'But why did the papers at the time say the killer could have been a woman?'

'No idea. That bothered me too.'

XXXII

THE SECATEUR WAS SITTING IN THE SHADE OF HIS TOOLSHED, SPOONING UP THE contents of the tin dish. Louis watched him eating for a few moments. Then he came to lean against a tree facing him, and took a sandwich out of its paper wrapper. The two men went on chewing without saying a word. The cemetery was empty and silent, the only sound the murmur of distant traffic. The Secateur had spread out on his satchel a clean white cloth with lace trimming, on which he had placed his bread and a knife. He wiped his brow, glanced somewhat anxiously at Louis, then went on eating, without paying him attention.

'Look out, a wasp!' Louis suddenly shouted, shooting out his arm.

The Secateur moved his spoon away from his mouth, and waved it in the air. The insect flew off it, buzzed a few times round his hair, then disappeared.

'Ta,' he said.

'You're welcome.'

The Secateur took another mouthful, looking thoughtful.

'There's a nest in the south wall,' he said. 'I nearly got stung three times yesterday.'

'You should call the emergency services.'

'Yeah.'

He scraped the dish noisily, then held it on his knees, as he reached for the bread.

'Nice cloth you got there,' said Louis.

'Yeah.'

'Looks like it's handmade.'

'My ma made it,' the Secateur muttered. 'Gotta look after it properly. It's a son-protector.'

'A *son-protector*?'

'You deaf or something? My ma, she made them for all of us kids. You got to wash it every Sunday and dry it properly if you want it to work. Cos what my ma used to say was, you wash the cloth every Sunday, you got to know what day of the week it is, so you've not got to drink too much. You've got to get up out of bed. You've got to have soap and water. And all that means a roof over your head. And to have a roof, you got to have enough money for the rent. So to keep the cloth clean, you got to have a *job*, you can't just sit about twiddling your thumbs all the days God gives you, knocking back the vino, that's what my ma said. And *that's* why it's a son-protector, see? My ma,' said the Secateur, tapping his head with the handle of the knife, 'she thought ahead all right.'

'What about the girls then?' asked Louis. 'Is there a daughter-protector too?'

The Secateur shrugged at such a stupid question.

'Girls don't drink,' he said.

'And you wash all your stuff every Sunday?'

'Just the cloth will do, then it'll protect you.'

Louis waved away another wasp, finished his sandwich and brushed the crumbs off his jacket. The Secateur was lucky, he thought. From his own father, he just had that heavy quilt to hold him down in bed when he'd drunk too much.

'I brought you some wine from your region, Sancerre.'

The Secateur looked at him suspiciously.

'I bet that's not all you brought.'

'No, I've got a picture here, it's of a woman. A woman who's dead.'

'Yeah, might have guessed you'd have summat.'

The Secateur stood up, carefully folded the cloth into his filthy satchel, went inside the shed to rinse out his dish, then shouldered a rake.

'Some of us got work to do,' he said.

Louis held out the bottle. The Secateur put down the rake and pulled a corkscrew from his pocket. He uncorked the bottle, and took a few long swigs. Then he held out his hand.

Louis passed him the cutting, folded so as to show the photograph. The man looked at it for a while and had another drink.

'Yeah,' he said. 'So what's the catch?'

'You recognise her?'

'You bet I do. I was still down in Nevers when that happened. Anyone from Nevers would recognise her, papers were full of it for a couple of weeks and all. Are you collecting them or what?'

'I think the scissors killer murdered her, same one. It could be you for instance.'

'Go fuck yourself. Think I was the only man in Nevers? The village idiot was around same time, could have been him.'

'But he didn't run off to Paris two weeks after that murder. Like you did. Right? You were scared?'

'I'm not scared of anything, except not looking after my cloth. There weren't any jobs in Nevers, that's all.'

'I'm going now, Thévenin,' said Louis, putting the cutting in his pocket. 'I'm going back there again, to your home town.'

The Secateur started to rake the gravel path, looking sombre.

'I'm going to see the man that *chased* the murderer of that girl,' Louis added.

'Leave me be, why don't you?'

Louis walked slowly across the cemetery, along a sun-baked alleyway, and went back to his car which was stiflingly hot. He sprayed water over Bufo before putting him on the passenger seat. He wondered where would be best to put the toad during the journey, if Marc Vandoosler did decide to come. In the glove compartment perhaps? Louis moved out the road maps and other odds and ends and looked at the small space. He didn't know how Marc could be so allergic to amphibians. But then he didn't understand Marc at all, and vice versa.

At two o'clock, he pushed the door of the dosshouse. Lucien was drinking coffee with Vandoosler senior and Louis accepted his fourth cup of the day.

'Did you talk to the cops then?' Lucien asked.

'About Nerval? Yes I did, and they didn't give a toss.'

'You're kidding!' Lucien cried.

'Nope.'

'You mean they're not going to do anything about the fourth woman at risk?'

'Well, they're not going to stake out your streets anyway. They're waiting for the people who are sheltering Clément to make a mistake and let him roam. Poor saps, they call them.'

Lucien had gone bright red. He gave a sniff and tossed back his hair.

'They're not *my* streets, for Christ's sake!' he shouted. 'And what are you going to do about it?'

'Nothing. I'm going to Nevers.'

Lucien stood up, pushing his chair back noisily, and left the room.

'See what I mean?' commented Vandoosler senior. 'St Luke is a hothead. If it's Clément you want, he's downstairs with St Matthew. St Mark is in his study working.'

Feeling angry himself, Louis set off up to the second floor and knocked at the door. Marc was sitting at his desk, surrounded by his medieval accounts. He had a pencil in his mouth and made a wordless sign with his head.

'Come on,' said Louis, 'we're going.'

'Mone mine anyming,' said Marc without taking his eyes off his manuscript.

'Take that pencil out of your mouth, can't understand a word you're saying.'

'Won't find anything,' said Marc, without the pencil, and turning to look at Louis. 'And in particular, I'm not keen to leave Lucien just now.'

'What do you mean, just now? You're not afraid he'll let Clément go wandering the streets again, are you?'

'No, it's something else. Wait here, I've got to go and talk to him.'

Marc went up to the third floor two steps at a time and returned ten minutes later.

'OK,' he said. 'Let me get some things together.'

Louis watched as he stuffed some clothes into his rucksack and added a bundle of photocopies – of his medieval manuscripts – as he did every time he left his study, refusing to be parted from them for even one night. Louis thought that Marc was perhaps in need of a son-protecting cloth to combat his vertiginous plunges into the deep well of history.

XXXIII

MARC HAD TAKEN THE WHEEL, WHILE LOUIS HAD A NAP ON THE BACK SEAT. WAKE me up when we get to the Loire, he had said. By about half past three, Marc had passed Montargis, and he felt in the glove compartment for a road map. His fingers touched something dry and hot and he had cried out, as he braked sharply and pulled on to the verge. Venturing to peep inside the open compartment, he had seen Bufo sleeping on a damp rag. Oh God, he had touched the toad! In disgust, he turned round to shout at Louis, but the German had not even woken up.

Marc, stammering various curses, had very slowly closed the glove compartment again, summoning up the image of the Courageous Pastry Cook to give himself the nerve. A guy who gives chase to the scissors killer can't run away because of a wretched toad. Dripping with sweat, he drove off again and didn't calm down for quite a while.

By half past four, his shirt clinging to his back, he was driving along the banks of the Loire. He decided to wait a while before waking Louis up and showering him with abuse. About thirty kilometres from Nevers, he braked, did a U-turn and parked the car on the main square of a small medieval town, leaving the German and his toad to sleep in the car, while he went on foot to the church. He enjoyed himself exploring it for half an hour, then sat for a long while on the square outside the west front, looking up in admiration at the facade and the high tower. When its bells began to strike six o'clock, he stretched, stood up and went back to the car. Louis was waiting for him, leaning on the bonnet.

'OK, Let's be on our way,' said Marc, lifting a hand in apology.

He took the wheel, and headed back to the N7.

'What the fuck were you doing, stopping here?' said Louis. 'Have you seen what time it is?'

'We've got plenty of time. I couldn't pass without going to greet Cluny's eldest daughter.'

'You what?'

'A girl I've always been in love with. Over there,' he added, pointing to the right, as the car passed in front of the church again. 'One of the most beautiful Romanesque daughters there is. Look at her, look at her!' he cried, waving his arm. 'She'll be gone by the time we're round the corner.'

Louis sighed, turned his head to took and settled back down, grinding his teeth. It wasn't the moment for Marc to plunge into one of his historical wells, and since the previous day, Louis had felt he was on the slippery slope.

'Right, fine,' he said, 'now put your foot down, we've lost enough time as it is.'

'It wouldn't have happened if you hadn't put your filthy toad in the glove compartment. I needed some spiritual cleansing after an unwanted contact of the flesh.'

The two men remained silent as they covered the final kilometres and Louis took the wheel as they entered Nevers, since he knew his way around the town to some extent. He nevertheless needed to consult a street plan several times before they found the way to the shop owned by Jean-Michel Bonnot, outside which they parked. Marc was the first to speak, suggesting they might need a stiff drink before breaking in on the domestic life of the Courageous Pastry Cook.

'Are you sure he'll be home?' Marc asked, as they sat down with their beers.

'Yes. It's Monday, he won't have opened the shop today. Anyway, I called his wife this morning to give them notice. Do you think you could do a drawing of the Secateur and Clairmont?'

'Well, more or less.'

'Get going now, since we're not doing anything else.'

Marc took out his sketch pad and pen from his satchel and started drawing. Louis watched as he worked for about fifteen minutes, a frown on his face.

'Shall I draw the bee as well?' Marc asked, without stopping his drawing.

'No! Instead do a general full-length outline of how they look, as well as the face.'

'All right, but that counts as a supplement. The bee would have been thrown in free.'

Marc finished his sketch and passed it over.

'That do you?'

Louis nodded several times to show his approval.

'Off we go then,' he said, rolling up the sheet of paper. 'Gone seven o'clock.'

Bonnot's wife asked them to wait in the sitting room. Marc sat on the edge of a large sofa with a crocheted lace cover and embarked on his second sketch. Louis had seated himself comfortably in a large plush armchair, stretching out his long legs. He hated to keep them bent because of his knee. Jean-Michel Bonnot came into the room. He was a short pot-bellied man, with very red cheeks, a doubtful expression and extremely thick glasses. Marc and Louis stood up politely and he shook their hands awkwardly. Through the open door they could hear the sound of children eating a meal.

'I'm sorry we've arrived rather late,' Louis apologised. 'My colleague here had to stop on the way to see an old friend.'

'It doesn't matter. My wife didn't say an exact time.'

Louis explained at length to the baker the chain of events which might link the murder in Nevers long ago to the current tragic string of killings in Paris.

He put it to him that his help might be decisive in tracking down a murderer whom he had bravely chased eight years before.

'Oh, it was nothing,' said Bonnot modestly.

'That's not true,' said Louis, 'you were very brave. All the papers said so at the time.'

'I thought the Paris police were already looking for a man – they've published an identikit picture.'

'That's only one of their leads,' Louis lied. 'But they *are* pretty sure that the murderer, whoever he is, comes from Nevers.'

'You're not from the police, are you?' asked the baker, glancing suspiciously at Louis.

'I work for the Ministry of the Interior.'

'Ah.'

Marc was busy with his pencil, looking up from time to time at the Courageous Pastry Cook. He wondered how Bonnot would have reacted if Louis had put on the table the Repulsive Amphibian (which he had surreptitiously slipped into his pocket as they left the car). He imagined that Bonnot would have contemplated it without fuss. Perhaps one day he himself would be able to react without fuss, there was no need to despair.

'The man in the identikit picture, did you recognise him at all?' Louis was asking.

'No-o,' said Bonnot, with a slight hesitation.

'Not sure?'

'Well, the other day, my wife was joking that he reminded us of this man who lives here, he's a bit simple. We see him now and again, he plays his accordion in the street, and we sometimes give him money. I told my wife we shouldn't make fun of people like that, the simple-minded. Or murderers either, come to that.'

Just then Madame Bonnot came in with a bottle of pastis and a large dish of pastries.

'Help yourselves,' said Bonnot, jerking his chin at the pastries. 'I never eat cakes myself. If you're a baker, you have to be self-disciplined.'

He helped himself to a drink, at which point Louis and Marc both gave him to understand that they would be quite interested in the pastis too.

'I'm sorry, I thought the police didn't drink on duty.'

'Ah, but we're from the Ministry,' said Louis, 'and we don't have rules like that.'

Bonnot glanced at him doubtfully once more, but filled their glasses without comment. Marc passed over the sketches of Clairmont and the Secateur, and helped himself to a large cream cake, before beginning a sketch of Clément Vauquer in outline. He hadn't particularly warmed to Bonnot, and managed to take little part in the conversation.

Bonnot was now examining the sketch of the Secateur alongside Louis, fiddling with his glasses. He pulled a face.

'Doesn't look very nice, does he?'

'No, not very,' Louis agreed.

Bonnot then turned to the drawing of Clairmont.

'No,' he said after a minute. 'But how do you expect me to remember? You know what happened. It was in February, the murderer was covered up with a scarf and a cap. I didn't even think to try and see his face, I was so shocked. And then after being pushed over, and running after him, all I could see was his back. I'm really sorry. If I had to choose between these two, by the outline, the shape of the body, I'd vote for this one,' he said, pointing to Clairmont. 'The other one looks a bit too broad-shouldered. But to tell you the truth . . .'

Marc tore off another page and put the sketch of Clément in outline in front of the baker. Then he took a coffee éclair, and went back to his drawings. This guy was certainly a good pastry cook, no question. A fusspot like Lucien might think the pastries were a bit gross and lacking in sophistication, but they were exactly what Marc liked.

'No-o,' said Bonnot. 'I don't know, this one looks a bit too thin.'

'How did he run?'

'Not fast, he didn't go that fast, he flapped his arms and he stopped every now and again for breath, no, he certainly wasn't a sprinter.'

'How come he got away from you then?'

'Well, I'm no good at running myself, and I had to stop to pick up my glasses when they fell off, and the man got away then. That's how it happened. Simple as that.'

'And nobody else ran with you, nobody else saw him?'

'No.'

'And you were alone when he attacked the woman?'

'My wife was in.'

'And she heard nothing?'

'No, but you see, I was on my way upstairs. I reached the landing just as it was happening.'

'I see.'

'Why are you asking me all this?'

'To explore your reaction, which could be helpful. Not many people would have run after a murderer.'

The man shrugged.

'I promise you, they wouldn't,' Louis said. 'And you weren't afraid?'

'Well, I can be as afraid as the next man. But there's one thing men aren't afraid of, isn't there?

'What do you mean?'

'Women! What do you think? And when I saw this man, I really thought it was a woman! So I ran after "her" without thinking. Simple as that.'

Marc nodded, still scribbling on his pad. The 'Moderately Courageous Pastry Cook', he thought to himself.

So this visit hadn't been in vain, the man was reassuringly normal.

'Like the cakes?' Bonnot asked, turning to Marc.

'Excellent!' Marc replied, waving his pencil. 'Very filling, but excellent.'

Bonnot nodded in approval and turned back to Louis.

'The police told me I must have been wrong. A woman wouldn't have had the strength to knock our neighbour out like that. She was quite young and strong our neighbour, I have to say.'

'I'd really like to know, though,' said Louis, pointing a finger towards the pastis bottle, 'what made you think it was a woman. Did you see a face, a body, even for a second?'

Bonnot shook his head slowly, and poured out a second glass.

'No, like I said, he was completely covered up. A big dark overcoat, ordinary trousers, like anyone, man or woman, might wear in winter.'

'Hair poking out from under the cap?'

'No, or I didn't see any. Really, I didn't see a thing, I just thought it was a woman, a bulky sort of woman, mind you, not young or agile. I just don't know why. Not because of the clothes or the shape or face or hair. Maybe something else, but I don't know what it was.'

'Try and think, it could be very important.'

'But they told me it was a man,' Bonnot objected.

'Yeah, but what if it was you that was right?' suggested Louis.

An evasive smile flitted across the baker's face. He put his chin in his hands and thought, muttering to himself. Louis picked up the drawings, and gave them back to Marc, who slipped them inside the pad.

'No, I can't think of anything,' said Bonnot, sitting up. 'It's all too long ago.'

'Well, it might come back to you,' said Louis, standing up. 'I'll call you later tonight to give you my number at the hotel. And if anything at all occurs to you about this woman, or about the sketches, just leave me a message, I'll be here all tomorrow morning.'

Marc and Louis walked through the streets of Nevers, looking for somewhere to eat. It was still very warm, and Louis carried his jacket over his arm.

'Not much luck there,' commented Marc.

'No, he's not particularly engaging, is he?'

'Waste of time my doing the sketches. The Only Very Moderately Courageous Pastry Cook is blind as a bat anyway.'

'But that bit about a woman was interesting. If it's true.'

'Hard to tell, he doesn't seem very forthcoming.'

Louis shrugged.

'That's how some people are. Look, let's eat here, it's the sort of little restaurant Clément used to play his accordion in.'

'I'm not very hungry,' Marc admitted.

'What were the cakes like?'

'Really, really good. Whatever else, he's a fantastic baker.'

Louis picked an out-of-the-way table.

'Tell me,' he said, as they sat down, 'what were you drawing in the possibly Cowardly Pastry Cook's place, after the other sketches? Churches, flowers, cakes?'

'Old Clairmont would tell you that all of those are just substitutes for women. No, none of those.'

'What then?'

'You really want to know?'

Marc held out the pad and Louis pulled a face.

'Yuk, what's that? One of your rotten little demons?'

'It's an enlarged portrait about forty times of the bee in Clairmont's bonnet,' explained Marc with a smile.

Louis shook his head, disappointed. Marc turned the page.

'And here's another insect,' he said, 'a worse one.'

Louis turned the pad around, trying to make sense of the tangle of features and black holes.

'I can't see what that is at all,' he said, handing back the pad.

'That's because it's impenetrable,' said Marc. 'That's the bee in the killer's bonnet.'

XXXIV

AT SIX THAT EVENING, LUCIEN, IN A STATE OF HIGH EXCITEMENT, HAD HURRIED back from giving his lectures and down to the cellar. Mathias and Clément were working on a piece of flint with a roll of sticky tape.

'Are you ready?' Lucien asked.

'Just finishing up,' said Mathias calmly.

Lucien drummed his fingers on the table, while the hunter-gatherer finished sticking his pieces together. Then Matthias took the flint from Clément's hands and laid it carefully in a container.

'Hurry up!' said Lucien.

'OK, OK. Have you got some food ready?'

'A veggie sandwich and a bottle of water for you. And for me a take-away chicken curry and a beer.'

Mathias made no comment and went upstairs, propelling Clément gently ahead of him.

In the refectory, Lucien took the broom and banged hard four times on the ceiling. A fragment of plaster fell at his feet and Mathias made imperceptible signs of disapproval. The attic door slammed and Vandoosler senior appeared soon after.

'Already?' he asked.

'I'd prefer to be there by seven,' Lucien replied firmly. 'Lack of preparation in military matters inevitably results in a bloodbath.'

'All right,' said the godfather. 'So which street are you taking?'

'Mathias will be in the rue du Soleil, and I'll take the rue de la Lune. Too bad about the Soleil d'Or – there are only two of us.'

'Are you sure about this?

'About the poem? Sure as I can be. I've got Marc's sketches of the two guys and he's described them to me in detail.'

'Could be a complete stranger.'

Lucien sniffed impatiently.

'Have to take our chances. You disagree?'

'No, no, not at all.'

The older man saw them to the door, locked it behind them and pocketed the key. That evening he would be spending many hours alone with Clément Vauquer.

XXXV

AT THE HOTEL DE LA VIEILLE LANTERNE IN NEVERS, THEY DIDN'T SERVE BREAKFAST after 10 a.m. Louis was used to being a victim of the rule, since he belonged to that suspect category group of people who get up late, between eleven and twelve: the night owls, oddballs, refugees, criminals, layabouts, bachelors, hippies, bohemians and people of doubtful morality. At reception, there were two messages for him. Opening the first, Louis recognised Marc's writing, which was not good news.

Greetings, son of the Rhine. I'm leaving at eight to see the eldest daughter I told you about, and the surrounding buildings I didn't have time to see yesterday. I'll be back between 2.30 and 3.30 this afternoon on the old bridge. If I don't see you, I'll take the train back. If your toad has a sudden urge to visit the banks of the Loire, please don't stand in his way.
Marc

Louis shook his head irritably. How anyone could get up at dawn to go and see a church you'd already seen the day before was beyond his understanding. Marc was plunging into his wretched Middle Ages, and wouldn't be any help. The other message was much shorter. Jean-Michel Bonnot asked him to call by his shop as soon as possible.

Louis found his way back quite easily to the shop of the man they were now calling the Craven Pastry Cook. Madame Bonnot took him to the stiflingly hot kitchens in the basement, smelling of butter and flour. He remembered that he hadn't had any breakfast. Bonnot, redder than ever in the face, and bursting with impatience, gave him two croissants.

'Something's come back to you?' asked Louis.

'Absolutely,' said Bonnot, rubbing his hands together to get the flour off. 'I just couldn't get a wink's sleep last night, thinking about our poor neighbour, Claire, she was haunting me like a ghost. I'm worn out.'

'Yeah,' said Louis, 'I know the feeling.'

'My wife said it was because of the moon, but no, I knew it was because of the neighbour. Had to be, after you'd been round talking about her.'

'Sorry.'

'And then suddenly, about two in the morning, I got this flash of recall. Then I realised why I thought the killer was a woman.'

Louis stared hard at the baker.

'Go ahead,' he said.

'You're going to be very disappointed, but you did say to tell you as soon as –'

'Go ahead,' Louis repeated.

'If you really want this. When I went into the room, the killer was crouching down beside Claire's body, in his big coat. I could see blood, so I panicked and kind of choked. He heard me and didn't even turn his head, just jumped up and pushed me over hard. But just before that, in a split second, he picked something up off the carpet. And it was a lipstick!'

Bonnot stopped and looked up at Louis.

'Go on,' said Louis.

'Well, that's all. What with the lipstick, and a stocking on the floor, I must have put two and two together. I started running after *her*, without thinking for a moment that it could be a man.'

'Yeah, I see what you mean.'

'But still, I ask you, if it *was* a man, what was he doing with a tube of lipstick?'

Both men fell silent for a few moments. Louis munched his second croissant slowly, as he thought.

'This lipstick, where did he pick it up from?'

The man hesitated.

'Near the head? Alongside the body?'

Bonnot looked at the floor and fiddled with his glasses.

'Near the head,' he said.

'Sure?'

'I think so.'

'Which side?'

'To the right? Near the face.'

Louis felt his heartbeat get a bit faster. Bonnot was staring at the ground again. With his foot, he was drawing circles in the flour.

'And from the front door,' Louis insisted, 'you could really see that it was lipstick?'

'Well, not exactly,' Bonnot admitted. 'But from a distance, you can recognise some things. It was red and silver, and made a little metallic sound when he picked it up. As if it was hitting against rings on his fingers. Just like my wife when she picks up her lipstick. She keeps dropping it, don't ask me why. So I didn't see it clearly, but I glimpsed a flash of colour and I heard the click. And if that had been in my house, well, it would have been lipstick. Anyway, that's why I thought it was a woman.'

'Well, thank you,' said Louis, still looking preoccupied, and holding out his hand. 'I don't want to keep you any longer. I'll leave you my number in Paris just in case.'

'No need,' said Bonnot as they shook hands. 'I've told you what you wanted to know, I can't help you any more. The pictures you showed me yesterday, they still don't mean anything to me.'

Louis walked slowly back to the car. It was only midday, so he had time to call in at the police station and see Pouchet. He considered it only fair and necessary to keep him informed of his progress. They could discuss the matter of horse–donkey reproduction, and the Nevers murder. There was a good chance that Pouchet had been the officer questioning Bonnot at the time.

Louis picked Marc up at three fifteen. He was leaning over the parapet of the old bridge and dreamily watching the Loire flow by. Louis hooted and leaned over to open the passenger door. Marc jumped, ran to the car and Louis pulled away without comment.

More to break into Marc's dreams than to inform him, Louis reported in detail on that morning's conversation with the Craven Pastry Cook, and his lunch with Pouchet. Yes, he had indeed questioned the witness at the time. But no, he had never mentioned seeing a lipstick. Louis had paid for four beers and they had drunk the health of all future baby mules.

'You what?' asked Marc.

'We had a bet on the mystery of where mules come from: you know, they're like big donkeys.'

'What mystery?' said Marc innocently. 'A mule's a cross between a male donkey and a mare. And the other way round it's called a hinny. So what was the bet about?'

'Nothing,' said Louis, watching the road.

XXXVI

AFTER DROPPING MARC OFF IN FRONT OF THE DOSSHOUSE, LOUIS WENT STRAIGHT to the rue de l'Université. Old Clairmont's voice answered the buzzer.

'Kehlweiler,' said Louis. 'Isn't Merlin there?'

'No, he's out this evening.'

'Excellent, because it was really you I wanted to see.'

'And what might that be about?' said Clairmont, with the superior tone he sometimes affected.

'Claire Ottissier, a woman who died in Nevers.'

A short silence.

'Name doesn't mean anything to me,' came the voice.

'She's facing the clock in your studio, you carved a statue of her.'

'Oh, that one. I'm sorry, I can't remember all their names. So what about her?'

'Can you open the door?' said Louis more forcefully. 'Unless, that is, you want to discuss your penchant for necrophiliac art in front of the whole street.'

Clairmont released the door and Louis went to join him in the studio. The carver was sitting on a tall stool, bare-chested, a cigarette clamped in his mouth. He was working on his current statuette, carving the hair with a small chisel.

'This won't take long,' said Louis, 'because I'm in a hurry.'

'Well, I'm not,' said Clairmont, chipping away. Louis picked up a pile of photographs from the workbench, and sat on another stool facing Clairmont: he began to leaf through them quickly.

'Make yourself at home, why don't you?' said Clairmont ironically.

'How do you choose the women you're going to use as models? Do they have to be pretty?'

'Doesn't matter. All women come down to one in the end.'

'With or without lipstick?'

'Doesn't matter. Why, is that important?'

Louis put the photographs down.

'But you prefer it if they're dead? Women who've been murdered?'

'Not necessarily. But I have immortalised some victims, yes. I don't make any secret of it.'

'Why do you do that?'

'I think I told you before. To make them immortal, or to honour the fact that they went through an ordeal.'

'Does that give you pleasure?'

'Yes, it does.'

'And how many victims have you . . . honoured that way?'

'Could be seven or eight. There was a woman who was strangled on the station in Montpellier, two girls in Arles, and some women from Nevers, from the time I lived there. I haven't done any lately, I think I'm getting over it now.'

Clairmont hit his chisel with a hammer to chip out a fragment of wood.

'So what else is bothering you?' he asked, treading out his cigarette end in the sawdust.

Louis made a gesture and the old man passed him a cigarette.

'It's my intention presently to have you arrested for the rape and murder of Nicole Verdot and the murder of Claire Ottissier,' said Louis, lighting his cigarette from a match offered him by Clairmont. 'Pending raising a few other charges.'

Clairmont shook out the match, smiled, and went back to work.

'That's just ridiculous,' he said.

'Never mind. The statuettes of two of your victims and your presence at the time would be quite enough to convince Commissaire Loisel, especially if I ask him. He's on the case of the scissors killer, and he needs an arrest.'

'What's that got to do with me?'

'Claire was the first victim of this killer. After Nicole Verdot, but Nicole doesn't fit the sequence. She was just the beginning.'

The sculptor looked slightly worried.

'You want to try and pin all that on me? Because of my statues? You really must be nuts.'

'You don't understand my plan. As you say, the charges won't stick and they'll have to let you go after forty-eight hours, which may not be very pleasant ones. But when you get back, the damage will be done. Your stepson will always suspect that you were a party to the rape of Nicole Verdot. Scandal, rumour – mud always sticks. So much so that he'll chuck you out – that's if he doesn't attack you with your own chainsaw. And since you depend on him for money, you'll be on the streets.'

Louis stood up and walked round the studio, hands behind his back.

'And what if I don't like your plan?' said Clairmont, now looking anxious.

'In that case, you'll tell me all you know about the night Nicole Verdot was raped, and I would then forget about my plan, for the moment. Because you *do* know something. Either you were there yourself, or you know about it. Your barn was only a matter of about twenty metres from where it happened.'

'My barn was behind the trees and I was fast asleep.'

'Well, it's up to you. But make your mind up, because I haven't got all night.'

Clairmont pressed both hands down on the head of the statue he was working on and sighed, looking at the floor.

'This smacks of police brutality,' he muttered between his teeth.

'Yep, correct.'

'I didn't have anything to do with *either* that rape *or* any murder.'

'And your version is . . .?'

'It was Rousselet, that student who drowned in the Loire. And the gardener.'

'You mean Vauquer?'

'No, not the idiot, the other one.'

'Thévenin? The Secateur?' asked Louis with a start.

'Yes, that's it, the Secateur. And another man.'

'Who?'

'I didn't recognise him. It was Rousselet that raped Nicole, the Secateur didn't have time, and the third man didn't do anything.'

'How do you know?'

Clairmont hesitated.

'Come on, let's have it,' said Louis, gritting his teeth.

'Because I saw it all from my window.'

'And you didn't rush out?'

Clairmont clung on to the wooden statue.

'No, I was watching through binoculars.'

'Bravo, what a hero! And that's why you didn't say anything to the police?'

'Of course.'

'Even when Vauquer was under suspicion?'

'They released him right away.'

Louis walked once more round the room, slowly, and without uttering a word.

'So what is there to prove that you weren't the third man yourself?'

'It wasn't me!' said Clairmont forcefully. 'It was some stranger, a voyeur, perhaps someone the Secateur knew. If you go and find him, you'd probably find your answer there.'

'What do you know about him?'

'Two days later, I saw the Secateur in a cafe in Nevers. He was pissed and throwing money about in the bar. I was intrigued, so I kept an eye on him for a while. All the money disappeared within a month, unless he put some aside. I always thought he'd been paid for the rape, and Rousselet too, and that the third man, the voyeur, was the one who paid, because he held the girl down.'

'Bravo, deserve a medal, don't you?' repeated Louis.

Silence fell once more. Louis was twisting a piece of wood in his hands which were shaking, and Clairmont was looking at his feet. When Louis headed for the door, the sculptor glanced up in alarm.

'Don't worry,' said Louis, without bothering to turn round. 'Paul won't be hearing about how bravely you defended his fiancée. Unless it turns out you were lying.'

Clenching his teeth and with his hands gripping the wheel, Louis drove fast back up the rue de Rennes, cut in on a bus and made straight for the Montparnasse Cemetery. It was only when he was parking in the rue Froidevaux, just as a heavy rainstorm broke out spattering the windscreen, that he realised that it was well past eight o'clock and the gates of the cemetery would have been shut long ago. Without Marc, he wouldn't be able to climb the wall. Louis sighed. He had to get Marc to do so many things: drawing, running and climbing walls. But Marc had conspicuously taken himself off into another age, and Louis doubted whether he'd be able to drag him out of the house that night.

His car started to show signs of distress on the avenue du Maine and Louis looked at the petrol gauge. Almost out of juice. It limped to a stop near the Tour Montparnasse. He'd gone to Nevers and back without bothering to check the tank. He banged his fist on the dashboard and swore, then pushed the car alongside the pavement. He extracted his bag and shut the door. By now the rain was pouring down on his shoulders. Walking as fast as he could to the square, he plunged into the metro. It had been six months since he had last taken the metro and he had to scan the map to see how to reach the dosshouse.

On the platform, he took off his jacket, without disturbing the pocket holding the toad who, contrary to Marc's wish, had shown no inclination to rush off to the banks of the Loire. In fact Bufo rarely rushed off in any direction. He was a prudent toad.

Louis got into the train, shaking raindrops from his hair, and sat down heavily on a folding seat. The rattle of the carriages drowned out in his mind the atrocious confession of old Clairmont, and that was a very good thing for the next ten minutes. He had had to restrain himself from kicking the old man down into his piles of sawdust. In fact it was a good thing the cemetery gate had been shut as well. He wasn't certain the son-protecting cloth would have been much help to the Secateur tonight.

Louis took some deep breaths and fixed his gaze in turn on a woman with wet hair, on an advertisement for something or other, and on an eleventh-century poem translated from Arabic which was displayed at the end of the carriage. He read it conscientiously from start to finish and tried to understand what it was about, since the meaning seemed very obscure. Something about hope and disgust, and that suited his mood. But suddenly he stiffened. What in God's name was a medieval Arabic poem doing in the metro anyway?

Louis examined the poster. It was officially framed, alongside the advertisement. And the poem's two verses were printed there, followed by the name of the poet and his dates. Followed by the Paris Transport Authority logo and a slogan: *Verse on the move.* Stunned, Louis got out at the next stop and moved to another carriage. Here he found a little poem in prose by Prévert. By moving in turn to all five carriages of his train, he discovered five poems. He got out, waited for the next train, and repeated the operation. That made ten poems. He changed trains again, and ended up travelling in two more trains. When he finally got out at the Place d'Italie, he'd collected a grand total of twenty poems. The Arabic one had been repeated four times and the Prévert three times.

Feeling dazed, he sat on a seat on the platform, elbows on knees, head in hands. Why hadn't he known about this before, for heaven's sake? Because he bloody never took the metro, that was why. They put poems up in the trains and he didn't know, and how long had they been doing this? Six months? A year? Louis visualised the determined and frantic expression of Lucien Devernois. Lucien was right. It wasn't just some fancy literary puzzle, it was a frightening possibility. The whole thing took a completely different turn. It wasn't that a murderer had gone looking for a poem: a poem could have crossed the path of a maniac. A maniac who had sat in the metro, and found opposite him this poem which might have been written for him, had read and reread it, and imagined that it was a sign, a key. The killer didn't have to be someone well educated, he just had to travel by metro. And the text had fallen on him, as if destiny was sending him a personal message.

Louis went up the steps and knocked at the glass of the ticket office.

'Police,' he said to the clerk, showing his old card from the Ministry. 'I need to see someone from the station administration, anyone.'

The young man, looking intimidated, glanced at Louis's wet clothes, but yielded to the red, white and blue insignia on the card. He unlocked his cubicle and invited him inside.

'Some bother going on down there?' he asked.

'No, not at all. Do you know how long the Paris Transport Authority has been posting poems in the metro? I'm serious.'

'Poems?'

'Yes, in the trains, "Verse on the move".'

'Oh, that.'

The young man frowned.

'A year or two maybe. But what –'

'It concerns a murder. I need some urgent information about a particular poem. I want to know whether it was one of the ones posted, and if so, when. Someone in the administration must know that. You got a directory here?'

'Yes,' said the young man, opening a filing cabinet and pulling out a tattered book.

Louis sat down in one of the ticket sellers' seats and started looking through it.

'At this time of day,' the young man said timidly, 'you're not going to find them at their desks.'

'Yeah, I realise that,' said Louis wearily.

'If it's as urgent as all that . . .'

Louis turned to him.

'You've got an idea?'

'Well, it's just, I could call this mate of mine, Ivan. He sticks up posters, in trains and on platforms. So he might know.'

'Yeah, great, go ahead,' said Louis 'Call Ivan.'

The young man dialled a number.

'Ivan? Ivan? It's Guy here, come on, pick up! I've got your wretched answerphone! It's urgent, I'm calling from work.'

Guy looked apologetically at Louis. Then his friend apparently answered. 'Ivan? I've got a problem, about one of your posters.'

Louis took over the telephone and explained.

'What poem would that be?' asked Ivan. 'I might remember, you never know.'

'Shall I recite it?'

'That would help.'

It was Louis's turn to look in embarrassment at the young man. He tried hard to recall the four lines he had been looking at the day before, with Loisel.

'OK, then,' he said, 'ready?'

'Go ahead.'

Louis took a deep breath.

'*Je suis le Ténébreux, le Veuf, l'Inconsolé / Le prince d'Aquitaine à la Tour abolie / Ma seule Étoile est morte et mon luth constellé / Porte le Soleil noir de la Mélancolie.* It's by a poet called Gérard de Nerval and it's called "El Desdichado". I don't know how it goes on.'

'Can you repeat that?'

Louis did so.

'Yeah, that was posted up,' said Ivan. 'Yeah, I'm sure it was.'

'Terrific!' said Louis gripping the phone hard. 'And would you be able to say when it was up?'

'I think it was just before Christmas. Yeah, must be, just before Christmas, because I remember thinking it wasn't very cheerful for the festive season.'

'Quite agree.'

'But it stayed up a few weeks, after that, they all do. You'd have to ask someone in the administration.'

Louis thanked the poster-sticker warmly. Then he tried unsuccessfully to contact Loisel.

'No, no message,' he told the duty officer. 'I'll call back.'

He shook hands with young Guy, and ten minutes later was back at the door of the dosshouse. The bolts were drawn and there was no sign of life. He put down his bag and went round the side. From the back, you could reach up to the three tall windows of the refectory, which gave on to a slightly larger bit of garden than in front. Marc called it the plantation, as opposed to the fallow patch, because it had been cleared somewhat, and Mathias had planted a few potatoes. Louis banged on the shutters, calling out his name so as not to scare Clément's minders.

'OK, I'm coming,' came the gruff voice of Vandoosler senior.

He welcomed Louis with a bottle of wine in his hand. 'Ah, here you are, Louis, we're playing dice here, 4/21, the three of us.'

'Which three of you?'

'Us three, Marthe, her kid and me.'

Louis went into the refectory where Clément was sitting astride the bench, alongside Marthe. On the table were wine glasses and cards for marking points.

'And where's everyone else?' asked Louis.

'The evangelists? Out for a walk.'

'Really? All together?'

'Don't ask me, that's their business. Do you want to play?'

'No, but I'd like some coffee if there is any.'

'Help yourself,' said the godfather, settling down to play again. 'There should be some in the pot.'

'Vandoos,' said Louis, pouring himself a cup, 'there's a good chance the Secateur really *was* there at the rape, the second man.'

'Tsk, tsk,' said Clément.

'And there's a good chance too that both he and Rousselet were paid for it. The third man, who was probably the one who paid them, is still a mystery. And he could be the most dangerous. He must be someone known to the Secateur.'

Vandoosler turned to face Louis.

'And there's something worse,' said Louis. 'I've made a big mistake. Lucien was right.'

'Ah,' said the godfather in a non-committal voice.

'But how was I to know that "El Desdichado" had been posted up for anyone to see, in this series of poems they ran, both in the metro and in the suburban trains, last December?'

'Is that important?'

'It changes everything. The murderer didn't go looking for a poem, it hit him between the eyes.'

'I see,' said Vandoosler, shaking the dice.

'Six hundred and sixty-five,' Marthe announced.

'Six, six, five,' Clément chanted.

Louis looked across at Marthe's protégé. He seemed quite happy in this house now. Louis could understand that. The coffee was better here than anywhere else, even cold, as it was this evening. It was a basically restful coffee. Perhaps it was the water, or just the house.

'I've tried to contact Loisel,' he said, 'but he's not at the station. Unreachable.'

'What do you want with him?'

'I want to convince him to keep a watch on the streets. But now, dammit, we can't do anything till tomorrow night.'

'If it's any consolation, the evangelists began the watch last night. Tonight, all three of them have gone out. St Luke is eating a chicken curry in the rue de la Lune, and St Mark and St Matthew are eating sandwiches in the rue du Soleil and the rue du Soleil d'Or respectively.'

Louis stared in silence at the elderly cop, who was shooting dice again, with a smile, and at Marthe, who was pulling on her small cigar as she shot a glance in his direction. He ran his hands through his dark hair, still wet with rain.

'Three, three, one,' whispered Clément.

'It's mutiny,' Louis said, sipping his cold coffee.

'Exactly what Lucien said. He said it reminded him of 1917 and the mutinies in the French army. Everyone has been watching out for the Secateur and the old sculptor. But if it's the third man, how would they recognise him? The cops ought to check out all the young women who live alone in these three streets. And then lay an ambush.'

'Why didn't they say anything to me about this?'

Vandoosler shrugged.

'You were against it.'

Louis nodded and had some more coffee.

'Is there any bread?' he asked. 'I haven't had any supper.'

'It was my day to cook so I made my special gratin dauphinois. I could warm up some for you if you like.'

A quarter of an hour later, feeling satisfied and more relaxed, Louis helped himself to a generous portion. If the mutineers were watching the streets after all, he felt reassured. Still, Vandoosler was right. If it was the third man, it would be impossible to recognise him. Unless the killer visited the streets to stake them out for several nights in advance. The streets in question were quite small, one of them was hardly more than a mews. It should be quite easy to work out who lived in them. But it had become essential to enlist Loisel's help.

'Are they armed?'

'Last night no, they didn't have anything. I advised them to carry something tonight.'

'Your gun?'

'No fear! They'd be capable of shooting themselves in the foot. Lucien has the sword-stick that belonged to his grandfather . . .'

'Very discreet.'

'He insisted, you know what he's like. Mathias has an Opinel pocket knife, and Marc wouldn't take anything. He's allergic to knives.'

'Oh, that doesn't sound great,' sighed Louis. 'If something really tough comes up . . .'

'They're not as vulnerable as you might think. Lucien has his passion, Mathias his integrity and Marc his subtlety. Not bad, believe me, I've a lifetime in the police behind me.'

'When will they be back?'

'About two.'

'I'll wait for them, if that's OK.'

'Yes, go ahead, you can replace me on watch. But make up the fire, you'll catch your death in those wet clothes.'

XXXVII

IT WAS LATE ON WEDNESDAY MORNING WHEN LOUIS WENT IN THROUGH THE GATES at Montparnasse Cemetery. The previous night's rain had refreshed the atmosphere a little and the paths through the cemetery were soft and smelled of wet earth and lime blossom. The night before, Louis had waited until two thirty for the evangelists to return. Vandoosler had seen Marthe home before going to bed himself. Clément didn't want her to go, and put his head on her shoulder. Marthe tousled his hair.

'Go and have a shower before you go to bed,' she'd said to him gently. 'It's important to take a shower regularly.'

Louis thought that Marthe was quite capable of inventing son-protecting cloths like the Secateur's mother. Then he had remained alone in front of the log fire, gazing into the flames, his thoughts unfailingly returning to the scissors killer. Oddly enough, the three images that kept running through his head were the much-magnified picture of the bee in the murderer's bonnet, Lucien's chicken curry, and the Craven Pastry Cook's foot tracing circles in the flour. He must be tired. And then Lucien had burst in, noisily and excitedly waving his sword-stick. None of the men had seen anything in any of the streets.

Louis walked in a leisurely way through the cemetery, a bottle of Sancerre in his hand, but didn't find the Secateur. The shed was empty.

He looked in the other section, across the rue Émile-Richard, but again with no luck. Feeling slightly anxious, he came back to the gates and asked the janitor.

'First time anyone's asked for that one,' he said irritably. 'He didn't turn up this morning. What's it about? If you're bringing him more drink,' he said, pointing to the bottle, 'it can wait, he's probably sleeping off a hangover as it is.'

'That happen often?'

'No,' the janitor admitted. 'Must be off sick. I've got to do my rounds now. With all the nutters you get in here.'

Louis went off down the street, starting to worry. If the Secateur had bolted, he was losing control all over the place. He had to warn Loisel. He jumped on a bus for Montrouge and spent some time wandering through the nondescript streets before he found the Secateur's address. Wedged between a waste patch and a cafe with frosted windows, the small house was losing its plaster in chunks. A neighbour pointed out which was Thévenin's room.

'But he's not there now,' the woman said. 'Seems he's got a place where he can stay at work. Lucky for some.'

Louis listened at the door for a few minutes without hearing anything. He knocked a few times and then gave up.

'Told you he wasn't there,' said the woman, grumpily. 'And you see, he's not.'

Still clutching his bottle of Sancerre, Louis took a couple of buses to reach Loisel's headquarters in the 9th, at the other end of Paris. He wanted to put him on the track of the three streets, without mentioning either the Secateur or Clairmont, that is without interfering with the machinery so far. He would have to say something about the two women who had died at Nevers, there was no avoiding that. Anyway, sooner or later, Loisel would have heard about the rape in the institute grounds, if he hadn't done so already. The job now was to get him moving away from Clément, and towards the poem about the black sun. Finding the best angle of attack would not be easy. Loisel wasn't stupid.

'Got anything more on those marks on the carpet?' Louis asked him as they sat down. Loisel offered him one of his strawlike cigarettes.

'Not a thing. Fingers, certainly, but that's all. No abnormal substance on the carpet.'

'No trace of lipstick?'

Loisel frowned as he blew out smoke.

'You wouldn't be doing a Lone Ranger act, would you, my German friend?'

'Why would I? I don't have a job any more, remember.'

'So what's all this about lipstick?'

'Well, I don't really know. But I think this killer had already had a go at several people before coming and specialising in Paris. I think he was behind the death of a certain Nicole Verdot, who was killed soon after being raped, and also of a student called Hervé Rousselet: he was involved in the rape and might have talked. And I think this killer got a taste for it, and strangled and stabbed another young woman less than a year later, one called Claire Ottissier. You'll find their names on file, as unsolved crimes.'

'Where was this?' asked Loisel, grabbing a pen and notepad.

'Where do you think?'

'In Nevers?'

'Correct. Eight or nine years ago.'

'So. Clément Vauquer then,' said Loisel.

'He's not the only man in Nevers. But he was there when the rape happened. You'd find this out sooner or later, and I'd prefer to tell you myself. It seems he was a witness who tried to rescue the girl, neither a rapist nor a killer.'

'For God's sake, Louis, don't be an idiot. Are you defending this man?'

'Not specially. I just think he fell into our hands a bit too easily.'

'Right now, I've got nobody in my hands. Where d'you find all this?'

'The Claire Ottissier affair was one I already had in my archives. It rang a bell. Because of the MO.'

'And the rape?'

Louis had foreseen this. Loisel's tone was aggressive and his features hostile.

'It was in the local paper. I did a bit of research.'

Loisel gritted his teeth.

'Why, what were you looking for?'

'An explanation of why someone might actually have it in for Vauquer.'

Loisel paused for a moment.

'And the lipstick?' he began again.

'In the Claire Ottissier case, there'd been an eyewitness. So I went to see him yesterday in Nevers.'

'Oh, don't bother telling me anything, will you!' cried Loisel angrily. 'I suppose you couldn't get through to me on the phone?'

Louis put his hands down flat on the table and stood up calmly.

'I don't like your tone, Loisel. I've never been in the habit of giving a detailed account of my inquiries when they're still at an early stage. Now that I think I have something solid, I've come straight to you with it. If you don't appreciate my approach, and if you're not interested in my information, then I'll go away right now, and you can do your own inquiries.'

If you want peace, prepare for war, Louis thought to himself, although he had never been keen on the saying.

'All right, so tell me about it,' said Loisel shortly.

'This witness, Bonnot, he's a baker, but anyway he was a neighbour who stumbled on the crime. He saw the murderer picking something up by the victim's head. He couldn't see clearly, but it seemed to him as if it was a lipstick, so he actually thought at first the murderer was a woman.'

223

'Anything else?'

Louis sat down, now that Loisel was calmer.

'It's this poem I told you about the other day. It's become more serious, in fact very serious. Because that poem was actually posted up in the metro for about two months round about last Christmas. So I want you to put some men into the streets it might be connected to: rue de la Lune, rue du Soleil and rue du Soleil d'Or. And I would like it if you could warn any women living alone in those streets. There can't be many, they're quite small streets.'

'What's all this about the metro? I don't get it.'

'Well, suppose this killer is a madman, a maniac, obsessed.'

'There's not much doubt about that,' said Loisel with a shrug. 'But so what? You don't think he picked a poem just to find his way around Paris?'

'No, but the poem chose him. Suppose this guy wants to kill all the women on the planet but he isn't stupid enough to risk his own skin by embarking on a massacre. Suppose he's mad, but careful and calculating, so he decides to kill just a sample, but a significant sample so that symbolically they'll stand for all the women in the world: part for whole.'

'How do you know that's it?'

'I don't, but that was where *my* reasoning would take *me*.'

'Ah. Bravo. So what else would you do?'

'I'd look for a key, with some special meaning, so as to construct a series.'

'And that would be this poem?' asked Loisel.

'It could be this poem, that he might have seen four times in the metro, or anything else that Destiny threw in his path: let's say a drawing on sugar paper, or a kid's exercise book found in the gutter, a visit from the Jehovah's Witnesses, or a fortune-teller in the local market, the number of steps you find yourself going down three times in one day, or the words of a song overheard in a bar, or an article read in the paper . . .'

'Are you taking the piss?'

'Have you never thrown salt over your shoulder, or tried to avoid walking on the cracks?'

'No.'

'Too bad. But that's how people behave, and worse, if they have a bee in their bonnet. And this killer really has a big bee there, one that collects honey from every sign from Destiny encountered in daily life. He's sitting in the metro, he sees this poem, *Je suis le Ténébreux, le Veuf, l'Inconsolé:* I'm the prince of darkness, widowed, and disconsolate – it's quite a striking poem, isn't it? And then coming home that evening in a crowded carriage, there it is again. The prince of Aquitaine, the ruined Tower. And then the next day, the next, and the next. There's another line too, something about the sighs of the saint and the cries of the fairy – that would ring a bell for a rapist, wouldn't it? It's a weird text, it's cryptic and mysterious, nobody really knows what it means, anyone can hitch his crazy thoughts to it. He starts looking for it, he finds it, and in the end, it belongs to him, he's adopted it, he makes it the pivot of his urge for blood. That's how they work, bees in bonnets.'

Loisel was toying with his pencil and looking sceptical.

'You really must stake out those streets,' Louis insisted. 'And get men to call round to the residents in the buildings. Please, Loisel, for the love of God.'

'No,' said Loisel, firmly pressing the pencil end to his forehead. 'I've already told you what I thought about that idea.'

'Loisel! Come on!' cried Louis, banging his hand on the table.

'No, my friend, I'm not going for it, it's too far-fetched.'

'So that's it? You're going to let things take their course?'

'Sorry, old man. But thanks for the leads about Nevers.'

'You're bloody welcome,' said Louis, heading for the door.

Feeling angry and concerned, Louis allowed himself to gnaw the fingernails on his left hand, the hand of doubt and muddle. He stopped for a bite of something in a cafe. Loisel was a blessed idiot. What could the four of them achieve? If only he'd been able to lay hands on the Secateur this time. He would have poured the Sancerre into him through a funnel until he spat up the name of the third man. But Thévenin had vanished and all their leads had gone nowhere.

He returned to the dosshouse at about three in the afternoon, to report his lack of success with Loisel and the disappearance of the gardener. Marc was ironing, since he had got behind with his laundry work. Lucien was out teaching, and the hunter-gatherer was sticking flints together, aided by Clément who was developing a taste for it, while Vandoosler senior was weeding the plantation. Louis went out to join him and sat down on a tree stump. The blackened wood felt warm.

'I'm worried,' said Louis.

'I'm not surprised,' replied the godfather.

'It's Wednesday.'

'True. Shouldn't be long now.'

Towards seven that evening, the four men left the house to stand guard. Louis went with Lucien to watch the other end of the rue de la Lune. Time passed, slowly and monotonously, and Louis wondered how many nights they could go on like this. He reckoned that after about a week, they'd have to give up. They couldn't keep going out with takeaways forever. The locals were starting to give them funny looks. They didn't know what these men were doing there, standing around, several nights in a row. Louis got to bed at about three. He had to push Bufo off the mattress, and went to sleep instantly.

The next day, Louis tried another offensive with Loisel, but without result. He visited both the cemetery and the room in Montrouge, but the Secateur had not reappeared. He spent the rest of the day typing away without enthusiasm on his Bismarck translation, and in the evening he went to the rue Chasle. The other three were preparing to set out. Lucien was wrapping up his takeaway of beef and onions.

'You're spoiling yourself, aren't you?' Marc remarked.

'Soldier,' said Lucien without looking round, 'if the troops had been fed beef and onions every day, the face of the war would have changed.'

'Yeah, right, at the sight of you feeding your face, the Germans would have died laughing.'

Lucien shrugged disdainfully and rolled out three times as much kitchen foil as necessary to wrap his food. Vandoosler senior and Clément had begun a card game at the end of the table and were waiting for Marthe to join them.

'My personal turn now!' said Clément.

'Yes, go ahead,' said Vandoosler.

Tonight, Louis planned to go with Marc to the rue du Soleil d'Or. It was somehow reassuring to be checking the streets, and he tried to forget how pointless this vigil was turning out, almost grotesquely so.

The next day, Louis made what was getting to be his ritual trip to the Montparnasse Cemetery under the suspicious eyes of the janitor. The tall man with dark hair who came every day didn't look too reassuring to him. With all the nutters you get.

Then Louis went to Montrouge, where the neighbour looked at him equally suspiciously, and finally back to Bismarck. He attacked the translation with rather more enthusiasm than the previous day, which didn't seem a good sign. It was an indication that he was beginning to despair of ever getting anywhere in the case of the scissors killer . . . and in that eventuality, which seeemed more than probable, what in the world would they do with Marthe's doll? This looming question threw a shadow over all his thoughts. For ten days now, the three evangelists and the old policeman had been leading a life of sequestration, behind closed shutters, putting off all visitors, locking the door, sleeping on the bench, and for ten days Clément had been unable to go out in daylight. Louis didn't see how this could go on much longer. As for letting Clément stay with Marthe, that would hardly be any better. The guy would lose what wits he had, dozing on the red eiderdown, or else he'd run away. And then the cops would catch him.

That was always the point to which he returned.

In the end, Clément had had the benefit of a short reprieve. But there was no way he could hope to get out of the trap. And that was supposing Clément Vauquer really was who he said he was.

And he kept returning to that point as well.

The day went past and, having visited the cemetery and Montrouge, and worked a little on Bismarck, Louis turned up at the dosshouse again. He was a bit early. Marc was still out cleaning, Lucien at school. Louis sat down at the big table and watched Clément, who was now playing another game with Marthe. After the ten days of incarceration, the air was thick with cigar smoke and alcohol, and the shaded room felt like a gambling den. The kind of place you didn't go for fun, but to pass the time. Marthe tried to vary the distraction and change the games they played. That evening she'd brought along a game of knucklebones, one belonging to Clément, which he'd left behind on the bed that first night. He liked this game and played it with great dexterity, throwing the little metal pieces shaped like knucklebones up in the air and catching them like a juggler.

Louis watched for a while: he didn't know the rules, but it was fun to observe. Clément would throw the pieces up and catch them on the back of his hand, throw again and pick them up one by one, then two by two, and three by three, keeping the silver ones in his palm, but the red on the back of his hand. Marthe kept the score. Clément, playing fast and well, was almost laughing, but he missed at four by four, and the jacks fell on the floor. He bent down to pick them up and Louis gave a start. The flash of colours, red and silver, the click of the pieces in his hand. He sat still, watching as Clément started again. His fingers picked them up and threw them down, leaving greasy finger-marks on the polished wood.

'Death's Head!' pronounced Clément, showing the ones in his hand. 'Now, Marthe, shall I do Lucky Break, personally, I mean to say?'

Clément's lips were twisted with excitement.

'Yes, my boy, go ahead,' Marthe encouraged him. 'Nothing venture, nothing win.'

'What does Lucky Break mean?' Louis asked, his voice danger-ously tense. Just then, Marc came back in, and Mathias, punctual to the minute, emerged fom the cellar. Louis motioned to them to be quiet.

'Lucky Break?' said Clement. 'It's . . .'

He stopped and pressed his nose.

'It's the one that, well, it saves people,' he went on. '(a) The ship doesn't sink, (b) the cow gives milk and (c) the fire's put out.'

'It's like a jackpot,' Marthe summed up helpfully.

'It makes dangers go away, brings you luck,' said Clément, nodding seriously, 'and you get a hundred points.'

'What if you miss?' asked Marthe.

Clément made a gesture of cutting his throat.

'You lose everything, you're dead,' he said.

'So how do you play it?' asked Louis.

'This way,' Clément said. He put the red jack in the middle of the table, took the four silver ones and threw them down. 'Missed. I get five goes, what it is, they've got to be, like, face up, all four of them ...' He frowned.

'Do you mean they have to give you all four different sides, facing up, in one go?' asked Marc.

Clément smiled with relief, yes, that was what he meant.

'It's an old game,' Marc explained. 'The Romans played it with real knucklebones and they put all four signs on the timbers of a ship before it sailed. It protected you from shipwreck.'

Clément had stopped listening, but went on playing.

'Missed again!' said Marthe.

Louis stood up quietly and pulled Marc out of the room by his wrist. He climbed a few stairs in the dark.

'Marc,' he whispered, 'those knucklebones or whatever you call them, did you see?'

Marc stared at him through the dark, perplexed.

'Yeah, why? Lucky Break, it's as old as the hills.'

'Marc, don't you see? It wasn't a lipstick, it was a game of knucklebones, those metal ones, silver and red. The killer was playing with a set like that at the scene. The fingermarks! The stripes on the carpet. He was playing a game!'

'I don't get what you mean,' Marc whispered.

'It's what the Craven Pastry Cook was talking about. It must have been that game that the killer picked up quickly.'

'Ah, all right, yes, I see that, but why would he? What makes you think a murderer would stop and have a little game of knucklebones on the carpet?'

'Because of the bee in his bonnet, Marc. Games of chance, dice, knucklebones, going for broke, that's the kind of thing a maniac does. He was playing to see if Destiny would send a sign to justify the murder, get the gods on his side, bring him luck.'

'The Lucky Break,' Marc murmured, 'the one that saves the man. So . . . do you think Clément . . .?'

'Marc, I really don't know. You saw how good he was at it. He's been playing that game for years. It's his sphere of excellence, as Vandoos would say.'

A shout of enthusiasm reached them from the refectory.

'Huh,' said Louis, 'see, he's hit the jackpot. But whatever you do, keep mum, don't say a thing, don't give any sign, don't alert him.'

Lucien opened the door noisily.

'Hush,' said Marc preventively.

'What are you doing out here in the dark?' he asked.

Marc took him aside, while Louis went back into the room.

'We're on our way,' he said to Mathias.

Clément, sweat beading on his forehead, had passed the knuckle-bone set to Marthe.

XXXVIII

JULIE LACAIZE HAD JUST GOT HOME TO HER APARTMENT AT NUMBER 5 RUE DE LA Comète, in the 7th arrondissement.

With a sigh, she put down her three carrier bags of shopping in the kitchen, kicked off her shoes and flopped on to her couch. Tired after eight hours in front of a computer, she stayed lying down for a while, thinking how best to get out of those office lunches on Fridays. Then she closed her eyes. Tomorrow, Saturday, she'd do nothing at all. Sunday morning, same thing. Perhaps in the afternoon she'd take her nephew Robin to a puppet show: marionettes amuse children and people of discernment.

At about eight o'clock, she put a dish in the oven, had a long phone call with her mother, and switched the answerphone on. At half past, she opened the window on to the little courtyard, to get rid of the smoke, since she'd left the dish in a bit too long. At a quarter to nine, she was eating her supper, cutting off the bits of crust that had burnt, and was watching *55 Days at Peking*, curled up in an armchair with her back to the open window. The fresh air was welcome, but the light had attracted some large crane flies which stupidly got caught in her hair.

XXXIX

MARC, LUCIEN AND MATHIAS SEPARATED AT THE METRO, AND EACH HEADED towards his chosen street. That night, Louis was going to accompany Mathias to the rue du Soleil. The day before, worried whether they were at all on the right track, they had at Marc's request re-examined the poem and the street plan of Paris, but they felt sure their choices were the correct ones. Rue de la Lune, rue du Soleil or possibly rue du Soleil d'Or. Lucien was sure it would be rue de la Lune because the moon could be considered as the sun of the night, and therefore as the *soleil noir*, the black sun. Louis was inclined to agree, but Marc was doubtful. The moon, he said, was just a dead planet, it only reflected light, it was the opposite of the sun. Lucien would have none of it. The moon sheds light, full stop, it was the best candidate for the role of black sun.

Sitting in the metro, Marc was reading that month's poem posted up in the carriage, a meditation on ears of corn, which didn't provide any help on his personal destiny. He thought uncomfortably about Louis's hypothesis about the knucklebones. There was every chance that Louis was right about that, which made Marc despair. Because in that case, everything did point to Clément. His love of games, his habit (not at all common) of playing with those metal knucklebones he carried around in his pockets, his talent for the game, and then his credulous and no doubt superstitious mind, not to mention the circumstantial evidence against him, which they had all been trying to ignore for ten days.

Marc changed trains, disconsolately. He had grown fond of Clément, slow-witted though he might be, and this development pierced him to the heart. But who could tell in the end if he was really so simple? And what did it mean anyway? In his own way, Clément could be quite subtle. And he had other talents: he was a good musician. He was nimble-fingered. He was careful. He had very quickly picked up the skill of sticking flints together, which wasn't that easy. But he had never heard of the poem, Lucien was sure of that.

But what if Clément was clever enough to have fooled Lucien?

Marc got into another underground train where there were no seats and he had to stand, hanging on to the pole in the middle of the carriage, the one that two or three thousand passengers a day clung on to, so as not to be thrown about. Marc had always wondered why the metro had only two poles per carriage. Putting in any more would be too much like common sense, wouldn't it?

Two poles.

Two game players.

Clément and someone else. Clément wasn't the only person in the world for heaven's sake. There were probably thousands of players of knucklebones if you checked the whole of Paris. No, there weren't thousands. It was an unusual game and an old-fashioned one. But Marc didn't need there to be thousands. Two would do, just Clément and someone else.

Marc frowned. The Secateur? Did he play knucklebones? They hadn't seen any in his bag, but that didn't prove anything. What about the old voyeur, Clairmont? No. Marc shook his head. He couldn't see the two of them playing stuff like that. It didn't make sense.

Well, no, wait a minute, it did, they had both lived in Nevers, back in the old days. And you have to learn a game from someone. What was more likely than that the two gardeners and Clairmont had played that old-fashioned game round a table in the evenings, in the barn? Clément might have taught them perhaps. And he'd learned it . . .

And he'd learned it . . .

Marc stood still, hanging on to the pole.

He left the metro looking strained, and walked hesitantly towards the little rue du Soleil d'Or.

And he, Clément, had . . .

Marc took up his position at the street corner. Leaning on a lamp post. For an hour or so, he watched passers-by without seeing them, walking away from the lamp post and coming back every few minutes, in a radius of about five metres. His thoughts were clenched like his fists, and he tried to iron them out flat, like he did Madame Toussaint's skirts.

Because, after all, Clément must have had to . . .

At nine o'clock, Marc abruptly abandoned his lamp post, turned and began to run down the rue de Vaugirard, watching the traffic. He saw a free taxi and dashed towards it, waving his arm. For once his arm was effective and the taxi stopped.

XXXX

LESS THAN A QUARTER OF AN HOUR LATER, MARC JUMPED OUT OF THE TAXI. IT wasn't yet quite dark on this summer evening, and he looked anxiously for somewhere to hide. Just a newspaper kiosk, shut up for the night, but it would have to do. He leaned against it, feeling breathless, and began to watch. If he was going to do this every night, he'd need to find a less risky place. Louis's car for instance. He wished he could phone Louis, but the German was up in Belleville, the other side of Paris, rue du Soleil. He could perhaps find a phone booth and call the Ane Rouge to alert the godfather. But what if Clément were to run away in that time? And anyway, he couldn't take the risk of leaving his post for a few minutes. There wasn't a phone box anywhere in sight, and he didn't have a phonecard either. Poor strategic preparation, Lucien would call it. Cannon fodder, that's what they were, they'd get massacred.

Marc shivered and started to bite the skin round his nails.

When the man came out of the house about three-quarters of an hour later, by which time it was quite dark, Marc stopped panicking. He had to follow him discreetly. Not lose him above all. Perhaps he was only going out for a drink in a nearby cafe, but all the same, don't lose him for heaven's sake. And don't get spotted, stay at a safe distance. Marc followed the man, leaving other passers-by between them, walking with his head down, but his eyes peering up. The man walked

236

past a cafe without stopping, and then past the metro station without going down the steps. He wasn't hurrying, but there was something tense about the way he held himself, about the curve of his spine. He was wearing workman's overalls and carrying an old leather satchel. He passed the taxi rank, again without stopping. Obviously he was heading for somewhere on foot. It couldn't be too far. So it wasn't the rue de la Lune, the rue du Soleil, or the rue du Soleil d'Or, all of them too far away. Somewhere else. This man wasn't merely ambling about, he was striding ahead steadily without hesitation. But just once, he stopped and seemed to consult a map, before going on. So wherever he was heading, it was for the first time, apparently. Marc clenched his fists inside his pockets. For ten minutes now, they had been walking, one behind the other, on a course too determined for it to be a simple evening stroll.

Marc began to regret deeply not having brought any kind of offensive weapon with him. All he had in his pocket was a pencil sharpener, which he kept turning over and over nervously. He certainly wasn't going to accomplish anything with that, if, as he feared, things turned nasty. He began to glance around the pavements hoping to find something, anything, even a stone. In vain, since nothing was harder to come across in central Paris than a pebble, of the sort Marc liked to kick along. As they turned into the rue Saint-Dominique, he saw, not fifteen metres away, an imposing builder's skip, with the irresistible instruction *Keep Out* painted in white on its green metal side. Normally there might be a few people hanging around it, looking for copper wire, mattresses, clothes, anything worth selling. But tonight, nobody. Glancing ahead at the man he was following, Marc sprang up on the side of the skip and leaned in. He pushed aside a few lumps of plaster and rolls of carpet, then found several pieces of lead piping. Choosing a short solid one, he jumped back down. The man was still in full view as he crossed the Esplanade in front of the Invalides. Marc ran on about thirty metres, then skidded to a halt.

Their progress went on for about five minutes, before the man lowered his head and turned left. Marc didn't know this district. Looking up at the street name, he involuntarily brought his hand to his mouth. The man had just started down the narrow rue de la Comète. A comet! How could they have missed that one? Poor research. They hadn't scanned the four thousand street names in Paris, they'd just looked for sun, moon and stars. An amateur attempt. Nobody had thought of a comet, a shooting ball of ice and dust with light shining from it, a black sun. And for good measure, the little street was but a stone's throw from the crossroads called La Tour-Maubourg. The abolished tower, the comet, surely this wouldn't have needed a bee in the bonnet, an ordinary housefly could have guessed it.

Marc then realised with certainty that he must be following the scissors killer, without a gun, without anyone to help, just a stupid bit of lead piping. His heart began to beat fast and his knees wobbled. He had a clear feeling he wouldn't be able to manage the last few metres.

Julie Lacaize jumped when her doorbell rang at five past ten. She didn't like to be interrupted in the middle of a film.

She went to the door and looked through the peephole. It was dark, and she couldn't see anyone. From the little courtyard, a firm and reassuring male voice explained that there was a gas leak just opposite the building, and he was doing an urgent check of all the flats.

Julie opened the door without hesitation. Firemen and gas fitters were sacred beings, looking after the fragile destinies of pipes, underground conduits, chimney fires and explosions in the capital.

The man looked serious and asked if he could see the kitchen, which Julie showed him, shutting the front door.

Then two hands gripped her neck. Unable to scream, she was dragged backwards. Her own hands felt for the man's arms in a desperate and convulsive movement, but in vain. On the television, gunshots from the Boxer rebellion were making a huge din.

Marc pressed the end of his lead pipe hard against the killer's back.

'Let her go, Merlin, you bastard,' he yelled, 'or I'll blow your guts out.'

He had shouted as loud as he could, feeling that he would be quite incapable of blowing out anyone's guts, or brains. Merlin released his grip and turned round, his toad-like features full of hate. Marc felt himself being grabbed by the neck and hair. He jerked the lead under the killer's chin. Merlin fell to his knees, clutching his jaw and groaning. Hesitating to hit him on the head, Marc waited for him to react, calling to the girl to phone the police. Merlin held on to a chair to stand up again and Marc moved towards him, the pipe gripped in both hands. Merlin stumbled backwards and Marc pinned him down with the lead bar across his throat. He heard the girl's alarmed voice as she told the police her address.

'Tie him up, his feet!' Marc yelled as he tried to hold the large man on the floor. He was still pressing the bar downwards, but his hands were trembling badly. The man was strong and was struggling to get up. Marc felt desperately slight by comparison. If he let go, Merlin would quickly overcome him.

Julie had no rope in the house, and was scrabbling about, frantically trying to wind sticky tape around the man's legs. It was a few minutes later that Marc heard the sound of the police bursting in through the open window, the same way he had.

XXXXI

SITTING ON THE COUCH, ARMS DANGLING AND LEGS TWITCHING, MARC WATCHED as the police manhandled Paul Merlin. He had asked them to call Loisel and to get someone to pick up Louis Kehlweiler from the rue du Soleil in Belleville. Julie, sitting alongside him, seemed, while not exactly perky, in better shape than he was. He asked her if she had any painkillers to deal with the atrocious migraine which had attacked his left eye. Julie gave him a glass of water and passed him three tablets one by one, so that a cop who had arrived late thought Marc had been the person attacked.

When the migraine began to fade a little, Marc looked at Merlin, now pinioned by two policemen and moving his batrachian lips in an incoherent automatic way. Bee in the bonnet, well, there was certainly some monstrous insect in there, like the one he'd drawn in Nevers. The sight confirmed Marc's dislike of toads, although he vaguely realised that was irrelevant. Julie was impossibly pretty. She was biting her lips, looking alert, her cheeks pink with emotion. She hadn't taken any painkillers or anything else, and Marc was frankly impressed.

They were all waiting for Loisel. He arrived quickly, with three men as his escort, followed soon after by Louis, who had been picked up by police car. Louis rushed towards Marc, who indicated with annoyance he wasn't the victim, it was this young woman sitting beside him. Loisel took Julie into another room.

'See where we are?' asked Marc.

'Rue de la Comète. What dopes we were.'

'And see who it is?'

Louis looked at Merlin and nodded gravely.

'How did you get here?'

'It was the knucklebones. I'll tell you later.'

'Tell me now.'

Marc sighed and rubbed his eyes.

'I followed the trail of the knucklebones,' he said. 'If Clément played them, who taught him? That was the right question. Not Marthe, she didn't know about them before. In the institute there was someone who played games with him, dice, card games, simple things . . .'

Marc looked up at Louis.

'Remember what Merlin told you. Clément used to play games with him. And Merlin played knucklebones, I'm sure. When we were in his office, he was fiddling with coins in between his fingers, remember that? Then he collected them in his palm and moved them again. Like this,' said Marc, showing Louis with his own fingers. 'So I went to his house and waited outside.'

The police were now taking Merlin away and Marc stood up. Nobody had turned off the television, and Charlton Heston was in mid-battle on the walls of the fortress. Marc picked up the lead piping from the floor.

'You brought that with you?' asked Louis, somewhat taken aback.

'Yeah. My trusty weapon.'

'Just a poxy bit of lead?'

'It's not a poxy bit of lead, it's the sword-stick of my great-great-grandfather.'

XXXXII

IT WAS ALREADY WARM AND MARC WAS IN THE BACK GARDEN OF THE dosshouse, sitting cross-legged on a railway sleeper he used for this purpose, in the shade of the tree of heaven, the only one worthy of the name in the plantation. He was stirring his coffee as fast as he could without spilling any, while an old transistor radio speckled with paint crackled at his feet. Every half-hour, he retuned it to catch the latest news. The arrest of the scissors killer had already made the headlines. The young woman with bright eyes was called Julie Lacaize, as Marc was pleased to learn. He'd admired her, and was wondering now whether he hadn't made a big mistake in asking her for painkillers after his brave action. In the ten o'clock bulletin, he had been described as a 'courageous history teacher'. Marc had smiled and pulled up some grass while rewriting the report himself to read: 'Heedless of danger, the hysterical house cleaner pounced on an amphibian'. There's glory for you. Glory is built on ignorance, Lucien would have said.

Louis had called Pouchet earlier that morning and had headed off to Loisel's station to be present as Paul Merlin was being interrogated. He was regularly phoning the cafe where Vandoosler senior was passing on the information. Loisel, in cooperation with the Nevers police and the families of the victims, was putting together the information with which to charge Merlin.

By eleven o'clock, it had become clear that Merlin had himself organised the rape of Nicole Verdot, although they had not yet managed to make him confess to it, or to obtain the names of the people he had hired. Merlin had become delirious and uncontrollable at any mention of the young woman. By midday it had become easy to map the course of his growing desire for and then hate of Nicole Verdot, who, after imprudently agreeing to a one-night stand, had later rejected his advances and threatened to leave the school. *Mon front est rouge encore du baiser de la Reine / J'ai rêvé dans la Grotte où nage la Sirène.* My brow is still red from the kiss of the queen / I have dreamed in the cave where the mermaid swims.

From behind a tree, Merlin had witnessed this punitive rape. Perhaps he was hoping to go to the aid of the young woman after the attack, or even to rush to her rescue and through his attentions win back her goodwill. But then that wretched Vauquer had charged in like a madman, brandishing his hosepipe, and had laid waste all the pleasure and all the plans of the head of the institute. Worse still, he had unmasked Rousselet, so Nicole Verdot had recognised one of her attackers. Rousselet was a brute and a coward, who would surely talk, and give away the name of the man who had hired him. Consequently, that night, Merlin killed Nicole at the hospital, and drowned Rousselet in the Loire. Clément Vauquer was going to have to pay for that.

Ma seule Étoile est morte. My only Star is dead.

At three in the afternoon, Merlin had confessed to the murders of Claire Ottissier, Nadia Jolivet, Simone Lecourt and Paulette Bourgeay. Louis explained that Nicole Verdot's death throes had triggered a process of pleasure and satisfaction derived from murderous violence, summed up by Vandoos senior as 'the guy got a kick out of it and couldn't stop'. The poem's next verse had the line: *Les soupirs de la Sainte et les cris de la Fée.* The sighs of the Saint and the cries of the Fairy. Merlin had seen the poem three times one morning while in the metro after a sleepless night. It had shown him the way.

At four thirty, Louis reported details of the simple and clever way Paul Merlin had identified his victims. He had an administrative post in the Vaugirard District of the French Inland Revenue Office. He had checked the computer records for the streets he had chosen, and then picked unmarried women with no children, aged under forty.

Merlin had planned two more murders after Julie Lacaize: one in the rue de la Reine-Blanche, and the last one in the rue de la Victoire. With a frown, Marc went to get the Paris street map, which was still lying on the kitchen sideboard, and returned to sit on the sleeper. Rue de la Reine-Blanche: Street of the White Queen. *Mon front est rouge encore du baiser de la Reine*: . . . 'the kiss of the queen', yes, a perfect choice, the white queen, immaculate purity, it was obvious. Obvious that is to that horrible insect buzzing in his bonnet with its many-faceted eyes. And rue de la Victoire to close the sequence. *Et j'ai deux fois vainqueur traversé l'Achéron* : 'twice, victorious, I crossed the Acheron'. Yes, you could see how the insect's mind worked all right. Marc looked at the map for the 9th arrondissement: rue de La Victoire was very near the rue de la Tour-des-Dames, which itself crossed the rue de la Reine-Blanche, and both were no distance from the rue de la Tour d'Auvergne, which crossed the rue des Martyrs. And so on. Marc put the street map down on the grass. A terrifying board game, in which everything made sense and fitted together unfailingly, to the point of vertigo. The relentless logic of an insect, reducing Paris to pulp.

Five o'clock. Marc tuned his radio. Clement Vauquer's part in this had been worked out with care. He was to be kept hidden in Merlin's own house after the first three murders. Merlin would then have 'suicided' him after the rue de la Victoire. But the village idiot had escaped, there is a god who looks after the simple of heart. Merlin had had to press on, taking more risks. Once the final crime had been committed, within the rules, with the Lucky Break to sanction it, his plan was to lay down his arms and glory in his memories.

Louis, Loisel and the psychiatrist who was present all thought that in fact the man would never have been able to stop.

A single insect can reduce Paris to rubble, Marc observed to Lucien, who was preparing their evening meal.

Lucien nodded. He had retrieved his scissors from their hiding place and was cutting up herbs. Marc sat and watched him in silence.

'That woman,' Marc began after a long pause, 'Julie Lacaize. She was charming to me. Given that I'd just saved her life, that's quite normal of course.'

'And since then?'

'And since then nothing. And frankly, I didn't think I was going to get anywhere with her.'

'My friend,' said Lucien without pausing in his work, 'it's not possible to accomplish an act of intelligence and courage *and* expect to pick up a girlfriend as a bonus.'

'Why not?'

'Because then it wouldn't be heroism, it would be musical comedy.'

'Ah, yes,' said Marc in a low voice. 'But given the choice, I think I'd prefer musical comedy.'

XXXXIII

BY LATE AFTERNOON, LOUIS HAD LEFT THE POLICE STATION FEELING BOTH STUNNED and relieved. He would leave it to Loisel to tie up all the loose ends. But he had some unfinished business of his own.

The Secateur was raking paths in the north of the cemetery. As he saw Louis approach, he froze.

'I thought you'd resurface,' said Louis. 'You heard that the killer's been caught, didn't you?'

The Secateur tapped the rake pointlessly on the ground.

'So you thought it was safe to poke your nose out of doors again? That I wouldn't be coming to collar you? But there's still that rape, isn't there? Have you forgotten the rape?'

The Secateur gripped the rake.

'It wasn't me,' he snarled. 'If the boss is saying it was, he's lying. There's no proof. Nobody'll believe a murderer.'

'You *were* there,' Louis insisted. 'With Rousselet and some mate of yours that you'd recruited. Merlin paid you.'

'I never touched the girl.'

'Only because you didn't have time. You were already on top of her when Clément Vauquer drenched you with water. And don't waste your breath. Merlin didn't say anything, but there was another witness. Clairmont was watching you through field glasses from his studio.'

'That old bastard,' growled Thévenin.

'What does that make you then, eh? What kind of a man are you?'

The Secateur threw him a look full of hostility.

'I'll tell you what kind of man you are, Secateur. You're full of shit, and I could easily get you arrested. But Nicole Verdot is dead, and we can't do anything for her now. There is just one thing that's worth saving about you, and that's the cloth your mother gave you. And because of that, and *only* because of that, do you hear me, I'm going to leave you in peace, to honour the hope your mother must have had in you at one time. You're very lucky that she's protected you.'

The Secateur bit his lip.

'And you can keep this fucking bottle of Sancerre I've been carrying round every day while looking for you. So when you drink it, think of Nicole and try and manage some sincere regret for her.'

Louis put the bottle down at the Secateur's feet and went off down the central avenue of the cemetery.

That evening, Louis went to have supper at the dosshouse. When he walked into the refectory, he found it empty and dark, and peering out through the slits in the shutters, he saw Marc and Lucien sitting on the sparse grass of the plantation.

'Marthe's doll, where's he gone?' he asked as he joined them. 'Has he flown out into the daylight with his little wings?'

'No, no,' said Marc. 'Clément hasn't been out at all. I said he could go for a walk in the streets. But he explained quite calmly that no, he personally preferred to go and stick bits of stone together in the cellar.'

'Ah,' said Louis. 'We'll have to get him used to the great outdoors gently.'

'That's right, gently does it. We've got plenty of time.'

'You haven't opened the shutters.'

Lucien looked up at the house.

'Fancy,' he said, 'nobody thought of that.'

Marc jumped up and ran into the house. He opened wide the windows of the refectory and pushed back the wooden shutters. Then he released the metal bar holding the shutters of Clément's bedroom and let the hot sunshine flood in.

'There!' he said to Louis, sticking his head out of the window. 'See?'

'Excellent!'

'Right, and I'm going to close them all now, else we'll all die of heat in here.'

'What's the matter with him?' asked Louis.

Lucien held up his hand.

'Don't cross the heroic rescuer,' he said. 'He was hoping for a romantic outcome, and he's just got a pile of laundry to iron.'

Louis leaned on the tree and shook his head. Lucien sniffed and put his hands in his pockets.

'Always a melancholy business,' he mumured, 'the return of soldiers from the front.'

XXXXIV

FROM THE DOORWAY IN THE RUE DELAMBRE, GISÈLE DECIDED, EXCEPTIONALLY, TO carry her bulk along the thirty metres separating her from young Lina, a newspaper under her arm.

When she reached her, she waved the paper under her nose.

'See?' she cried. 'Who was right, then? Was it Marthe's little lad killed those girls, or wasn't it?'

Lina shook her head, apprehensively.

'I never said he did, Gisèle.'

'Oh no? Few days ago, there you were, sorry to say so, but there it is, you wanted to go to the cops about him. And who had to stop you, one more time? So pay attention, young 'un. Learn a lesson, if you can. Marthe's little lad, he'd had an education, right? And he belonged to Marthe, right? So what was there to discuss?'

Lina looked at the ground and Gisèle moved off, muttering to herself.

'Comes to something,' she grumbled, 'when you got to yell at people to tell 'em what's what.'

FRED VARGAS was born in Paris in 1957. A historian and archaeologist by profession, she is now a bestselling novelist. Her books have sold over 10 million copies worldwide and have been translated into 45 languages.

SIÂN REYNOLDS is a historian, translator and former professor at the University of Stirling.